Urban Dragon

Volume 3

by

JW Troemner

First Edition December 2016

Copyright © 2016 by JW Troemner.

All rights reserved.

Cover design by Deranged Doctor Designs

ISBN 978-1-945182-02-0

For Andrew, who gave me hope,

for Tane, who gave Arkay her chair,

and for the woman with knitting needles on the edge of the

circle

Table of Contents

Book 7:

Crusader Non Grata

Arkay

"Uh… guys?" The voice in my earpiece belonged to a rakshasa named Yash. He was new around here, which was saying something with this group. I was second in command on this mission, and I'd only been with the Hoarde for a little more than two years. "Is she singing the Spider-Man theme?"

Nadia didn't answer him, except with a very loud and long-suffering sigh.

"Of course not," I said. "I'm *humming* the Spider-Man theme. It's much more professional. Why? Are you a fan?"

"A bit, yes," he admitted. "But doesn't this sort of thing call for…" I could hear him squirming. "…you know, silence?"

"Yash, honey, it's four in the morning and I'm stuck to the side of a fourteen story building. Anyone who's awake to hear me is in no condition to notice." They would most likely assume I was part of some dream, or the spillover of a neighbor binge-watching cartoons late at night.

Nadia finally broke in. "Except perhaps the Orderlings who are actively conducting surveillance in this area. Arkay, could you *please* try to focus?"

"Focus on what, exactly? I haven't moved an inch in fifteen minutes." A cold April wind ruffled my hair and sent a fresh chill through my fingertips. "I can't actually feel my hands anymore, so if you guys could hurry up and do your thing, that would be swell."

"We've got everyone inside," said the other rakshasa. "Tomasi's got the defensive runes up and ready. We're good to go when you are."

"We'll actually be needing silence out there," Nadia said. "Arkay, give us sixty seconds to get into position. We'll move when you give the signal."

Normal protocol was to rush in with guns blazing and mow down the Order goons before they could put up a real fight. But this time around, they'd set up on the fourteenth floor of a cheaply made apartment building in New Jersey. It wouldn't take much for a stray bullet to rip through the walls and hurt an innocent bystander, especially with the massive caliber the Order liked to use in their firearms.

Thus our current plan.

I inched along the side of the building and perched on the absurdly narrow ledge above the window. I wanted to dig my claws into the brick for better leverage, but the people inside would hear that. The less opportunities they had to grab their guns, the better.

I counted down at a mutter: *one macarena, two macarena, three macarena,* and I jabbed an EpiPen full of Styx into my thigh.

My team got into position in the hallway. There'd been too much surveillance in the apartment building itself, so instead of taking the elevator like actual sane people, we'd wound up bringing the entire team to the top of the office silo next door so they could zipline into the only empty apartment on this floor.

And guess who had to climb fourteen stories by hand, just so I could open the damn window for them? And, of course, supply a distraction.

Fifty-eight macarena, fifty-nine macarena, sixty.

With a single stroke of a ball-peen hammer, I shattered the window. Shouts of surprise and alarm joined the sound of breaking glass. I dropped onto the windowsill and tucked into a crouch, bursting through the pane and landing in a bedroom that looked more like a barracks. Three military-style cots stood against the far wall. Two were buried in neatly organized equipment and duffel bags. The third was occupied by a man who looked like he'd only just jolted awake. The door sprang open, and another three figures rushed in. Ignoring them, I sprang on top of Sleepyhead, pinning him to his cot before he had a chance to get up. They couldn't shoot me without hitting him.

I sank my teeth into the exposed flesh of his neck and poured electricity into his veins. His spine arched so hard he nearly bucked me off, his limbs flailing as every muscle and nerve in his body lit up at once.

A gunshot hit me like a punch in the kidneys. My body armor caught the bullet before it could do major damage, but the force of it threw me backwards. I fell into the pile of supplies, and one of the cots flipped and landed on top of me.

A spray of bullets rained down around me. I flattened myself against the floor, sheathing myself in scales. The thin canvas of the upended cot made a shitty shield, but at least it hid me well enough to throw off the shooter's aim. A few bullets grazed my legs. Another two sliced past the compromised vest and into the scales of my abdomen. Even slowed down, the impact burned like hellfire, but it wasn't enough to kill me.

A metallic click warned that the person who'd fired was reloading.

"That won't be the only one," a woman barked. "Check the windows."

"I don't see anything," called another voice from the next room.

"What about this one?" Footsteps crept closer to the pile of debris that hid me from view. "Is it dead?"

"It sure as hell better be," muttered the woman.

A hand grabbed the shredded canvas close to my face.

Any day now, Nadia.

My cover was yanked away. A second barrage of bullets peppered the ground as I sprang, tackling the woman to the floor.

My whole body burned, too saturated with pain to distinguish any one source. I shoved it aside and raked my claws across the woman's abdomen. Blood and sewage curdled the air as I opened her insides, and she fell back, her eyes wide and unseeing.

One of the men shrank away in horror; the other lunged at me. A combat knife flashed in his hand. No time to roll away. I could only grab onto his wrist as he bore down on top of me. Cold steel glinted a bare inch from my face. I had a dragon's strength behind me, but he had weight and leverage and animal fury.

But before he could cut my face off, he gave a soft, sharp gasp, and his whole body shuddered and went limp on top of me. His chest bloomed red around the point of a second knife. A pair of pale, slender hands pulled him off me and tossed him aside.

My rescuer was tall and corded with muscle, her long blond hair braided into a tight crown around her scalp. Blood splattered the stark white of her fatigues— more blood than she should have gotten from that one *coup de gras*. I glanced past her athletic calves. Two bodies lay just outside the door, and a growing pool of gore suggested more just out of sight.

I frowned, counting on my fingers. "I thought this was supposed to be a two-bedroom apartment."

"It is." Nadia caught me by the arm and hauled me to my feet. I swayed, but managed to stay standing. Damn bullets.

"And they had— what, six people living here? Eight?"

"Nine," she said.

I tsked. "Nobody respects fire code anymore. It's a damn shame."

Nadia rolled her eyes. "Are you going to be alright?"

"I'll get over it," I said. The Styx was already repairing the damage, leaving behind an uncomfortable heat and pressure around the wounds. That shit still made my skin crawl, but damn if it wasn't useful.

Satisfied, Nadia turned away from me and returned to her team. "Tomasi, get on those computers and see if the hard drives have been wiped. Melissa, bring the van around front. We'll take the elevator down. Jordana, get Kanti and Yash calm and start collecting what you can. Move fast. Police are already on their way."

I leaned heavily against the wall and focused on my breathing while the Styx did its work. In the other room, Kanti and Yash hissed and snarled, still coming down from the high of bloodlust. Unlike the rakshasa on the rest of Nadia's strike teams, these two could rein in their fury enough to leave survivors. Some of the time, anyway.

Okay, so we had yet to bring anyone in alive. At least we were working on it.

A gasping cough pulled me out of my thoughts. The man I'd electrified dragged himself upright. His gaze swept over the carnage around him before he turned to me.

"Morning, Sleepyhead." I flashed a smile. "You slept right through the fight. Sorry about that. But on the plus side, you get to live."

Sleepyhead scrambled away from me. One arm groped at the scattered mess beside his cot.

On the other side of the open door, Nadia frowned and glanced my way.

Sleepyhead yanked a Desert Eagle from a duffel bag and flipped off the safety. His hands twitched as he pointed the enormous handgun at me.

"Calm down, dude," I said. "It's a noble effort and all, but you're surrounded. There are a lot more of us than there are bullets in that little thing. So how about you put it down and sit tight for a while? I promise nobody's going to hurt you."

He glanced at the bodies on the floor and smears of blood from the next room. Sweat beaded on his forehead. "You— you want to take me prisoner."

"It's really not as bad as it seems. We're under new management, so now we do the whole rules of engagement thing. We're practically Geneva Convention certified and everything."

Maybe I'd mixed up my historic treaties, because the color drained from his face. His hands started shaking. "No. You won't take me."

"You can call me a liar, but that won't make it less true." I stepped forward, still smiling cheerfully. "Now let's put that thing down before you hurt someone."

Nadia appeared in the door. "Arkay, get away from him."

My gaze flicked to her face for just an instant. When I looked back, he had the gun pressed to his temple.

"Hold on a second!" I leaped at him. "No, wait!"

The single gunshot felt louder than the entire firefight had been. I recoiled as blood and gray matter splashed the wall behind him.

The rest of my team poked their heads in just in time to see his body fall.

I stood frozen, staring. I could still taste his blood in my mouth.

"Back to your assignments," Nadia snapped, and they retreated even faster than they'd come. She caught me around the waist and yanked me out of the room. "You, too, Arkay. We don't have time for this. Let's go." I didn't get a chance to protest before she slung an overburdened duffel bag across my shoulder and shoved a box of papers and notebooks into my arms. She grabbed another pair of bags and yanked the door out of its splintered frame.

"Elevator's this way." She pushed me in front of her, through the hallway and into the elevator. The nylon straps of the bags pushed my vest into my wounds.

"He shot himself," I said quietly.

Nadia glowered at the far corner of the elevator. "He did."

I took a deep, ragged breath. "Is this going to keep happening?"

"Give it time," she said. "There is always a spike in suicides after an Orderling defects. Eventually it goes back down again."

I ran my tongue over my teeth. "Any idea how long these spikes are supposed to last?"

"Only a few years," she said.

A few years of suicides.

"We could tie them up or something so they can't shoot themselves," I pointed out. "Or you could do that hypno-eye thing that you do. If we could keep them alive long enough to give them some decent therapy—"

"Then you would have a hospital full of dead therapists on your hands," Nadia said. "This is a war, Arkay. There are going to be people you can't save."

The elevator doors opened and we stepped into the lobby. The doorman stared at my bullet wounds and Nadia's bloodstains with bulging eyes. I put down the crate and dug through my pocket.

"Hey." I tried to flash a winning smile, but it felt strained and wrong on my face. "The police are already on their way. We've got some more people coming down on the next elevator. Don't bother trying to stop them, and everything is going to be great." I slapped a twenty on his desk. "And maybe get yourself a drink. You look like you need one."

Meph

We'd chosen a coffee shop for our rendezvous point. It typically served a college population, but the end of the semester meant that the large cafe was nearly deserted. A barista polished the espresso machine. A young coed lounged in an armchair, her latte forgotten on the small table beside her. Another student eyed her from his perch across the room.

I sipped at my own coffee, black, and didn't look up when Mara walked in and sat in the booth behind mine. Her cane tapped an uneasy pattern into the tile floor.

"I take it you found something?" I asked.

"I wouldn't be here if I didn't." The vinyl booth cushion squeaked as she sat back. "Shit."

"Do you know how many?"

"At least two," she said. "The Hoarde breaks into our network periodically, but they're kicked out again before they can get much out of the system, and most of it is menial detail. Surface stuff. But someone else is accessing our data. Someone more experienced. More professional. It's hard to spot, because they don't do anything to it, and they use too many proxies to trace, and…" She hesitated. "And they know our passwords, Meph. Top-level passwords. RSA authentication. Shit you never had access to."

"Which means?" I prompted.

"Which means you can't be the mole. Or you can't be the only one."

It was the closest to vindication as I was ever going to get.

"When the Contessa made her offer, she was talking like she could get me a high rank. She said she'd done it before."

"They'd have to be pretty high up there to get that kind of access." The tapping of Mara's cane gained a jagged rhythm. "How could they do that to us? How could they betray us that way?"

"Maybe it didn't feel like a betrayal from where they're standing," I said quietly. "Dragons are insidious. They get under your skin, make you see the world their way until you can't see anything else. Giving up everything you ever believed in seems easy when a dragon asks you to do it."

"Except for you?" Her voice was more bitter than my coffee.

"Especially for me. The difference is that you and I are both aware of their influence, and we can compensate. Keep fact checking what I say. Keep making sure it makes sense. The best defense against a dragon is the truth."

The coed in the corner finally rose out of her armchair, leaving her coffee and her book to vanish into the bathroom.

The other student stood and stretched, glancing around with forced nonchalance. I averted my eyes to my own beverage.

Mara let out a heavy breath. "Do you think you're ever going to get past this, Meph?"

"I can kill them," I said. "And then it won't matter how many hooks they have in me."

The student crossed the cafe and bent over the coed's chair, pretending to read the cover of her book. The distracted baristas didn't notice him tipping a packet into the spout of her drink.

I threw back the last of my coffee. "I need to get going."

Mara tensed beside me. "What is it?"

"Just a bit of monster hunting," I said. "Do me a favor, will you? Make sure the girl in the bathroom gets home in one piece."

I'd learned the hard way: not all monsters had claws.

Arkay

It was a long, quiet ride back to the Felldeep. I used baby wipes to scrub the gore from my face and hands, trying not to think too deeply about who the blood belonged to. Yash attempted to start up a conversation about comic books, but it fizzled into one-word sentences and awkward silence before it could get very far. We had a long night behind us. I wanted it to be over as soon as possible.

The movements of the van grew bumpy as we left the highway and turned onto a dirt road in the middle of a thick forest. The sky lightened from a brooding charcoal to the color of a fresh bruise by the time we pulled up in front of a crumbling shed. I climbed out and stretched, my legs stiff from three hours of being crammed into the back of a van.

The dry blood under my clothes had started to slough off into an itchy powder. I wanted to peel off the body suit and brush off the debris, but no such luck. Nadia was already organizing the rest of the team, and she motioned for me to get on with it.

She insisted that I always be the first person to go inside. It was supposed to be symbolic of leadership or something, but mostly, it came across as stupid. We all knew where we were going. Still, I tried hard not to roll my eyes as I led the file into the dilapidated shed.

It was barely big enough to lay down, with a few emergency supplies to tide over whatever unfortunate soul found themselves this far into the middle of nowhere. The entire team wouldn't have fit inside all at the same time. The only point of interest were the doors: it had two on the inside; on the outside, there was only one, so big that it took up the entire wall.

I pressed the secret latch and jiggled the knob a few times, and finally the door opened into a gaping black abyss. I stepped through, and the world went as dark as spilled ink. Slowly gradients of shadow emerged, revealing a pair of oni dressed in overalls. They carried lanterns, the glass tinted dark so as not to attract living shadows, and the faint light barely reached the path before their feet. Behind them walked a cave troll who squinted her huge eyes against the faint illumination.

The oni waited beside the door for the rest of our team to file through. Their tusks caught the light as they exchanged words in Japanese and chuckled. I didn't miss the quick glance in my direction. The cave troll stayed behind, looking at her feet to avoid the brightness of the doorway. She was nearly twice my height, but she wasn't as broad or muscular as the other trolls I'd met. Nadia dismissed the rest of my team, and they started to dissipate. I would have joined them, but the troll was directly in my way, and her awkward shuffling made it impossible for me to step past her.

As it turns out, that was deliberate.

"Um… hello, ma'am. Arkay. Ma'am." She stumbled over the words.

I tried not to look too nonplussed. "Hi?"

"Hi," she squeaked. Before that moment, I did not know trolls could squeak. It sounded like a pair of boulders scraping together. Her head bowed so low that it almost retreated between her shoulder blades. "I… um… we're here for the pick-up. I mean, we were told you would be here and you had stuff that needed… um… picking up… but you knew that." She wrung her enormous hands, and I noticed pink sparkles in her chipped nail polish. "I just wanted to tell you that I—um—"

"Ey! Dagny!" One of the oni stepped back through the doorway, a stack of boxes leaning in his hands. "Hurry up, there's more here!"

"I-think-you're-really-cool-okay-thanks-bye!" The troll got the words out in half a breath and fled to the oni's side, determinedly avoiding my stare.

It took me a few seconds to figure out what she'd been trying to say. "Er… thanks?"

But she'd already vanished into the woods. The oni was back on the other side of the door, out of earshot. My entire team had vanished.

I was alone.

I tilted my head back and inhaled. The safe paths to the common areas had been marked by occasional dabs of scented oil— peppermint for the hospital wing, clove for the bazaar, and rose for the residential areas. I couldn't remember exactly what oil had been used for the armory, but it hadn't been reapplied in years. All you had to do was follow the smell of sweat, gunpowder, and blood.

Dagny's interruption hadn't been a particularly long one, and so it didn't take me more than a few minutes to catch up with the rest of the team.

Unfortunately, that was long enough for them to think they'd missed me altogether.

"...and then the guy shot himself," Kanti said to the sayona who drove the van. "The boss freaked the fuck out."

"It's not a very pleasant thing to see," her cousin Yash muttered over his shoulder. He walked at the front of the group, carrying another tinted lantern to guide the way.

"It's not like it's the first time this has happened," Kanti continued. "But you should have seen her, Melissa. She got all broken up about it. My money says she was saving that one special."

"Gross." Melissa made a face. "Hoping to add him to her harem?"

Yash paused. "Wait. The boss has a harem?"

"Why?" Kanti laughed. "Are you wanting to join?"

"Might as well ask her," Mellissa said. "It's not like she's going to turn you down."

"Better wait your turn, though." Their giggles grated my nerves. "Did you see her with that porter back there? Three guesses where they'll be tonight."

"Don't be disgusting," Jordana muttered from a little further on. "A *troll?*"

Really? I narrowed my eyes. *Everything you've just heard, and **that's** where you draw the line?*

There was a time when I'd threaten to break someone's jaw for talking that way in front of me. But these were my subordinates. I had no right to abuse them, even if they did deserve it. Besides, I had enough trouble gathering teams who were onboard with taking living prisoners; I couldn't afford to alienate them just because they were slut-shaming, racist shitheads.

I drew back, seething. Not mauling half my team would be a lot easier if I couldn't hear the rest of their conversation.

A shadow skittered behind me, accompanied by the sounds of sucking and cracking knuckles.

"You okay, boss?" asked Terry, our resident eldritch abomination.

"There is absolutely nothing wrong with trolls," I grumbled.

"Of course not, boss. Some of my best friends are trolls." As the local gossip, Terry was personally responsible for the entire Hoarde knowing the details of my job history. They hadn't done it in malice. In fact, they probably didn't even realize at the time how much harder that bit of information could make my life. At least they had the decency to be ashamed of what they'd done, if not a little sycophantic.

"Seriously, though," I said. "Did you see Dagny's nails? Super cute."

"Oh, yes. She has this friend who paints them for her. A djinn—Hammed, have you met him? He's quite talented." This was the kind of gossip I could actually get behind.

"Yeah?" I asked. "What else has he done?"

Terry regaled me with tales of Dagny's nail art, and by the time we reached the door to my apartment, I actually felt a little bit okay.

As soon as I got inside, I shucked off my body armor and tossed it into the pile of laundry in the far corner. In short order the bullet holes would be patched, and the shattered ballistic plates would be replaced, and the armor would be etched with new protective runes, and I'd be ready to go out and kill a bunch of other brainwashed cult victims.

Dried blood had plastered my clothes to my skin. Bits of fabric had been incorporated into the healing wounds, and so when I peeled off my shirt, it brought fresh scabs with it. Underneath, the skin was raw and half-mended, but at least I wasn't bleeding anymore. I stepped into the shower and washed off the grime of the night, revealing dull stretches of words written in blue sharpie on my skin. Most of the marks were only a few hours old, but already they were faded.

My name is Arkay

Protect Rosario Hernandez

The Hoarde = mine

Mephistopheles = ~~friend enemy frenemy brainwashed~~ it's complicated

Help him anyway.

Order of . . . chel of the Sun = bad people.

DO NOT TRUST THEM.

That last instruction had been interrupted by a bullet, but the point came across nicely enough. A list of names crawled down my right leg. I read over them carefully, trying to place their faces, their voices, the way we'd met.

No blank spots so far.

My shoulders sagged in relief, and I started shampooing my hair.

Nadia had toned down the overprotective schtick over the past year, but I still wasn't allowed to leave the Felldeep without a case of Styx in my pocket. For the most part, it was a reasonable safety precaution, like an all-purpose EpiPen. Only instead of beestings and peanut butter, the syringes of Styx protected me from little things like gunshot wounds. And where a dose of epinephrine might give a person nausea and heart palpitations, Styx's major side effect was completely erasing your memory and identity.

Every time I took a dose, I risked losing part of myself. And worse, I would never even know it.

"Fuck that." I pulled myself out of the shower, toweled myself dry, and dug a sharpie out of my duffel bag and traced over the faded words.

My name is Arkay.

Protect Rosario Hernandez.

I didn't get much farther than that when I heard a knock at the door. One of the doors, anyway. Back when this was ThreeClaw's apartment, it had been meant as a central hub of the Felldeep. The walls were lined with enchanted doors that led to every essential area in the compound, plus a few to the further reaches of the Hoarde. Nadia had locked most of them when I first got here, partly to keep me contained and partly to keep me from getting hopelessly lost. As much as I appreciated her lifting my house arrest, there was no saving me from the winding hallways full of identical doors. I only managed to keep them straight thanks to the generous application of post-it notes and door hangers. Not that either of those were particularly helpful in this situation.

I yanked on a bathrobe and started the tedious process of unlocking and opening every single fucking door in rapid succession. There had to be a better way than this. A peephole or something.

On my seventh try, I opened the door to the security wing. The dim hallway beyond was blocked by a figure so tall that the top of the door only reached about halfway up his barrel chest. The black of his fur and the dark blue of his tailored uniform blended seamlessly into the shadows.

I pasted on my most chipper smile and stepped through the door. "Hey, Ives. What's shakin'?"

The minotaur glared down at me, though maybe that was just his default expression. I'd never seen him not glare at anyone. Ivan Pandev was the Hoarde's head of security and one of the most intimidating people on staff. He was only a good eight feet tall— short compared to some of the oni and trolls in the loading bays— but between his rigid posture and the arc of his horns, he seemed to tower over them just as effectively as he did over me.

Nadia did the same thing, come to think of it. I'm not sure if ThreeClaw sought out people who had a straight-edge shoved up their ass, or if that was part of the initiation to her inner circle.

"There's been an issue regarding the bodyguards assigned to Miss Hernandez," Ivan said. "It requires executive oversight."

Immediately I straightened. "Yeah?"

Ivan's nostrils flared, but his expression remained otherwise stoic. "I believe this is a matter better discussed in private." He gave me a stern look. "I believe you would feel the same."

"What kind of issue are we talking?"

"Her security detail abandoned their posts. She has not come to harm," he added, probably in response to the static electricity sparking from his horns like they were Tesla coils. Somewhere between the two sentences, all his fur started standing on end.

"That answers my first question," I said evenly. "Next question: why?"

"For coffee." He had amazing composure for a guy talking to a pissed-off dragon. "She invited them inside her home."

Just like that, my anger deflated. "Oh. That's different."

"It is not," he said. "My teams pride themselves on their discretion and discipline. The fact that she became aware of their presence in the first place is shame enough. That they left their posts on a mere whim is unforgivable."

"Or it would be, if I didn't tell them to do that," I said. "I really appreciate you keeping me updated, Ivan, but that sounds completely in line with… Ivan?"

Have you ever seen a bull having an aneurism, all twitching ears and bulging eyes? It somehow straddles the line between disturbing and hilarious.

"Why… exactly… would you tell them to abandon the woman that you assigned them to protect?"

"Well, that would be stupid," I said. "I just told them to do what she says."

"Why was she informed about the surveillance team in the first place?"

"Because conducting surveillance on her behind her back is creepy as fuck. Just because I want her safe doesn't mean she's not entitled to privacy."

He let out a sound between a bellow and a growl, as only a part-bull can make. "Is that why the indoor cameras are offline?"

"Wait, you didn't know about that?" I frowned. "Ivan, she's been moved into her new house for almost a month already. If you thought there was a legitimate problem, why did you wait until now to tell me about it?"

His shoulders shook. He looked like he would have strangled me, if he could fit his enormous hands around my neck.

"Listen, I can see you're stressed, so how about we just drop that. I'm sure you had your reasons."

"Thank you," he grated. "So much. For your *leniency*."

I smiled. "No problem."

Meph

There was too much blood on my jacket to wear without attracting attention, so I left it in a nearby dumpster. As soon as I stepped out of the shelter of the alley, I regretted the decision. A cold wind blew across my back as I trudged back to the vacant house I'd been using as a base camp. With numb hands, I fumbled the sheet of plywood that covered the broken window and I climbed inside.

It wasn't this cold before. I'd spent the winter months in Arizona, tracking Arkay's agents through a network of caverns in the Superstition Mountains, but that had gained me nothing but wasted time and a patchwork of new scars. Now intelligence told me that she was focusing her attention on the

Midwest, which meant I had to do the same, even if it meant enduring the last cold snap of a Wisconsin April.

Out of the bitter wind, I sank to my knees and threw a mildewed blanket over my shoulders, cracking a chemical hand warmer to bring some heat back into my bones.

A patch of darkness shifted in the corners of the house, and I drew my gun. "Who's there?"

The darkness detached itself and stepped into the thin sliver of light that leaked from the front window. In the shadows, all I could see were his hunched shoulders and his hawkish glare.

"Dammit, Gage," I muttered. "Ever hear of knocking?"

"Do you seriously think I'm going to stand around knocking on the front door of this shithole?"

Commander Gage was once the Grand Master of this region, before he'd backed the wrong dog in a fixed race. Just like that, a lifetime of devoted service was wiped off the slate, and he worked as little better than a clerk. The only way he could regain his position and prestige was if his failed protégé actually amounted to something worthwhile.

Unfortunately for both of us, that protégé was me.

"How'd you find me?" I asked, curling again under the blanket.

"I tracked your phone."

I frowned. I was sure I'd turned off the GPS. But that was beside the point. "What have you got for me?"

He swooped past me, blocking out the sliver of light. In the dark, his fingers dug into my blanket and dragged me close enough to smell his breath. "Listen here, you ungrateful little shit—"

"Don't pretend you're doing me any favors." I twisted out of his grip. Even in his prime, he had nothing on dragon claws. "I don't want you here any more than you want to be here. So how about you do what you came here to do?"

He'd told the High Synod that my repeated failures were an elaborate strategy to nab him a dragon. It was utter bullshit, but it was bullshit he could sell them, provided that I delivered on his promise. And when he went back to complacency in a cushy desk job, I could start my investigation in earnest.

"Word is that the Hoarde's hacked our network again," he said. "We're using top-of-the-line encryption, but they're waltzing through it like it doesn't exist."

"Tell me something I don't know."

"The account they hijacked spent an awful lot of time looking at mission plans," he continued. "This mission in particular."

He tossed me a file. It was short enough that it barely needed a paperclip to hold it together. A contract job. "You said this was the kind of job that would attract her attention."

I skimmed the details. A small number of agents, a big payoff, and a low-income area. "Yeah, this has Arkay written all over it." I glanced at the address. "If I jack a car, I can get there by morning."

"Then find yourself a fast one," Gage said. "Get over there, and get me that dragon."

Arkay

The Order of Saint Michael of the Sun was not a small organization. They had agents all over the world, and they depended on a vast network of doctors, armorers, weapons manufacturers, and mechanics to help them deal with the most basic functions of their job.

Keeping all that straight required one hell of a network. In the case of the Order, it was a digital network, like Facebook for fascists. Unlike Facebook, though, it had top notch security and a knack for identifying fake accounts, which made it annoyingly difficult to break in and find out what was trending among the Axis of Evil.

But we had an experienced hacker on staff, and even the most secure systems had a way in. Like a computer that was already logged into the system, thanks to some naughty little Orderling who didn't like typing in their password every time they turned the computer on. And thanks to that surprise raid in Jersey, they hadn't had a chance to fry the hard drive before we got to it, along with all their saved passwords.

This leads us to the other thing that vast and powerful organizations need a lot of: money.

And as much as the Order encouraged generous charitable donations and the liberty of being a tax-free religious institution, tithing wasn't enough to keep the doors open and the bullets flying. Sure, there were records of sales, most of them labeled with codewords and serial numbers, but even those didn't get the Order all the way into the black.

So they put on their best puppy faces and gave a heartfelt request for donations.

"Everybody get down! I see a single one of you move and I blow your head off, you hear me?"

By which I mean they hired a bunch of masked goons to rob a bank.

"I said get down!" repeated the guy in the Frankenstein mask. Even if we didn't hear him the first time, it wasn't like anybody had missed the gush of bullets he'd fired into the ceiling. The rest of the brute squad— one dressed like Dracula, the other like what might have been a wolfman— dragged the tellers and patrons into a panicked crowd.

I caught slight movement coming from behind the blinds in the bank manager's office. The lights were off; hopefully the robbers wouldn't think to check inside.

Frankenstein pushed me to my knees on the wheelchair ramp that led down from the entrance, close to the little desk that held all the deposit slips.

"Over there, by the railing. All of you in a line." He pinned my wrists to the bronze railing and fastened them in place with a pair of...

That couldn't be right.

Zip ties? Really? This had to be some kind of joke. But the other masks were doing the same damn thing on either side of me, and the other hostages whimpered and cowered like they were bound by tempered steel and carbon fiber, instead of tiny strips of cheap plastic. I bowed my head, mostly to keep the masked brigade from noticing the look on my face.

Seriously, you could find better restraints in a sex shop.

An unfamiliar knee nudged against my hip. I opened my eyes to glance at one of the other bank patrons, who was leaning as close to me as his zip ties would allow. "Hey, don't cry. It's gonna be alright. The police are on their way."

"No, they're not." I popped my head up. "But thank you for saying so. It's really sweet of you."

"Of course they're coming," said one of the tellers on my other side. "They're gonna save us. They have to." Her voice faltered. "What's going to happen to us if they don't?"

"You're gonna be just fine," I said. "And you're gonna get out of here in one piece." I yanked my hands down, and the zip ties snapped apart like old rubber bands. "Just stay calm and keep quiet. The guys with the guns aren't playing around."

That was a lie. This whole event was a performance, meant to be big and flashy. Then the police would come to investigate, and Order goons would pack up even more cash in evidence bags. Classic misdirection, worthy of a stage magician.

I preferred action movies.

A grunting question was tossed around behind the bank counter, and heavy footsteps moved toward us.

"Shh. Not a sound." I rolled onto my hands and knees and scurried behind the deposit desk.

"What the hell is going on back here?" Frankenstein demanded. "Who said you people could—" His head canted forward as he looked at the empty space where I had been. "What the hell? Where's the kid—" The rest of the words were muffled by my hand over his mouth.

I latched onto his back, my legs wrapping around his waist. With one hand I muffled his cries for help, and with the other I wrenched the rifle out of his grip and tossed it across the room.

Frankenstein kept thrashing against me, gnashing his teeth in an attempt to bite through my hand.

I pulled his head to one side and sank my teeth into his exposed neck. A few thousand volts of electricity later, he dropped to the ground, smelling mildly of cooked meat and ozone.

That was one goon out of the way. I could hear the other two arguing in the back. Apparently that hadn't caught their attention yet.

"Where was I?" I patted the hand of the guy who'd tried to comfort me, and my claws sliced through the zip ties on his wrists. "Right, right. There's more guys in the back, and they're armed, so it's super important that you keep quiet."

"Are you with the police?" asked one of the tellers as I cut her free.

"Not exactly— hey, you, don't touch that!" One of them started crawling toward the rifle. I darted past him and snatched it off the ground before he could grab it. "That's mine now."

The teller recoiled. "Wait, what? You're not—" She glanced at Frankenstein, still unconscious and twitching. "Are— are you robbing us?"

"Of course not," I said. "The assholes in the mask are robbing you. I'm robbing *them*. It's completely different."

"How is it different?" the teller started upright. Before she could rise to her feet, I stepped over her and pushed her back onto her ass.

"We're staying put, thank you very much. There's guys with guns out there, remember?" I smiled with all of my teeth. "Besides, what do you care if this place gets robbed? The money's insured, and you can probably argue for a pretty hefty compensation package for living through all this. So how about you worry about getting out of here, and I'll worry about the costume party?"

For some reason, that didn't seem to persuade the rest of the hostages to trust me. They stared at me like I was one of the masked weirdos. Even the blinds in the manager's office swung skeptically.

"Yeah, let's get you guys out of here. Exit's this way, folks." I marched to the door and pushed against the glass. The door didn't open. I tried again, with identical results. I tried pulling, in case I had somehow misinterpreted the sign on the door. Still nothing.

"They locked the door when they came in," the teller said. "And…" She pointed at the lock. The key had been snapped off inside the lock, jamming it shut.

"We're locked in," one of the patrons said. "We're trapped!"

"Are not," I scolded. "Just stand back, I've got this."

It was all the warning I gave before I slammed the heel of my hand into the glass.

"*Motherfucker!*"

To be fair, the glass *did* crack. As did, I suspect, a few of the bones in my wrist.

I winced and glanced back at the teller. "Bulletproof?"

She gave a quick, frightened nod. "There's another way out, but it's through there. And you need a key."

"Do we have the key?" I asked.

The masked robbers continued to argue, but their tones had changed. Apparently they'd heard my little outburst. The crowd of hostages huddled closer together.

The teller lowered her voice. "It's in my cash drawer. Third station from the right."

"Shouldn't be a problem." I vaulted over the counter. "You show me which way is out, and I'll take care of whoever's waiting for us." I pulled out a tray of cash and groped around until I found the key taped to the underside of the desk. "Got it."

I stuffed the key into one pocket, and tossed a stack of twenties into the other.

The teller gave me a disapproving look.

"What? You're insured, remember?"

"What about him?" asked one of the other hostages, peering anxiously at Frankenstein. "What if he wakes up?"

"I dunno," I said. "Tie him up or something. Sit on him. There's one of him and five of you. Figure something out." I rolled my eyes and marched down the hall, past the darkened blinds of the manager's office. "These guys are wearing Halloween masks, for crying out loud. It's not like they're—" The muzzle of a rifle swung out of the dark and pointed right between my eyes. Behind it stood the guy in the wolfman mask. "Hi there."

"What were you saying?" He advanced, and I retreated a step. "Frank?" He narrowed his eyes. "What the fuck'd you do to Frank?"

"It's a funny story, really." I could probably duck into the manager's office or dive under the counter, but either one would put hostages at risk. There had to be a third option. "See, he was coming by to check on us, and then—"

"I don't want to hear it." Wolfman's hand tightened around the stock of the rifle. His fingers tightened around the trigger.

And then he froze. Probably because the muzzle of another gun was now digging into the underside of his jaw.

"Do it, and they'll have to pry your molars out of the ceiling," came a low, rasping growl.

The gun was a .50 caliber Desert Eagle, and the man who held it was tall and muscular, but as lean and hunched as a street dog.

"Aw," I said. "Meph. You do care!"

Wolfman attempted to turn, but he didn't get a chance before Meph pistol-whipped him unconscious.

He turned on me, and his lips parted into a snarl. "Nobody gets to kill you but me."

"So you keep saying. And yet…" I ducked just in time to hear four gunshots fired inches from where my face had been. The screaming hostages were barely audible over the ringing in my ears.

Before Meph could adjust his aim, I grabbed the grip of the Deagle. The next three shot fired harmlessly into the ceiling.

"Don't be like that, Meph," I said, springing right into his personal space. "No shooting at the audience. This is a dance, not dinner theater."

He bared his teeth. "We're not dancing."

"Are you kidding? That's all we ever do anymore."

I didn't know what else a rational person could call what we did.

Not fighting, because I had no intention of hurting him.

Not sparring, because he genuinely intended to kill me.

Not brawling, because to date, only one bystander had gotten killed during our little spats, and that was because the guy had fled into oncoming traffic. Gone were the days that I flailed wildly at my opponents. Now I had daily training sessions with a woman who considered ballet a relaxing way to cool down after her workout.

Meph grabbed a combat knife out of his belt and slashed at me, and I swung away without letting go of his other hand. The single point of contact turned my dodge into a twirl, and I rammed my elbow into his gut before he could swipe at me again.

He rocked back, the breath knocked from his lungs. I stepped in again, closing my other hand around the blade of the knife. We were hand in hand. Add a bouncy little beat, and you'd think we were doing the jitterbug.

With his hands caught, he kicked at me. I sashayed past his left foot, then his right. And just to be an ass, I dropped to the floor, diving between his spread legs with both feet and dragging him along behind me. He toppled, tumbled, and rolled into a graceful arc. But he couldn't do that without letting go of the weapons.

By the time he sprang to his feet, I had the Desert Eagle leveled at his chest. He froze. Like I would actually shoot him.

"Ladies, gentlemen, et cetera," I said. "This concludes tonight's entertainment. Please follow the lovely bank staff to the nearest exit, and have a *great* day."

The hostages stared in dumbfounded silence.

I rolled my eyes and twitched the gun at them. "Any time now, folks."

Maybe it wasn't a great idea to take my eyes off Meph. In that instant, he closed the distance between us and kicked the gun out of my hand. He drew a second knife and brought it in for the kill. I barely parried the attack before he struck again.

"I'm sensing a lot of anger." I blocked a jab that was meant for my heart. "Do you want to talk about it?"

He made a sound between a bark and a roar.

"That's good. Just let it all out."

He drew yet another knife, and I had to spring away to escape a flurry of flashing steel. I rolled behind the counter, putting heavy wood between him and me.

"So let's talk sources," I said. "Who are you really mad at?"

"*You*!" One of the knives sailed past my ear and embedded itself in the wall behind me. Another knife followed right behind, and then a third.

What I wanted to know is how he got that many weapons into a bank in the first place.

"Why?" I twisted around him. "Why are you mad at me?"

"You ruined my life!" He whirled, but I darted around him, keeping at his back. "You fucked with my mind!"

"Get specific, Meph," I hissed. "If you're gonna kill me, then at least let me know what I'm dying for."

The words were a script, plagiarized from Hoarde therapists and thrown around alongside punches, knives, and miscellaneous blunt objects. He'd resisted the witty banter the first few fights, but the more we fought, the faster he answered me, and the more honest he got. Maybe one day we'd get to some actual introspection, preferably before he put a bullet between my eyes.

"You did this to me!" He spun, catching my ankle and throwing me off balance. "You made me like this!" He brought his knife down over my head. I blocked the blade, but I stumbled. I fell one way, the knife fell the other. He pinned me down with a foot to my collarbone. His knife glinted silver in the fluorescent light. "You made me like you!"

A gunshot split the air. Then a second. Then a third.

With each crack, Meph shuddered.

His contorted features smoothed into a look of blank surprise. Of shock.

"Meph?"

He staggered. Fell to one knee. His eyes were fixed on me.

I sat up. "Meph?"

Three bullet wounds bloomed across his back.

A man in a Dracula mask stood at the end of the hall, a rifle in his hand.

I grabbed the knife out of Meph's hand and sheathed myself in scales.

Dracula took aim.

So did I.

A hail of bullets ripped through dragon scales and into the soft tissue of my chest. But I'd been shot before. I knew the pain. It was familiar. It was something I could live through.

Dracula couldn't say the same thing about the knife in his throat.

I glanced back at the hostages. "The fuck are you waiting for? That's all of them. Get out of here!" I didn't spare them enough attention to make sure they obeyed.

Meph was bleeding— fuck, there was blood everywhere.

I tried to make sense of it. Bleeding meant heartbeat. Heartbeat meant alive. But this fast— was this too fast? Too much blood all at once? Had he hit a major artery?

I scrambled at the case of Styx that I was contractually obligated to carry with me at all times, and my wet fingers slipped on the zipper. I fumbled the EpiPen.

First aid had to be administered fast. With every moment I wasted, he lost that much more blood. And when he lost enough, when he hit that certain tipping point, then the brain damage would begin, and…

I stabbed the EpiPen into his back and grabbed another. Right now he needed action, not a panic attack. More importantly, he needed another dose of Styx.

I dug a second out of the case. It felt leaden and heavy. It felt wrong.

Too much Styx, and I'd erase him.

But he needed more.

But I couldn't risk an overdose. Not again. I couldn't do that again. My head was spinning. It was getting hard to think.

"Shock," I whispered aloud. "I'm in fucking *shock*."

Meph wasn't the only one who was bleeding. Better take care of that.

I jabbed the second dose into my thigh with a hiss. Then, with shaking hands, I wrenched my phone out of my pocket. It wouldn't cooperate. The touchscreen wouldn't obey my blood-soaked fingers until I wiped the phone against my pants.

"Hello?" Doctor Magbantay's voice buzzed from the speaker. "Arkay? Is that you?"

"Hey, Quinn." I couldn't tell if my voice sounded calm, or just empty. "I need your help."

Meph

I woke up staring at a blank white ceiling, and immediately I knew something was wrong. Where was the cracked paint and water damage? Where was the creeping mold that dominated the southeastern quadrant of the room? Where was the barking of the overgrown Doberman from two doors down? Where was the smell of dust and dry rot?

I noticed a pressure around my wrist. A coldness when I moved. Handcuffs. I'd been handcuffed to a hospital bed. The fact sent a surge of adrenaline through me, and I jolted out of my doze. Something rattled beside me. A black woman in medical scrubs replaced an IV bag full of clear fluid. She looked oddly familiar.

"What is that?" I asked.

"You're awake." She fixed me with an odd, tightlipped smile that didn't look anything like the real thing.

"What are you putting in me?" I asked again.

"This?" She tapped the IV grip hooked up to my arm. "Just saline solution. You lost a lot of blood."

Blood? Oh. Wait. That was right. "I got shot."

"You're lucky to be alive." She pulled out a phone and tapped out a quick text message. God, why did she look so familiar? I'd seen her before, but where?

She glanced at a digital panel beside my bed and jotted down the readings on a clipboard. It was such a slight change of expression, but suddenly I remembered.

A would-be drug lord and his oversexed little brother. A wall full of photographs taken from the unnatural angles of a hidden camera. She was from the club where Arkay used to work. Another one of the dancers.

"What the hell are you doing *here*?" I demanded.

She glanced at me from the side of her eye, but her voice remained nonchalant. "I'm checking your vitals."

I sat up. I'd suffered multiple gunshots to the back. Moving at all should have been impossible, or at least unbearable, but all I felt was sore.

This was wrong. This was all wrong.

People didn't just magically heal from traumatic injury. They died, or they were crippled for life. I shouldn't have been recovered already.

Unless…?

Ghouls were known to heal quickly. So were wendigos, and their affliction could be transmitted. Vampirism came with advanced healing, but vampires were extinct, weren't they?

Weren't they?

"What did you do to me?" I demanded. She stepped away, but I caught her wrist with my free hand before she could escape. "I said, *what did you do to me?*"

Her stare hardened, and she grabbed my middle finger, bending it back to the point of pain. "I'm doing my job. You can either let go of me, sir, or I can treat you for a broken hand."

The door swung lazily open, and a small figure sauntered in, carrying a fruit basket.

"I'd believe her if I were you," Arkay said. "Rebecca is a certified badass."

"I knew it was you." I released the nurse's hand anyway. I'd made my point.

"You know me." Arkay grinned. "Always doing dastardly things like giving people proper medical attention. If I had a mustache, I'd be twirling it right now."

The nurse took shelter behind her dragon. "Should I call security?"

"Nah, he's basically harmless. Thanks, Becky." As soon as the nurse left, Arkay deposited the oversized fruit basket on my bedside table. "I brought you a present. Lots of Vitamin C for a speedy recovery."

This had to be a joke.

I sneered. "Do you really think a fruit basket will change anything?"

"It'll do wonders toward preventing scurvy."

"I'm going to kill you." I said it slowly, annunciating each syllable with careful precision.

"You'd be a whole lot more intimidating if you weren't in a paper gown."

I bared my teeth. Couldn't she even pretend to take this seriously? "Where are my clothes?"

"In hazardous waste. Do you have any idea how much blood was on those? It's unsanitary." She waved a hand, dismissing my protests before I could form them. "Don't worry, I'll get you some new ones. Maybe something sturdier. It looks like your old stuff was getting a bit threadbare. I'm pretty sure your shirt would have dissolved if I tried bleaching the blood out."

Once again, a dragon wanted to dress me. "Fuck you."

"Well, if you're gonna be like that, then I'm gonna take your pear." She snatched a piece from the top of the basket and took an exaggerated bite out of it. Her teeth sank into the soft flesh, and its juices seeped down her chin. "No pear for you."

It went to show what a dragon's mercy was worth. First she handed you food, and in the same breath she took it away.

The joke was on her, though. I didn't even like pears.

Arkay

Raised voices echoed from inside the conference room. That was unusual; normally the people in charge kept their conflicts restricted to passive aggression and glaring before I arrived. It was especially surprising, given that the voices belonged to our two resident avatars of discipline and protocol.

"It's beyond wasteful," Ivan snarled. "It's *frivolous*. We are strained enough for resources without catering to her guests."

"He is not a guest," Nadia said. "He's a prisoner."

"He's her nemesis! He should be *dead*. Instead, I'm hearing reports that she's bringing him fruit baskets."

"She has tapped this source for information before. He is the reason we know about the Order's networks in the first place. There is no telling what other intelligence he could give us."

"And how do you intend to get it?" Ivan stomped his enormous hoof. "By plying him with produce?"

"That Arkay's methods are unusual is not news to anyone. We have to trust that she has a plan."

"A plan is what I'm afraid of," Ivan said. "First she brings him into our home, then she brings him into her bed, and then she invites the entire Order to join them. And then—"

I knocked a shave-and-a-haircut rhythm into the open door. Nadia tensed. Ivan whirled to face me.

"Look at you guys, getting all passionate about stuff." I showed off my widest, toothiest smile. "Seriously, we need to invest in a debate team."

"Arkay," Nadia started.

I didn't let her finish. "Oh, and while we're tossing around pointless discussions, I've got another one for you: Deadpool and Spider-Man: bromance or romance? Be sure to cite your sources."

"There is nothing pointless about this," Ivan said.

"I disagree," I said. "It's important for teenagers to have positive representations of same-sex relationships among their role models."

Unfortunately, Ivan couldn't take a hint. "You brought an Orderling into the Felldeep. You made no preparations. You didn't even consult me."

"I was kind of in a hurry. Besides, up until about…" I checked the timestamp on Becky's text. "Twenty minutes ago, he was unconscious."

"Every person in that hospital is in mortal danger so long as he's there."

I rolled my eyes. "He's fucking handcuffed to the bed, Ives. You put a security detail at the door. What more do you want from me?"

"I want you to get rid of him."

"And I will, as soon as he's cleared to leave by a trained medical professional. Do you have an MD after your name? Because the last time I checked, that was a no."

Ivan's nostrils flared. "I want you to end this nemesis farce. I want you to kill him."

"And you wonder why I don't consult you on this stuff." I flopped into my armchair.

"The Hoarde is getting restless," he said. "Our people don't feel safe with the likes of him in here."

"Then assure them that you have this under control."

"You're asking me to placate them with *lies*." He spat the last world like a curse. "Nothing about this situation is under my control, because you insist on cutting me out of the chain of command at every opportunity."

"Tell you what. You come up with some strategies that don't involve war crimes, and *then* we can talk about putting you back in the loop."

The floor shook under his hooves as he marched toward me. "While you campaign for humans' civil rights, the rest of us are fighting a war for the right to survive. You prioritize privacy while our people are dying in battle."

My expression didn't change an iota. "I'm out there fighting right next to them."

He snorted, and a blast of foul breath filled my nose. "You're given the safest missions and a vein full of Styx. You are coddled and spoiled, and the Hoarde is suffering the consequences." He turned and stormed away, slamming the door behind him.

I watched him go, running my tongue over my teeth.

The Hoarde was suffering. Didn't I know it.

It seemed like there wasn't a minute of the day the Hoarde *wasn't* suffering. They needed money, they needed jobs, they needed better healthcare, they needed better trade agreements, they needed a morale boost, and they all expected me to provide it for them.

Whatever happened to beating up stalkers and drug dealers? I liked doing that. I was good at it.

But the Hoarde didn't need me to be heroic, or just, or merciful. They didn't need me to be the kind of person Rosa could call her friend. They didn't even need me to be all that sane.

They needed a leader.

They needed a lifeline, even if it was a noose around my neck. And I could feel it tightening.

Nadia broke the silence. "Ivan is not entirely wrong. You should have sought his opinion on this."

"Is that what ThreeClaw would have done?" I asked wearily.

"She would," Nadia admitted. "But then, ThreeClaw would have had him made into shashlik for speaking to her that way."

I tried for a lighter tone. "I never said that option was off the table. If he keeps this up, I'm breaking out the skewers."

Nadia offered a small, thin smile. I didn't push it further. We'd maxed out her sense of humor for the day.

"He would have told me not to bring Meph in," I said.

"Maybe you should have listened to him."

I slumped into my armchair. "He was dying, Nadia. I didn't have much of a choice."

"I know." She sighed. "Maybe it would have been for the best. A mercy killing—"

"Is not an option." I didn't have the energy to be mad at Nadia for the suggestion. Unlike Ivan, she wouldn't act on it without my say-so.

"Then win us over," she said. "Persuade the Hoarde that the benefits of keeping him alive outweigh the risks. There may still be information he can give us."

"He's been kicked out of the Klan, remember?"

"And yet he has been following our movements and spoiling our plans for the past eighteen months. He's better informed than we are, at times. He has to be getting his information somewhere. Start with that. Find his source."

Meph wasn't going to talk to me.

Which wasn't to say the guy was impenetrable. He could be downright chatty when he got comfortable. But that was the problem. He had to be comfortable enough to spill his secrets, and that wasn't going to happen while we were dancing the masochism tango. And no way was I letting anybody else near him, either. He was fucked up enough without sampling any of the Hoarde's advanced interrogation techniques.

So I got creative.

He had a phone on him when I brought him in, and the poor dear hadn't changed his lock screen passwords since he'd traveled with me. He had enough sense to refer to all his contacts by nonsensical codenames, but there were little details he'd failed to account for. Somebody had activated his phone's GPS, and some finagling informed me that he'd spent a lot of time in an abandoned building not far from the bank. Maybe I'd get lucky, and he'd have a conveniently labeled serial killer collage tacked up across a wall, like in the movies. Maybe he'd have all his important information stored in tidy little documents. Maybe he kept a nifty little flash drive stowed away behind an electrical outlet that was just a little bit askew.

Though, once I saw the house, the chances of finding such an outlet seemed an awful lot less like Sherlock Holmes and an awful lot more like finding a needle in a stack of straight pins. The house was a wreck. It looked like one of those old Sears Roebuck houses that they built at the turn of the century, the kind that got ordered from a magazine and delivered in pieces by train. The rest of the houses in the neighborhood looked like they'd come out of the same catalog; they were almost identical, except for their paint jobs and their states of disrepair. Meph's was one of the nicer abandoned houses on the block, not too unlike the foreclosures Rosa and I used to huddle in when it got too cold to sleep outside. I used to spend those nights big and scaly, coiled around Rosa like she was a space heater. She'd pet my face and tell me stories that got steadily more nonsensical as she drifted off to sleep.

It was weird to feel nostalgic for bare floors, sub-zero drafts, and a complete absence of running water.

I had always favored the upper windows for my entrance, but Meph wasn't nearly as adept at climbing. I found a loose sheet of plywood over a window in the porch, and I slipped in.

The boarded-up windows left the inside wreathed in shadows, and I skulked through carefully, listening hard for the sounds of company. A pile of Goodwill blankets formed a nest in the front room, and beside it lay a pile of discarded clothes, too bloodstained or too rank with sweat to be worn in public. There was something wrong about it, an inorganic neatness to the piles. It was a display of occupancy, meant to ward off other homeless people from making camp here, and maybe give potential thieves a satisfying place to search before they moved on. But this wasn't where Meph slept. There were too few vantage points, and too many opportunities for ambush.

I climbed the stairs carefully, so as not to disturb the quiet. Meph had picked out a room along the corner and covered both windows with heavy blankets to insulate against the cold. The air was stuffy, oversaturated with blood and body odor and gun oil. He kept weapons in here, and supplies to take care of them, but they were nowhere in sight. The entire room was bare, aside from a meticulously rolled sleeping bag and a duffel full of clean clothes. It would have been easy to miss them in the dark, if I wasn't looking for them. It would also have been easy to miss the body-sized patch of floor that had been worn free of dust. He'd made a habit of sleeping in front of the closet, so it would be impossible to open the door without waking him.

Classic Meph.

The closet itself was empty, except for an attic access. And just inside the attic...

"Jackpot," I muttered, dragging down a sports bag. Inside lay an assault rifle and enough ammunition to stock a gun store. And more importantly, notebooks. More than a dozen of them, ratty and thick from overuse, their pages smeared and waterlogged and stained by dirty hands. If this was a movie, I would have flipped open to a random page and found shocking details of something important. Instead I found abbreviated names and incomplete addresses and annotations written in an unintelligible shorthand. The only part I could make sense of were the doodles in the margins.

It was about time he got a hobby that didn't involve shooting people.

The early books contained mostly drawings of eyes and awkward anatomical studies. But as the books progressed, so did his skill level. As the sketches became more detailed and recognizable, I realized he had a favorite subject.

He was drawing me, over and over again. Sometimes it was just my face, sometimes my entire body. In several of the drawings I was maimed or dead; in others, I was contorted in poses that wouldn't have looked out of place at a strip club; in some, I couldn't tell if I was meant to be sexy or suffering.

I'd been hoping for a serial killer vibe. I just hadn't expected one like this.

I stepped into the impenetrable dark of the Felldeep and kicked the door shut behind me. The huge sports bag hung from a strap across my chest, and the ammo inside rattled against my ass with every step I took.

With as much noise as I was making, it didn't take long for the groundskeeper to notice my arrival. Within a few minutes, a series of bone-shattering pops and cracks faded into an insectoid skittering.

"Hey, boss." I got Terry's voice in stereo as they scurried around me. "Ooh, who do you have there? Is it another—" They paused, and then said carefully, "Another prisoner?"

I recognized the odd silence of Terry's hesitation. Usually I heard it when they started telling me a joke before remembering that I was the punchline.

"It's a duffel bag, not a body bag." I couldn't blame them for the mistake. The duffel was huge enough that I could have fit inside it without too much effort. "Do I want to know what they're calling prisoners these days?"

"I don't know," Terry admitted. "I suppose it depends."

"Depends on what?"

"What's a piñata?"

The hairs on the back of my neck prickled. "What?"

"That's the word they kept using when I asked, anyway. Which reminds me, they're throwing a party in the receiving chamber. I heard Kanti talking about it, so I don't know if you got an invitation or not. I know you two don't really get along."

"A party," I repeated slowly.

"It's not like one of those crazy illegal raves or anything." Terry's sigh would have sounded a lot more wistful if it hadn't come out of all those orifices. "Ivan's going too, so it's all perfectly legitimate. I'm sure they'll clean it up after they're done."

But Ivan didn't attend parties. He was the antithesis of a party animal.

"Terry?" I asked slowly. "What kind of shindig are we talking here?"

Their blinking eyes glittered in the dark. "Didn't I tell you? A piñata party."

Meph

Half a dozen monsters dragged me from the hospital room. By the time we left the fluorescent halls of the hospital, they numbered more than twenty, and the group kept growing. Down another hallway and through a door, I found myself in the kind of impenetrable darkness that had become the substance of my nightmares.

I thought I could take advantage of the dark. I thought I could lose myself in the crowd long enough to make a break for it.

I thought wrong. I didn't get more than five feet before I was caught. After that, my escorts elected to drag me by my leg. The fact that my ankle wasn't meant to bend that way didn't bother them in the slightest. They only let me get on my feet in order to march me up a goddamned spiral staircase, and then across an elevated walkway of some kind.

White-hot pain stabbed through my leg with every step I took. The ankle might be broken, but the clawed hands on my back shoved me forward. The walkway shuddered beneath me. When I veered too far to one side, my arm brushed a metallic railing and the edge of my foot hovered over empty space. Another violent shove sent me stumbling forward, but this time, my feet hit solid stone. Another push forced me to keep going, and another. I was too busy trying to keep upright to notice the receding darkness until all at once it was gone, and the mob poured into one of the circles of Hell.

Dragons. Everywhere, dragons. The one nearest to me was made of white marble, though it seemed almost alive under the shimmering blue light that flooded the room. Another dragon was cast from steel; another from bronze. They transformed into walkways and twisted into helixes. They stretched high and looped overhead, so densely intertwined that I couldn't see the borders of the room. Every direction I looked, there were more and more *dragons*.

Living monsters crowded the floor and climbed onto the statues for a closer look. Some of them reached out to help shove me along as I was marched up a scale-lined walkway. Some shrieked and howled, lost in the frenzy of an angry mob. Some stared, transfixed by fascinated pity.

Stop this, I pleaded silently, trying to catch their eyes. *Somebody, stop this.*

Nobody did.

I was dragged before the face of a steel dragon. It was frozen mid-roar, its mouth gaping wide as if to swallow me whole.

A rope hung from its antlers. One end was tied into a familiar loop.

The room swam. The statues seemed to come alive, writhing closer at the corners of my vision. I was going to be sick. I was going to pass out.

I was going to die.

The thought cut through my panic with a cold clarity.

These monsters were going to kill me. For all my struggles, for all my fighting, I would die handcuffed and helpless. I would swing at the whim of a mob.

A minotaur caught the rope in its enormous hands and widened the loop to fit around my head. I didn't watch. My attention was fixed on one of the faces in the crowd. It was a kid, a boy who looked even younger than me, with dark curly hair and a rakshasa's tusks in his open mouth. He was shouting, scrambling to break through the mob, but other arms dragged him back. His eyes, wide with horror, never turned away from my face.

He was trying to help. Failing miserably, but at least he was trying.

That had to mean something, right?

The noose was forced over my head and pulled tight around my throat. The minotaur was bellowing something unintelligible to the crowd. There were cheers. There were screams.

The boy's expression changed. His mouth was still agape, but it was with a different kind of shock. His stare fell to the empty air below my feet. To the place where I would hang.

The minotaur's hands caught around my shoulders and gave me one last push. I couldn't have resisted if I'd tried. I tipped forward.

Overbalanced.

Fell.

For an instant I arced through the air, waiting for gravity to drive me down. But before it could fully commit to that downward plunge, something hit me from behind, knocking the wind from my lungs.

I hung.

Not from the noose, but from a vice grip around my waist. It squeezed me hard, pinning my arms tight against my chest, but it held me just high enough to keep the rope loose around my throat.

Legs, I realized. Thin, muscular calves crossed under my sternum. Powerful thighs gripped me as tightly as they had once held a metal pole. Wiry arms stretched overhead, tendons straining as they clung to the sculpted arc of a dragon's jaw.

One of the hands slipped free, and we swung wildly to one side. The rope constricted, choking off my scream.

"Dammit, Meph," Arkay hissed from behind my ear. "Stop wriggling. This is fucking hard."

Other people were shouting now. The chamber echoed with howls of outrage and fury.

Arkay swiped at the rope, slicing through it with claws. The noose tightened around my neck before she pulled it loose, and finally I could breathe again.

"I'm gonna drop you now," she said.

"You're *what*?"

"Try to land on your feet."

That was all the warning I got before I plunged the last fifteen feet to the crowd below. My legs buckled as soon as I hit the ground, and I crumpled to my knees. Arkay landed far more gracefully beside me.

A wendigo rushed at me, its mouth stretched wide in a ravenous howl before an uppercut snapped its jaws shut. Arkay drove her knee into the creature's gut, and it collapsed with a wheeze.

"What are you waiting for?" she demanded. "Get up. We need to go."

"Working on it." I struggled to get my feet back under me, but having my hands cuffed behind my back didn't exactly improve my balance.

"For the love of..." Arkay knocked back an impundulu with a vicious roundhouse kick, then fell back. She grabbed my handcuffs and pulled. The metal hinge squealed and whined as it strained apart, but it was slow. Around us, the crowd was roiling, some scrambling to escape while others rushed closer. A fiery-eyed rakshasa lunged over the fleeing bodies, a knife in her hand.

"Hurry!" I yelped.

"I've almost..." My wrists were wrenched violently apart as the handcuffs separated. Arkay let out the beginnings of a whoop, but the sound collapsed into a gasp as the rakshasa tackled her. The knife flashed between them as they rolled across the floor, glinting first silver, then red. I tried to scramble upright, but collapsed again when weight bore down on my ankle.

God fucking dammit!

I gathered my good leg beneath me and lunged at the fighters. I couldn't get far, but I caught the rakshasa's legs in my arms. She kicked like a demon, but I refused to let go, clamping on tight until I felt the convulsions of an electric shock.

"Thanks," Arkay said, once she'd dislodged her teeth from the rakshasa's arm. Before she could expand on the thought, another rakshasa closed in.

I tensed. If I was fast, I could grab his feet out from under him. After that a few good punches to the kidneys…

But he extended a hand to help Arkay up. "You okay, boss?"

He was the boy who watched me hang.

"Hey, Yash." Arkay accepted his hand and swung herself to her feet. "I take it you're not with the Batshit Brigade?"

He shook his head, but his reply was drowned out by the crack of enormous hooves on the stone floor. The minotaur had leaped from the walkway overhead and landed beside us. Its bulk arched forward, its teeth bared. Its muscles rippled as it stormed toward us with enormous strides.

It let out guttural bellow, and Arkay shrank back against the rakshasa boy in an attitude almost like fear.

But I'd seen Arkay afraid, and it didn't look like that. She was muttering something to him, and tilted her head up at one of the statues.

A plan, then. An ambush?

Before I could guess the details, the minotaur lunged with another deafening roar. Arkay leaped to one side, and the rakshasa boy dove for me.

"Get up," he hissed, then grabbed me by the shoulder and pulled me upright.

My injured leg spasmed as my foot hit the ground, but the boy dragged me along before I had the chance to fall. In the next stride he was under my arm and supporting my weight.

"*I'm* the traitor?" Arkay snarled, and instinctively I turned my head to look. She had the minotaur by its horns, and forced its gaze away from our escape. "I'm not the one who invaded a *hospital*. I'm not the one who organized a fucking *lynch mob*. I'm not—" The accusation turned into a yelp as the minotaur tossed its head. Arkay had the strength to hold on, but she didn't have the weight to keep it down. Instead, she whipped wildly over the beast's head and crashed against its back. It tried to throw her again, but this time she twisted and wrapped her legs around its neck.

"Climb," the rakshasa said, and pulled me vertical. A steel dragon statue rose out of the floor in a serpentine arc, its mane spread like something between a ladder and a staircase. The rakshasa shoved me up the first few feet, but turned abruptly away. An incubus was rushing after us with a broken bottle. It managed two swipes before the rakshasa swept its feet out from underneath it. A stonecoat charged at us from the other side. It lunged, but I swung over, catching its neck between my legs and yanking it hard enough to smack its scaly head against the steel sides of the dragon. The stonecoat faltered, dazed, and I detached myself just enough to grab it by the back of the head and drive it into the steel again, and then again. My fist wouldn't do anything against the beast's armor, but with enough blunt force I could crush its goddamned skull.

My ankle twisted sharply to the side, and the world went white in a flash of agony. The stonecoat fell out of my grip as I howled in pain.

The rakshasa boy let go of my foot and started climbing.

"Keep going." Again he grabbed me by the shoulder and dragged me after him, and I had no choice but to follow.

"Jesus Christ!" I hissed once we were out of reach of the tallest monsters. "Who's side are you on?"

The rakshasa bared his teeth. "You're a genocidal maniac. Whose side do you think I'm on?" He hauled himself into the antlers of the statue and opened a panel in the ceiling. A trap door. A trap? "Now get up here!"

I recoiled, suddenly wary. "If you're not helping me, then what are you doing?"

"Hopefully, the right thing." He climbed into the trap door and extended his arm to me. "You may be an utter shitstain, but that down there? Nobody deserves that. Not even you. Now get up here before *they* do!"

More monsters were climbing the dragon's back. They'd be on us in seconds. Even if I had the higher ground, I couldn't fight them all.

I grabbed his hand and let him help me up.

As soon as I crossed through to the other side, he slammed the trap door shut and threw his weight on top of it. "Find me something sharp. A knife, a screwdriver, a pen—hurry!" The door rattled from the other side.

I looked around warily. I wasn't sure exactly what I'd expected, but this wasn't it. We'd escaped into the living room of an apartment, a few feet away from a big-screen TV. I grabbed a nail clipper off the coffee table and tossed it at the rakshasa. "Will that work?"

He twisted out the nail file and carved rough lines into the frame of the door. When he scraped the last line into the wood, the pounding of fists stopped. He held his breath and listened, and I did the same.

The only sound came from the humming of the refrigerator.

Slowly he wrapped his hand around the door handle and pulled it open. Where there'd once been a gaping hole, now there was only a square of carpet.

He let out a long breath. "We should be safe now."

"What about those?" I pointed at the row of doors that occupied nearly every inch of the apartment's walls. They were packed too closely to be anything but magical. Who knew where they led?

The boy climbed to his feet and locked them, each in turn. "Okay. *Now* we're safe."

Warily, I hoisted myself into the leather couch. "Now what?"

He crossed into the kitchen and sank into the chair of a dinette set. He sighed. "Now we wait."

I wished he hadn't said that.

I was still wired from a near-death experience. Every muffled noise that leaked through the doors sounded like the prelude to an angry mob. I wanted to pace the floor, but my ankle couldn't take any more abuse. As the adrenaline slowly leeched out of my system, the pain shooting up my leg became harder to ignore. It washed over me in waves, interspersed with a mounting exhaustion. It was the wrong mindset to be in right now. There could be danger at any corner. The last thing I needed was to be crippled and exhausted when the enemy arrived.

I tried at conversation. "So were you expecting a fight, or are you just paranoid?"

The rakshasa boy frowned. "What?"

"You're wearing body armor under your clothes."

For a moment he continued to look puzzled, and then clarity dawned on him. He rolled his eyes. "It's a binder, dumbass."

"Oh."

We fell back into awkward silence.

It seemed like hours passed, but according to the clock on the far wall, it was only forty minutes before something rapped a stuttering rhythm into one of the doors.

Tap ta-tap. Tap ta-tap.

I jumped. "What's that?"

Tap ta-tap. Tap ta-tap.

The rakshasa rose from his chair. "It's Spider-Man."

That must have meant something to him, because he unlatched the door and stepped aside.

Arkay stood in the doorway, and she took the invitation to enter. "Oh good, you made it." She tossed a canvas bag into the corner. Her side was exposed, the torn shirt hanging loose around a bloodstained gash. The fabric was perforated around more than a dozen smaller cuts, some of them still bleeding.

The rakshasa boy started forward. "Boss?"

She smiled, but it was a strained, weary expression. "Thanks for your help back there, Yash."

He hesitated. "Is everything…?"

"The cavalry finally arrived." She trudged to the kitchen and grabbed a can from the fridge. "You want a drink?" When the boy shook his head, she glanced at me. "What about you, Meph? Do you still drink Coke?"

I stared at her, dumbstruck.

She shrugged and emptied the soda into a glass, adding a generous splash of rum. "Nadia's enacting martial law until we get this shit with Ivan sorted out. She'd appreciate your help keeping the peace, if you're feeling up to it." She grabbed a set of kitchen shears from a knife block.

He bit his lip. "Boss, back in the—"

"The lynch mob?"

"That. I thought I saw…" He squirmed. "With the knife. Was that… Kanti?"

Arkay sighed. "Yeah." When his shoulders sagged, she added, "You can get that look off your face, Yash. Her ass is grass, but I'm not going to kill her or anything."

"Okay," he said quietly. And again, louder, "Okay. Thank you, boss." And he disappeared through the door.

Arkay worked in silence at the counter for a few moments, then turned again to me. "You sure you don't want something?"

When I said nothing, she plopped down on the armchair beside me, carrying with her a glass and a small sheet of aluminum that she'd liberated from the Coke can.

"Lemme see your hands," she said after a few long gulps of her drink. "Come on. I've had those things on me before. They're no fun."

This was a trick. She was trying to lure me into obedience.

"Gimme." This time she reached out and took my wrist. The movement was slow enough that I could have escaped her reach, but I didn't. I was too exhausted to fight anymore.

As she shimmed open the handcuffs, the fake cheer melted off her face. In its stead was a grim, weary silence. If I turned my hand just a little, I could touch her knee. I could let her know that things were going to be okay. But that was the trauma talking. Just trauma, and the lingering remains of her influence. I kept my hands balled into fists until she dropped them.

"Bathroom's over there," she said. "Go ahead and get cleaned up, if you want. You'll feel better once you soak that ankle."

I was bloody and dirty from being dragged by the mob, but the thought of being so exposed so close to Arkay was even more uncomfortable.

I kept my voice even. "You know your way around the kid's apartment pretty well, don't you?"

"It's not his place." She emptied her glass. "It's mine."

That couldn't be right. I took in my surroundings again. The furniture was practical, if somewhat dated. There were no bright colors, no cute trinkets, no video games. Not even a mess, aside from a pile of dirty laundry in the far corner. I'd seen barracks on inspection day that had more personality.

She climbed to her feet and stretched. "If you're not calling dibs on the first shower, I totally am." And just like that, she vanished into what I could only assume was the bathroom, and I was left alone.

Alone and unguarded.

The doors were locked, but only from this side. I could escape right now if I wanted to. I'd have to hobble, but I could probably get decently far before she found me. Then again, I'd be escaping into unknown territory full of hostile monsters. For all her twisted machinations, Arkay had a vested interest in keeping me alive.

I could take advantage of that. I could stay here and let her think I was hers again. I could sleep on her bed like a loyal pet, and then...

It didn't even have to be right away. I could listen in on all her secrets, learn all the weaknesses of the Hoarde. It would take some time, of course, before I could reasonably expect her to trust me. I'd have to eliminate all doubt.

It wouldn't be that hard, really. She already wanted me on her side.

Unless that was what she wanted me to think. Unless this was all a trap, meant to lure me into faking trust until it was real. It was the kind of thing the Contessa would do. But Arkay wasn't the Contessa. But they were both dragons.

And dragons always lie.

My skin was starting to crawl. Sweat beaded on my forehead and moistened my hands.

What if this was a trap? What if everything that had just happened to me was an elaborate plot? No, that didn't make sense— did it?

I leaned on the couch and hobbled toward the row of doors.

God, the walls were lined with doors. Who knew what was waiting behind them all? How many of these passages were hiding armed guards and angry mobs? How many led to torture chambers and prison cells?

My lungs felt suddenly too small in my ribcage. I could feel the noose back around my throat, tightening, cutting off all air. Something roared in my ears—blood? The mob?

The room was spinning. The doors were spiraling around me.

I needed to get out.

"Meph?"

I turned so fast that I lost my footing and fell back against the nearest door. Arkay stood at the edge of the room, dressed in an outfit more fitting for yoga than for combat. But clothing meant little to a dragon. She was as dangerous naked as she was in Kevlar.

"You do know that door leads to the cafeteria, right?" Her voice didn't sound quite right anymore. It was too loud, but it seemed to come from far away.

A stabbing pain arced through me as my ankle skidded across the floor. When I looked up, Arkay was on her knees, looming over me.

"Meph, breathe," she said. "You're okay. Nobody's gonna hurt you."

It was a lie. A goddamned lie. There were mobs and monsters out there, and they wanted to kill me, and I was here alone with a dragon, *and dragons always lie.*

"Meph, look at me. You're having a panic attack. You need to breathe." She leaned closer, filling my vision. A pressure closed on my palm, gentle but solid. Inescapable.

I hissed in a breath and yanked my hand away from hers.

"Shit," she muttered. "Okay, bad touch. Lemme just…"

Oh God. I'd pissed her off. She was going to lock me away and starve me and *Jesus Christ I couldn't breathe!*

Something pressed into my hand again. A rod?

A pen. Paper crinkled as it landed on my lap.

"Meph, listen to me now." Arkay's voice seemed to come from everywhere at once, but she stood at the far corner of the room. "You're going to pick up that pencil and you're going to draw me something. Can you do that, Meph?"

What?

"Nod if you can do that."

I gave a faint jerk of my head. Yes, I could do that. My fingers curled around the pen, and I tightened my grip on the paper.

"Good. You see that lamp in the corner? Draw me that lamp."

My hands shook, but I obeyed. My attention zeroed in on the shape, the color, the angle of the light. I was replicating exactly what I saw on the paper. Breathing came easier as the rest of the world faded into the backdrop. In increments my pulse slowed to something less alarming. The lamp was finished, and other images joined it on the crumpled paper. I barely saw them, lost in the flow of the drawing.

A glimmer of light caught my eye, and I looked up. A glass of water had been set down just out of my reach. Beside it sat a plate of microwaved pizza bites. After a few moments of mute staring, I brought the glass to my lips. The water was clean and lacked any chemical aftertaste, and it was mercifully uncarbonated.

"I figure you might be hungry," Arkay said. She sat cross-legged on the floor in the far corner. After an instant's eye contact, her head bowed over her phone. "You don't have to eat, though. I know some people get nauseous when they get like that."

I forced my eyes down. She wasn't supposed to see that. It wasn't supposed to happen at all. Goddamn it, why did this keep happening to me?

"There's other food in the kitchen, if you want something else," she added. "And there's a pillow and some blankets on the couch."

"You expect me to sleep on your couch?" My throat was raw from hyperventilating.

She gave an exaggerated shrug. "Well, there's always the bed, but you better be prepared to share." The attempt at comedy only lasted a moment. "Seriously, though, the bathroom's big enough to sleep in, if you prefer something with a lock."

"You could still break in," I said warily.

"Yeah, but it'd be more than loud enough for you to wake up and get some countermeasures together, so there's that. Personally, though, I think the couch is more comfortable." She climbed to her feet and tucked her phone into her pocket. "But I'll leave the decision making to you. It's not a super great idea to go out while the Hoarde is under lockdown, but whatever. I, for one, am going to bed."

I did wind up sleeping in the bathroom that night, or as close to sleeping as I could get while ten feet away from a dragon, with my head pressed against a pillow that smelled overwhelmingly of her shampoo.

The bathroom door was tightly locked, but I wondered if she'd locked her own door. Back when we'd travelled together, she forgot to lock up all the time. It was a dragon's overconfidence, too secure in her own power to worry about intruders.

Would she wake if I entered? And if not, what would it take to wake her? A flick of a light switch? A knife to her chest? Would she notice if I pulled the covers back and slipped in beside her?

I knew the answer from experience. She would mumble groggily and then curl up tight against me, like the bed wasn't warm enough without me in it. Like that was where I belonged.

I missed that feeling. I missed the warmth and the softness. I missed the safety of another body so near mine. I missed having her trust.

But that was pointless. All her warmth had been an illusion. That safety was a lie. If she ever trusted me, it was as her pet.

I couldn't be her pet anymore, even if I wanted to.

I had my own purpose now. I had to root out the corruption from the heart of the Order. But to do that, I'd need to get back in first.

And for that I would need a dragon.

I gave up on sleep and got up, disabling the traps I'd set on the bathroom door.

The kitchen was illuminated by the glow of the microwave clock. Six-thirty, it read. I assumed it meant AM, but it was impossible to tell in this hole in the ground.

Regardless, Arkay had gone to bed a little after twelve, and she wasn't an early riser.

The wooden block on the counter provided me with a chef knife with a decent edge. It would give me a clean cut. It would be quick.

I stalked down the hallway to her bedroom door. I could do this. It didn't matter that I'd hesitated before. I could do this. I had to do this.

I took a deep breath and opened the door, careful not to allow it so much as a squeak. Silently I crept to the edge of the bed and stared at the murky shadows of the sheets. I'd get a chance to administer a single cut. Better make it count.

But as my eyes adjusted to the near-pitch dark, I realized the flaw in my plan.

The sheets were messy, but uninhabited.

The bed was empty.

Arkay was gone.

Arkay

I sat at the edge of my armchair, my elbows braced on my knees, my head bowed. The conference table before me was entirely buried under papers. Every single one was a letter of resignation.

It was a premeditated display. An act of protest. It was probably meant to rile me up, but I didn't have the energy to feel mad.

I didn't have the energy to feel much of anything anymore.

The conference room door shut with a deliberate click. It was meant as a courtesy. Nadia's posture told me that she wanted to slam the door off its hinges.

"Have you actually slept?" I asked.

"I'll sleep when we're not in a crisis." If she got any more tense, her shoulder blades were going to overlap. "We've caught looters in the bazaar and the residential wing. Terry's helping two of my teams keep guard, but the Forest is saturated right now. We physically cannot stop them all from leaving."

"Then don't." I said. "Find out who the ringleaders were and focus on them. The rest don't matter."

"The rest could dramatically undermine public confidence in the Hoarde," Nadia snapped.

"You said it yourself, Nadia," I said. "You can't catch them all. Trying is only going to exhaust your teams. So just... don't." Nadia's strike teams were loyal— to Nadia, at least. Even Kanti had switched sides when her Fext had arrived. She hadn't hesitated to take a swing at me before that, though.

I didn't know why I expected otherwise.

I massaged my temples. "Any luck snagging Ivan?"

"I have all my soldiers on the lookout, but we aren't going to find him." She slumped into a chair at my right hand. "He was practically born in the Felldeep. He knows this place better than anyone."

"Maybe have somebody keep an eye on Twitter. The guy's eight feet tall, even without the giant-ass horns. It's not like he can just put on a trench coat and blend in."

"Not unless his transportation was already arranged for."

Her tone was dark enough that I lifted my head.

"You have something in mind?"

She scowled. "The Contessa wasn't shy about propositioning me for a job. I wouldn't put it past her to extend an offer to him, too."

"Fuck," I muttered. Ivan would be a sweet prize for her, too. As head of security, he'd had access to most of the Hoarde's top-tier information. Just like that, all our secrets were an open book to the Contessa. "We need to have revoke his clearance to our servers and change our passwords. We need to lock him out."

"Already done," Nadia said wearily.

Of course it was. Because Nadia had this handled. She'd always had this handled.

"How many people left with him?" I asked.

"It's hard to get a solid number when we're so short staffed."

"Guess." My tone left no room for argument.

"Like I said, we don't know. It could be as little as ten percent. It could be as much as a third."

A third of the Hoarde. Fuck.

I meant to crack a joke. Maybe something along the lines of 'You know you're having a bad day when getting decimated is the optimistic option'.

Instead, what came out was, "Is this the part where you say 'I told you so'?"

Nadia was silent.

"Because you did," I continued. "Multiple times, and on multiple subjects. If you want gloating rights, now would be the time to cash in."

"Arkay," she said softly. "This isn't your fault."

She really didn't get it, did she?

"Fine, pass up a golden opportunity." I forced lightness into my tone, but it didn't sound natural, even to me. "I'm guessing fixing this isn't an option. So how do we stop the hemorrhage? Do I need to go back to living under a rock?"

She shook her head. "Going completely off-radar would make it look like you're running from the problem. You can't afford to look weak right now. They need to see you acting like a dragon."

I stared blankly at her. I wasn't another one of her doppelgangers pretending to be ThreeClaw. "I'm never *not* acting like a dragon. I don't know how to be anything else."

Hell, if they wanted me to act any more *draconic*, I'd be torching this ridiculous hole in the ground and go back to doing a job I was actually good at with people who actually liked me.

"They need to see you taking charge," she corrected. "They need to believe you know what you're doing."

Except they didn't want me doing any of the things I actually knew how to do. They wanted a dragon, but without the libido or territorial instincts or trademark narcissism that all dragons were born with. They wanted a leader, but not one with a past or personal attachments. They wanted perfection, constant and natural and effortlessly performed.

Fuck, I was tired.

I climbed to my feet. Meph was still too unstable to talk to me, but he had a metric shit ton of notebooks. One of them was bound to have something important in it.

"Where are you going?" she asked.

"To figure out what I'm doing."

Meph

I woke up freezing. Cold stone leeched the heat out of my body, and even colder wind scraped across my side. The sky overhead was a stormy winter gray, only a few shades darker than the pale stone underneath me. I was lying on a wide octagon, hemmed in with ledges on every side. Beyond lay the distant expanse of a highway. I was on a tower of some kind.

But that didn't make sense. The last thing I remembered, I'd been in Arkay's apartment. Then a door had opened, and I'd seen a pair of striking blue eyes.

Footsteps moved across the tower toward me, soft but unmistakable. When I turned, I found myself cornered by a pair of rakshasa. I recognized the boy who'd helped me escape the mob, but he made no move to help as a tall blond woman sauntered toward me.

I'd only seen her in pictures, her features blurred and grainy from shitty security feeds, but I recognized her instantly. The dragon's first lieutenant. The immortal Fext. I would have been fascinated, but my attention was focused on the revolver in her hand.

"Good morning, Mephistopheles." She pointed the muzzle between my eyes. "I have some questions for you. I recommend you answer quickly."

I scrambled to my feet, belatedly noticing the lack of pain coming from my bad leg. The revolver followed me without hesitation.

"Question the first: what is the building behind you?" She took several purposeful steps forward.

I spared only a glance over my shoulder. The horizon was mostly an expanse of water. Before that lay a stark, beachless coastline. "Which one?"

The gun went off, close enough that its report left my ears ringing. It missed my face, but only by a few inches.

"Which one?" I repeated. "There's an entire fucking city down there, and—"

A powerful hand grabbed me by the chin and turned my head. The woman pressed close against my back, pinning my arms to my side as she held me still, forcing me to look at a particular stretch of the shore. The pistol pressed into the corner of my jaw.

"That one," she said into my ear.

I didn't have any choice but to stare at the line of sharp angles and twisted architecture that made up the industrial sector of the city. Several large, nearly-windowless buildings huddled close together, surrounded by grassless grounds and barbed-wire fences.

Her accent grew more pronounced. "What is it?"

I swallowed, and my Adam's apple pressed painfully into a ring of cold steel. "It's a factory. A steel mill, I think."

"Do you recognize it, then?"

"It looks like another factory I've been to. But no. I've never seen this one in my life."

"Are you sure about that?" Her hand tightened on my jaw. I had to fight her grip to give my confirmation. She leaned close, and her breath puffed against my ear. "You're lying."

I didn't get a chance to plead my case before a violent shove against my back sent me sprawling. I stumbled to the edge of the tower. Fext grabbed me by the collar and yanked me further out, until my shoulders hung over empty air.

"Jesus Christ!" I yelped as she pushed down on my shoulders. My hips left the ground as my balance shifted over the ledge, and I grabbed onto her. I would have at least a hundred feet to fall if she decided to let go.

"Think carefully about your answers."

"I don't know anything!" I shouted.

"That address was marked in your personal notes as an Order stronghold. I want you to tell me everything you know about it."

I stared, wide-eyed. My notebooks. She knew about my notebooks. But why did that even matter? Most of the information there was about corruption within the Order, not anything the Hoarde would care about.

"I don't know!" I kicked at the stone, trying to drag myself back onto solid rock.

"What is it?"

"I swear, I don't fucking know! Gage gave me addresses sometimes," I said. "Safehouses. Boltholes. Drop-off points."

"Drop-off for what?" Fext pressed down ever so slightly. Any more, and I'd fall.

"For Arkay," I said at last. "If I caught her, I was supposed to bring her there." Her body, specifically, but this wasn't the right time to bring up that particular detail.

"Why?"

"Because they wanted proof," I said. "They weren't just going to believe me if I said so."

"What's inside?"

"I don't know. I don't know!" I could feel my center of gravity shifting. "For the love of God, *I don't know!*"

She leaned in close. "I actually believe you." When she pulled away, she yanked me back from the ledge, leaving me gasping on the floor. "I have no further use for you. Get out of my sight before I change my mind."

Arkay

"Nadia!"

I burst into conference room. She hadn't been in the training hall and she hadn't been in the bazaar and she hadn't been in her room and if I didn't find her I was going to go postal.

But there she was, hunched over a mountain of charts and forms and talking on the phone.

Right then, I didn't care.

"Nadia?" I tried to clamp down on my panic. I couldn't ask for help if I went non-verbal. "Nadia, I need your help. Like, yesterday."

She lowered the phone, courteous enough not to look annoyed with the interruption.

"Meph is gone." Fucking hell, if something happened to him— if Kanti or somebody got to him— "He was in my room this morning, but now he's gone, and there's no sign of a struggle, and *I need to find him.*"

"Calm down," she said, like it was that easy. Like I could just shut it off on my own like that. I wanted to throttle her, but I kept my hands at my sides. "I'm the one who took Meph from your room."

"Then where is he?" I shrieked.

"If he's smart, he's halfway to Chicago by now." She held my gaze, utterly steady while I reeled. "I questioned him and I let him go. Yash and Kanti will have spread the word by morning. And you running around in a panic will corroborate the fact that you had nothing to do with his release."

"Why?" I asked. "He was hurt. He was all kinds of messed up, Nadia. And it's fucking April. And—"

"And he's a distraction," she said. "The Hoarde needs its dragon. We need you to be unflinching and focused and strong. But you cannot do that if you are living in fear for his life. And he will never be safe here. His best chance at survival is out there, where the majority of people don't intend to kill him."

Fury and anxiety drained away, leaving me empty and exhausted.

"I could protect him." The words tasted like ash in my mouth. Nadia didn't bother pointing out the lie.

"I dosed him with Styx and stuffed his pockets with money while he was unconscious," she said.

I slumped against the doorway.

"That's smart," I said dully. And I meant it. Nadia was good at this sort of thing. Even if it did hurt to have him gone again. I sat down. "Okay, then. Let's get back to business."

The building was meant to look like a refinery, hidden in what had once been a major city in the steel belt. Even now when the city's economy had collapsed and most of the buildings in the area lay abandoned, it still blended in almost seamlessly. Only the little details gave it away.

Based on heat signatures, the walls were reinforced a few times over, likely concrete and cinderblock. What few windows were needed for ventilation were close to the ceiling, impossibly narrow, and fitted with iron bars. The grounds were rocky and covered in an asphalt mulch, but when the light was just right, hidden coils of razor wire glinted from among the rubble. Anybody who tried to cross the grounds on foot would either have to pick their way through an inch at a time, or else risk turning their legs into hamburger. After that, the barbed wire fence that surrounded the property was more of a courtesy than anything. The only road to the factory split off, one branch pooling into a small parking lot, the other leading to the docking bay of a massive warehouse. It was a relatively straight shot— assuming, of course, that you survived the sniper nests.

Pillboxes, guard houses and turrets would be too obvious in a town like this, but lost jobs and shitty industry meant that a third of the houses in the city were left to rot. Half a dozen of those empty buildings had been purchased and repurposed as security outposts. The only thing that marked them as unusual were the open windows on the upper floors, and the occasional glint of sunlight on a scope. The sniper nests were each within clear visible range of one another; the only way to take down any one of them was to take down all of them simultaneously.

We dedicated three strike teams to the task, each one split between two nests, each one working with the kind of perfect synchronicity only Nadia's elite could manage. Nadia herself barked out orders from inside an armored van a few blocks away, surrounded by a fourth team.

Four teams. Twenty combatants, including Nadia and myself. That was all the volunteers we could muster for this mission. The rest of her forces were back in the Felldeep, too busy or too exhausted or too apathetic to be lured by the promise of a raid. Even without Meph in the picture, tensions were high.

We needed a win right now.

Nadia fell silent, and her earpiece crackled with voices as each split team, in turn, gave the signal that they were in position.

"Melissa, start driving," I said quietly.

The sayona put the van into gear and pulled out onto the road. A gate house perched on the edge of the fence. At least four sniper rifles would be trained on us.

The van picked up speed.

"On your mark," Nadia said.

I found a good handhold.

"Now!"

In a single moment, our strike teams converged on six sniper nests. Two rounds of anti-material fire punched holes through the armor plating of our van. A third round shattered the supposedly bulletproof windshield. It would have hit Melissa, if she hadn't picked that time to introduce the gas pedal to the floor. The engine roared, and the van leaped forward, accelerating as fast as its eight-cylinder engine could take it.

The chain-link gate flew open as we barreled through. Rows of spikes lifted out of the ground, which might have been an issue, if not for the van's military-grade airless tires. We tore down the long road toward the docking bay when abruptly Melissa put on the parking brake and twisted the steering wheel. The van skidded into a turn that no vehicle that size had any right to make. With a sick lurch of shifting inertia, the van was speeding backwards. Yash and Jordana threw open the back doors, and I leaped out before the van stopped moving. As I hurtled through the air, I transformed, carried by sheer momentum into the garage doors.

Those doors were reinforced by concrete and steel. But they couldn't stand up against a forty-foot dragon moving at fifty miles per hour.

I ripped through the doors like an oversized cannonball and landed on a loading dock full of terrified workers. Some of them ran screaming. The stupid ones drew their sidearms and started shooting at me, but their bullets might as well have been BBs against my scales.

One idiot got it in his head to hit me across the nose with a cattle prod. That was hilarious. Almost as hilarious as his face right before I opened my gaping jaws and flooded the room with lightning.

Here's a hint: when your entire loading bay is lined in steel, wear lots and lots and *lots* of rubber.

The light bulbs burst overhead in a shower of sparks, and the room plunged into darkness, lit only by the gaping hole I'd made through the door. That light was eclipsed as the van pulled up behind it and my team poured inside to finish securing the loading bay.

Melissa was the last one out, climbing through just as I got small.

"Are we expecting backup?" she asked.

"No. Why?"

"There's a motorcycle coming this way. Are they one of ours?"

Nadia frowned at me. "I didn't send for anyone. Did you?"

"What makes you think I sent for anybody? You're the organized one."

We didn't get a chance to debate about the lone motorcyclist. More people were pouring from the doorways, and they were ready for a war.

Meph

The motorcycle's wheels squealed as I skidded to a halt in front of the factory's main entrance. Arkay was already inside the loading bay, surrounded by her agents. I had no hope of catching her, especially not without decent weapons at my disposal.

But I could still put a dent in her plan.

Nobody tried to stop me as I stormed through the front doors. Inside, workers were already scrambling, their panic illuminated in red by blaring alarms.

"What the hell is going on over there?" a well-dressed foreman shouted into her walkie-talkie. "Somebody answer me!" She switched channels frantically. "Monteiro, check the tanks. Shaffer, find out what kind of breach we're dealing with. I swear to God, if that minotaur wasn't secured—"

I grabbed the walkie-talkie out of her hand. "It's not a minotaur."

"Who the hell are you?" she demanded. "Davis, who the hell let him in here?"

I didn't have time for this. "You're under attack. This compound is surrounded by Hoarde strike teams. The Fext and a full-grown dragon are already inside. You need to evacuate before they kill you all."

The alarm lights washed like blood over the woman's paling face. "But— but we have guards. We have snipers—"

"Heard from them lately?"

She stumbled backward. "No. Wait. There's protocols for this. We need to destroy the paperwork. Activate safeguards. Flood the tanks."

"There is no time." I bore down on her. She was a small, heavy-set woman who'd obviously never seen a day of combat in her life. Pure middle-management: she called the shots, but only inasmuch as they were handed down to her. "I'm giving you a direct order. Evacuate the compound. Now."

She raised her walkie-talkie to her mouth. "Evacuate the building. Spread the word. We need to get everybody out, ASAP."

Arkay

There was too much a risk of friendly fire for me to get big and scaly again, but I didn't need to.

The five of us scattered, diving and weaving through the crowd. From the corner of my eye I glimpsed Yash picking up one of the armed guards and hurling her bodily into another two. Jordana whirled in a graceful dance. Nadia leaped and pirouetted, subduing them just as easily with her fists as with her eyes. The air grew warped and murky around Tomasi as he chanted, his eyes rolling back in his head, and the guards on him slowed to a standstill as time itself curved around them.

I wove between my enemies, pausing only long enough to slash through tendons before I moved on. I needed to get deeper into the compound, far enough away that only card-carrying Orderlings wound up extra crispy.

It looked like my first round of fireworks had hit a couple of the main electric lines. The deeper I went into the factory, the darker the halls became. Luckily, I had experience with navigating in pitch black. I moved quickly, maneuvering myself just right to trip running feet and then slice through Achilles tendons as more runners passed by.

In the absence of light, I lost the luxury of relying on my eyes. My past experiences with factories had taught me not to inhale through the nose, and this one wasn't a whole lot better. When I started breathing normally, my senses were assaulted by the sickly odors of industrial chemicals. They'd already coated my throat and made me want to gag, but now I got the full rainbow of stench. Molten iron, lime and fluorspar, burning magnesium and acrid sulfur, blood and fear and bone dust…

No. Wait.

I paused, taking deeper breaths.

I expected blood and fear. The former was all over my hands, and the latter was the inescapable scent of armed combat.

But even on the occasions when I'd been too aggressive with my claws and nicked bone, I hadn't hit hard enough to aerosolize the stuff.

When I started moving again, it was at a slower pace, my face lifted to get the full bouquet.

There was plenty of human blood, but it wasn't all human. The deeper I moved into the factory, the more distinctly nonhuman the scents became. I passed a branching corridor and other sounds rose over the footsteps: the drone of a generator and the slow whirling of a ventilation fan. I turned down the corridor. My pace slowed to a crawl as the scents were subsumed by the astringent smell of bleach.

That never ended well.

The hallway ended with an enormous steel door, if you could call it that. It wouldn't have looked out of place in a bank vault. I probably wouldn't have been able to get through it at all, but it had been left ajar. Most likely whoever had been inside had left in a hurry when the power shut off.

The echo of my footsteps told me that I was inside a larger chamber, but that was all I got. There were no windows, no exit signs, no source of light whatsoever. So I made my own.

I raised my hand over my head, and electricity arced between my outstretched fingertips.

I'd seen restaurants with less floor space. Concrete floors sloped noticeably toward a drain. Reinforced doors led out on every side, interrupting sinks and counters that lined the walls. They looked like workshop tables, and saws and knives hung from hooks on the walls, all of them within easy reach.

One table was dominated by a deer skull nearly the size of a minivan. An yggdradeer, just like Comet back in the Felldeep. Beside it hung a single detached antler, so huge and complicated that it took up most of the wall. Shadows danced in the contours of its fractal patterns. The stub of another antler lay on the next counter, along with the shadows of an industrial circular saw.

And beside the saw, bolted into the wall: an iron ring.

And another. Another. They were all over the room. Rings and clamps and handcuffs, their edges scratched and polished from repeated rubbing, the metal bent from a struggle. One of the rings nearest me was still wet with bleach. Apparently whoever had been in here had left before they had a chance to finish cleaning up the blood smeared behind it.

"Nope," I said, even though there was nobody around to appreciate my wit. I kind of wished that somebody else was around to be grim so I could lighten the mood. Or to start hyperventilating so I could focus on keeping them calm. Or to throw themselves at the equipment and try to tear it off the walls, so I could remind them that there was a time and a place to take apart the torture dungeon, but it wasn't in the middle of a raid.

I was alone, which placed the full burden of freaking the fuck out on my shoulders. But I had a job to do, and it didn't involve going feral.

Don't think about it, I told myself. *Just move on. Do your job now. React later.*

Next door, then. Two of the walls were occupied by more vault doors, but the last door was bigger and flatter, its cracks sealed with lines of folded rubber. I'd seen one just like it in some dude's basement a long time ago, attached to the front of his big-ass walk-in freezer.

I found the door latch and yanked it open.

In hindsight, that may have been a mistake.

The stench of blood and offal hit me like a wave, so thick it made my eyes water. I should have turned around right then and slammed the door behind me. I knew enough of what was in that room to justify horror and fear.

But that was the problem. I was afraid. And dragons do not run from the things that scare us.

Even with the brilliant light emanating from my hands, the room remained steeped in shadows, too huge for me to make out walls or a ceiling through the gloom. But slowly my eyes adjusted, and I could make out shapes in the dark.

Don't think about it. Move on. Move on. Move on.

I recognized the shapes, but they hovered at the edge of my mind, like a forgotten word on the tip of my tongue.

A forest of odd, lumpy trees, or... or heavy coats, hanging from chains?

I marched forward, my hand held over my head like an explorer's torch. I was too busy trying to make out the shapes to look down, and my foot plunged into something viscous and wet, and I almost fell. Aside from a narrow path, the floor was cut with gutters. The substance now squelching between my toes felt like egg white, but thicker, more goopy. When I yanked my foot out of the gutter, it came out stained a dark black. Not black, I realized when my eyes adjusted enough to pick out colors from the shadow. Not black, but dark, dark red.

Blood.

Which would make the things hanging all around me carcasses. Like the meat packing plant from the Rocky movies. But that didn't make sense, because they didn't smell like pork or beef.

They smelled like...

My mind tried to make the leap, but it couldn't. I'd built a wall around the conclusion, tagged with a warning. *Run. Don't think, just run.*

I followed the walkway past the lines of carcasses. Fuck, how many were they? Were they trying to feed an entire city or something? Up ahead, though, the lines abruptly fell away, and the walkway curved into a ring around an enormous pit. The blood inside reflected my light like a black mirror. At least, until the water rippled.

I tensed, searching the water for a sign of movement. Was this some kind of necromantic ritual, then? A blood sacrifice?

Now that I was paying attention, it was easier to see the next ripple when it happened. This time, I didn't miss the large droplet raining down to join the pool.

I looked up.

Its tail vanished into the shadows, but it was easily sixty feet long, with the same broad muscle that I'd seen on the Contessa. But it was all wrong. It was suspended from the ceiling by its limbs and tail. Its head hung limp, stained red-black from the blood still dripping from a long gash in its neck. Its mouth gaped open, but no teeth glistened from inside the broken jaws. Its scales were a deep forest green, where they hadn't been physically ripped out of the flesh.

The shapes dissolved back into darkness as the light in my hands died.

This was what the Order did to dragons. This was how they saw me: an animal to be slaughtered. A thing to be used and then thrown away.

I tried to force another light, but the electricity dissipated along my fingertips. I couldn't concentrate enough to keep it going. Instead, I fumbled for the flashlight on my belt and flicked it on, careful to rip my eyes away from the dragon.

Now I could see clearly. There were dozens of them. Hundreds of them. All of them bodies. Some were already skinned, others butchered, but I found identifying features.

Hands and feet. Hooves and scales. Trolls. Oni. Nymphs. Ghouls.

I wobbled, dizzy. I should have turned around, but I found myself moving to the other side of the dragon. There was another door there. It was a way out.

If I stayed in here much longer, I would pass out from the smell alone. The thought of waking up in this hellish place made me break out in a cold sweat.

Get out. You have a job to do.

If only I could remember what it was supposed to be.

I grabbed at the door and ripped it open. I couldn't smell anything but the reek of cruor clinging to my clothes and hair.

My pulse thundered in my ears. My vision blurred with a red haze. The room was spinning.

All at once, the lights went on and I reeled, blinded by the sudden brightness. A door slammed open. A trio of booted feet rushed toward me.

They shouted, but I couldn't make sense of the words. They were all jumbled nonsense.

But I recognized gunshots when I heard them, and I knew what they meant.

My lips peeled back from my teeth. Claws replaced my nails.

They knew about this. They did this.

It was their fault. Their fault. Their fault.

And they were going to pay.

Meph

The factory would have been difficult to navigate even if I'd had decent lighting; in the dark, it was almost impossible. I made another turn, glancing down at the map the foreman had given me. She'd marked the path in yellow highlighter, but under the glare of my flashlight, the line faded into the stark white paper. I'd probably taken a wrong turn somewhere along the way, because the room before me looked nothing like what it said on the map.

I was close, though. I smelled the faint sewer stink, and I could hear shouts and moans of combat. I just had to find the right passageway and hope I didn't run into the rest of Arkay's minions before I ran into her.

Dammit all. "Would it kill you people to install some windows in here?"

As if in reply, the lights turned on all at once. Apparently the foreman had gotten the generators back up and running. I blinked away the spots in my vision and tried to get my bearings. I was way off. This was one of the biggest rooms on the map, easily thirty yards square, though most of that space was occupied by large sunken metal tanks, topped by the kind of hatches that you'd expect to find in a submarine. Now that I knew where I was, I could find a detour to take me right to the loading dock.

But just as quickly as I'd thought of the new route, it slipped away.

I heard a noise. A raw, metallic cry. Not the sound of metal striking metal. Not the howls of combat. A sobbing, wailing sound. The kind a child would make.

And it was coming from behind me.

But that wasn't possible. This was a factory, not a daycare.

It came again: a long keen of misery. And then softer, rougher: *"Shut him up before they come back!"*

The second voice was nearly a hiss, so low I wouldn't have caught it if I wasn't already listening. But it, too, came distinctly from behind me.

Behind, and down.

I peered at the hatch door. Did this factory have a sublevel of some kind? Did the people down there not get the evacuation notice? Did they think they were trapped by the Hoarde's minions?

I grabbed at the hatch door wheel and threw my weight against it. There were probably protocols for this kind of thing, but there was no telling how long these people had before the strike teams showed up. They needed to get out of here now. I yanked the hatch open and staggered back.

The air was thick with sewage and infection. The smell hit me like a solid wall I turned away to throw up before dragging myself back.

There wasn't another floor below the hatch. Just the rest of the tank, nearly twenty feet down, and it was full of people.

People, packed so close together that they didn't have room to sit down. Some of them were missing eyes or limbs. Some showed obvious signs of infection.

At least one of them was a child, his sobs smothered into a woman's hip. He couldn't have been more than seven years old.

"Oh God," I whispered.

This couldn't be real. This couldn't be happening.

There were nine hatches in this room. Nine tanks full of people.

But that didn't make sense. There had to be a mistake.

But the number of people trapped inside, the placement of the tanks, everything about this was ruthlessly efficient. Planned and deliberate.

I'd seen similar in the workshops of serial killers, though nothing of this magnitude. Maybe the Order had confiscated it from a— from a—

Flood the tanks.

The foreman's words hit me like a brick in the chest.

She'd called the raid a breach. She'd talked about an unsecured minotaur.

There's protocols for this, she'd said. *We need to destroy the paperwork. Activate safeguards. Flood the tanks.*

I saw the valves now, set into the metal walls. Were they meant for water or for gas?

I wanted to vomit again, but there was nothing left inside of me.

They knew.

The people who worked here were Order, and they knew. They knew exactly what they were doing, and they were going to do it anyway. Murder men and women and children in the name of protocol.

And I— I'd been a part of this. I'd supported this.

Oh God. Oh merciful God, what had I done?

My hands shook as I gripped the edge of the tank.

"Hold on!" I had to say it twice to be understood. "Just hold on. I'm gonna get you out of there. Everything's..." I faltered. *Everything's going to be okay?*

I couldn't tell the lie. Nothing would ever be okay again.

I staggered back, shaking. I didn't know what to do. There was no ladder inside the tank. I'd need rope, or a pulley, or something. The workers needed to have a way to get these people in and out of the tanks, didn't they? A switch, or some kind of machinery, or something. I just needed to focus long enough to find it.

Sounds approached. Running feet.

What if the foreman had changed her mind about protocol? What if she'd decided to flood the tanks after all?

I drew a Desert Eagle from its holster. They wouldn't get past the door. I slowed my breathing, taking aim into the hallway. I could have them in my sights the moment they turned the corner.

Two figures turned into view, one long-limbed and pale, the other dark and stocky. Instead of the factory's uniforms, they wore modified dragonscale body armor in shades of blue and black. I knew their faces. Fext and the boy from before. Yash.

They froze.

It couldn't have been hard to see me, framed like I was by the mouth of the hallway, my weapon drawn and ready to fire. Fext moved with distilled combat discipline. Her eyes fixed on my hands, ready to judge the direction of my bullets before I pulled the trigger. Beside her, Yash sucked in a gasp, as though he'd been stabbed through the back. He looked betrayed, I realized dully, but not surprised.

He expected this of me.

The tension slumped out of my shoulders. The gun drooped to point at the floor.

You're a genocidal maniac, he'd said.

That's what I was to them. Just another one of the bastards who locked sobbing children in the cold and dark. Who crammed innocent people into impossibly tight corridors and murdered them without a thought if they became inconvenient.

Of course their people had been angry to see me brought in alive. Of course they would riot.

Of course they wanted me dead, if this was what they saw when they looked at me.

And they weren't wrong, were they? I was part of this. I was one of *them.* And there was nothing I could do to ever be clean.

"...help," I rasped, barely audible. I could feel my sanity tipping at the edge of a precipice. I wanted to cut off the words spinning through my head. To make them stop. *Please, for the love of Christ, make it stop.*

But there were still people behind me, trapped in those tanks. Desperate for help.

"Help," I said again, louder this time. I forced my teeth to stop chattering long enough to get the words out. "There's people— they need your help. I don't know how—" I couldn't order my thoughts, much less my words, but I needed them to understand me. "Rope. Do you have rope? We need to get them out of there. There's a *kid* in there."

Fext's eyes narrowed, scrutinizing me. Yash gave her a glance, but when she didn't direct him, he started toward me at a cautious run. "What do you mean, a kid?"

"In here." I dropped the gun and rushed to the open tank. Yash followed behind me, but paused as he stepped out of the shelter of the hallway, glancing at the ceiling as if looking for snipers. Of course he expected an ambush. Of course.

"This is Yash," I called into the tank. "He's from the Hoarde. He's going to help."

Voices erupted from below, starting as a murmur and breaking into a clamor when I mentioned the Hoarde. I caught a cry of "Thank God!" as Yash leaned over the pit. Horror dawned across his face as he took in this fragment of Hell.

"Fext!" he shouted over his shoulder. "Nadia, you need to see this!"

As she padded toward the open tank, I threw myself onto the next hatch, twisting the hatch door wheel with all my might. A scream rose from inside as I pulled the door open.

"Hold on!" I shouted back down. "We're gonna get you out of here, just hold on."

I turned to the next door, and found that Yash was already at work at another. Fext stood over the first, shouting orders into an earpiece. The distant sounds of footfalls announced another pair of feet heading our way— a tunda and a suangi, by the looks of them, but I didn't spare them more than a rudimentary glance. The former had pulled a length of chain from somewhere else in the factory, and when she arrived, she lowered it into the pit. I heard it clattering against the walls of the tank as Fext started to climb down into their midst.

"Wait!" I shouted, and she looked up. I opened my mouth to shout again, but the words stuck in my throat. Instead I rushed to her side. "Be careful about those valves on the walls. I don't know what's in them, but they're meant to kill the people inside. Don't set them off."

She grunted and resumed her descent, but this time she carefully avoided the valves.

The suangi glanced at me with suspicious surprise, but he didn't speak to me. Neither did the other teams as they poured in, already outfitted with ropes and harnesses, and started lifting out the survivors. They offered narrowed eyes and sideways glances as I joined them at the ropes, but beyond that they were entirely focused on their work. But even with more than a dozen people, the going was slow. There were injured among the survivors, and fae with nauseating burns on their legs who couldn't bear close contact with the steel walls. It took care and coordination to lift them out without hurting them even more.

We hadn't finished evacuating the first tank when a tremor shook the floor. A crash rattled the compound, and a crack appeared in the far wall.

"What the hell was that?" demanded a sayona in a bloodstained uniform. "Did they rig the place with explosives or something?"

Too many eyes turned to me, and I gaped helplessly. "I don't know. I don't know. I don't."

Another crash. Another. Dust rained down from the ceiling.

The suangi raised his head. "It doesn't sound right for explosives. It's too irregular."

Another groan of metal, and another fissure appeared on the wall. The same wall as before. Fext stared at it, and her expression clouded with distant horror.

"Where's Arkay?" she asked. "Tomasi, Jordana, did either of you see Arkay on the way here?"

The suangi and the tunda exchanged glances and shook their heads, but Fext didn't look at them. She was pressing frantically at her earpiece. "Arkay? Arkay, turn the damn thing on."

Fear washed over her. Not secondhand fear for the life of a teammate, but real, visceral panic. She was staring at the ceiling like she thought it might collapse.

And suddenly I understood.

There was enough in this Godforsaken compound to send a dragon into a rampage a dozen times over. But it would only take one true rage to bring this whole building down on top of us.

I let go of the rope and fumbled into my pocket for the foreman's map. There were only three areas in the factory large enough for a dragon to move around freely. This was one of them. Another was on the south side of the building, nowhere near the cracking walls.

"I know where she is," I blurted, and I started running.

I looked back only once, half expecting Fext to try to stop me. But her stare had turned to the floor between us, to the gun that lay forgotten at her feet.

"Keep going!" she shouted at her soldiers. "We need to move faster!"

I followed the trail on the map. With every corridor I passed, the noise grew louder. I felt like I was running through an avalanche, deafened by the sounds of tearing steel and crashing stone. And laced through it all like a melody, inhuman howls of rage and despair.

Jagged holes opened in reinforced cinder block. A steel walkway had been ripped out of the wall and embedded in concrete. Industrial machinery lay torn from its bearings and twisted beyond recognition. An entire wall had been torn away, revealing an enormous meat locker. Inside, bodies swung on their hooks, bumping into each other in a mad, swirling dance before they fell, a dozen at a time, their chains dropping with a crash around them.

Arkay was up there, ripping the beams from the ceiling to cut the bodies loose, and taking chunks of the roof and walls with them. The action was manic, crazed, and every lurch of metal came with another agonized roar.

There had to be more than a hundred bodies, all dead and mutilated beyond recognition. More than a hundred lives cut short without mercy or hesitation. More than a hundred people that she had failed to save.

"Arkay!" I shouted. Her snarl echoed off the metal walls and left my ears ringing. "Arkay, it's me! It's Meph. You need to—"

Blue bolts of electricity arced down from the ceiling. The dragon struck the floor mere seconds later, lunging at me with bared fangs. I leaped aside, barely escaping before her jaws snapped shut. She twisted with another furious howl and lashed out at me again.

She wanted to kill me.

For two years we'd been fighting. All this time she'd been holding back, humoring me out of some misguided attempt at mercy, and now that was gone. Now she genuinely wanted to kill me, and there was nothing I could do to stop her.

No. Not nothing.

I dove past her as she came around for another pass, and rolled to my feet. There was one vulnerable spot on a Japanese river dragon. Rosa had shown it to me the first time I met her.

I used the momentum of her turn against her and hauled myself up onto her back, then onto her neck, and I pulled myself into the shelter of her antlers. She grabbed at me, but her claws couldn't reach the one vulnerable spot on her neck. She turned and thrashed on the ground, but the antlers kept her head just far enough off the floor to keep from crushing me. In her natural habitat, she might have plunged into a river, but the gutters of blood on the floor weren't deep enough to drown me.

Abruptly she shrank, and the protective cage of her antlers disappeared. Before I could get my bearings, her fist connected with my stomach and I tumbled across the wall.

I wheezed, choking for breath. "Arkay, wait—"

She lunged at me, inhuman only in her fury. I barely managed to roll away from a kick that could have shattered my ribcage.

"Arkay, please," I pleaded between jabs. "You have to listen to me."

She snarled, and I ducked underneath a kick to my face. "Arkay!"

Madness gave her power, but it made her sloppy. I dodged every punch she threw, keeping just ahead of her. I led her, one lunge at a time, out of the icy tomb and into the narrow hallway, where she didn't have to see the carnage. My throat was raw from gasps for breath. My limbs burned. My chest ached with broken ribs.

But she was slowing down. Every blow took a little more out of her. Every kick came a little slower.

A punch caught me in the shoulder, hard enough to send me stumbling back, but not enough to kill.

This time I didn't leap out of the way, but into her. I threw my arms around her tiny frame and held on tight.

"Arkay," I said. "Arkay, I'm sorry. I'm so sorry."

She uttered a wordless scream. I pulled her closer and buried my face in the crook of her neck.

"I'm so sorry," I said again. "I swear, I didn't know this was happening."

Her claws dug into my back. She could cut straight through my spine if she wanted to.

But she didn't want to.

"I'm sorry," I whispered over and over again, rocking her gently. "I'm so sorry. I didn't know."

Arkay

It took a bus and four ambulances to get the survivors to the Felldeep. The factory collapsed into rubble and smoke as we drove away, courtesy of several bomb technicians and multiple cases of C4.

It seemed wrong, blowing it up.

There were so many bodies still left inside. We didn't know any of their names, or if they were spiritual, or what faiths they subscribed to, but at least some of them would have wanted proper burial rites. At least some of them would have been horrified to learn that their remains would be reduced to char and ash. Rosa would have worried about stuff like that. She would have wanted to go back in there and find ways to identify all the bodies, to give them the rites that they would have asked for, to find their families and let them know what had become of them.

But we didn't have time for that. Getting all of the survivors out took more than an hour, even after I joined the rescue. It was only a matter of time before the Order sent reinforcements to take back the factory. We couldn't allow it to remain standing.

We had to make sure nobody would ever use it again.

Before transports arrived to get us out of there, volunteers scoured the buildings to search for more survivors, and they came back gray-faced and hollow-eyed. But they had found paperwork and computers. It was a small victory, even if it didn't feel like one.

The next few days were a mad scramble to find enough hospital beds and supplies for the injured. We were short-staffed to start with, and meeting basic needs required double and triple shifts. Support poured in from our allies, and soon the hospital wing was crowded with volunteers and donated supplies. Quinn worked nonstop to make enough Styx for the survivors, but we were going to be tapped dry for a good month at least.

With the foreign aid came foreign scrutiny. Even the most sympathetic dignitaries wanted to know why we were suddenly so shorthanded. So while Nadia organized the volunteers, I wound up playing politics. Representatives from around the world were up in arms, some literally frothing at the mouth as they called for retaliation, for escalation, for revenge.

"Later," was the only word they would listen to. For now, the focus had to be on the survivors. They needed medical care, psychological treatment, and safe places to take them in. If we left them in the dust, then what was it all for?

The conferences dragged on endlessly. There were nights when I seriously debated curling up in my chair and sleeping there, too tired to face the fifteen-minute walk back to my apartment.

I knew better, though.

You would think that when somebody's faced with that kind of bone-deep, mind-numbing exhaustion, they wouldn't have enough left in them to have nightmares. But every night, without fail, I found myself back in that meat locker. Every night I found familiar faces hanging from iron hooks. Every night I ran frantically past them, tripping on gutters of blood, shouting desperately for Rosa. Because if I could just find her— if I could just get to her in time—

Sometimes I found her, floating in the pool of blood, under the shadow of a dragon.

Most nights, though, Meph woke me up before that happened, and he held me close and whispered soft nonsense into my hair until I stopped shaking.

He never asked me about my nightmares. I never asked him about his.

Meph

More than a week after the factory went down, my confiscated phone lit up with two messages, both from Mara.

Are you alive? and *Meet me. Same place as last time.*

Less than twenty-four hours later, I eased myself into the corner booth, careful not to jostle my broken ribs. I hadn't gotten comfortable before I heard the distinctive tap of Mara's cane. She paused and gave a low whistle.

"Damn. You look like hell."

"We can't all be blessed with your good looks," I said.

"More's the pity." She lowered herself into the seat across from mine, and I tensed. Since when did she acknowledge me openly? "Some real shit went down not too long ago. One of our compounds in a town called Gary. But I don't have to tell you about any of that, do I?"

I glanced at the exits without turning my head. I could outrun Mara if I had to. But if she meant to bring me in, she'd be packing heat.

"Close to a dozen witnesses put you at the scene," she continued. "Identified you from old photos we had on file."

I held my breath.

"They say you saved their lives. Evacuated the building before the Hoarde leveled the place."

Arkay said I'd cleared a path to get the survivors out safely.

"Search and rescue teams found security footage in the wreckage. Footage of you." Mara watched me with soldier's eyes, documenting every covered bruise, analyzing every wince when my clothes brushed against broken skin and broken bone. Arkay assured me that my recent injuries would heal as quickly as my ankle had, once they were treated properly, but for now I had to wait. All the Hoarde's medical supplies were earmarked for the refugees.

Mara's gaze returned to mine. "I've never seen anything like it."

I stared blankly at her. The footage had been pulled from the wreckage and then buried again exactly where we'd found it, edited to remove a few key scenes. "They showed you a bunch of security footage?"

"They're showing it to everyone," she said. "Adam, you forced a feral dragon out of its true form. No one on record has ever done that. Not even the Archduchess. Gage is telling them that you've been in deep cover studying dragons all this time. Do you understand what this means?"

She called me Adam.

Not Meph.

Adam.

"The High Synod wants you to come back to Chicago to reopen your case." She caught my hand and gave it a squeeze. "They sent me here to bring you home."

Book 8:

Remnants and Revenants

Monica

The night was thick. It was the only word for it. March had ended with an abrupt heat wave that turned the last inches of melted snow into heavy fog. Light pollution spilled out from the city and left a haze of orange-purple smeared across the sky, but this far on the outskirts of town, the streets were nearly black. Streetlights loomed like scarecrows over the parking lot, and gave off just about as much illumination. Of nearly a dozen, only three still worked, each one surrounded by a puddle of murky light.

What I'm trying to say is the place looked creepy as hell.

The weeds that jabbed through the cracked blacktop grew taller and thicker as they got farther away from the security fence, where it yellowed and collapsed into a hay-colored mat. In drier climates, the overgrown grounds might have constituted a fire hazard. Even in upstate New York, with all the rain and moisture in the air, it wouldn't take much more than a few sparks to catch.

I suspect there were a few people who wouldn't mind watching this place burn. Until it did, though, I had a job to do.

The path I walked was well-worn from years of repeated use. A perfect circle, a little more than a mile in circumference, closing in nearly fifty acres of industrial wasteland. I could have followed it by feel and memory, if not by moonlight, but that left too many openings to make a mistake. I used my flashlight to follow the line of mineral and sediment, and slowly added another layer to the circle. Black salt and brick dust. It was the kind of thing my Gramma used to tell me about, usually with a grin and a wink. *Nothing but superstition and mumbo-jumbo, but there ain't nothing wrong with hedging your bets.*

That's what this was. One last hedge against the thing that lay inside. Whatever the hell it was. I'd asked plenty of times when I'd been assigned here, but HQ didn't like me enough to throw me any bones. I wasn't sure how much I could blame them. The last team I'd been part of had collapsed when two agents were killed and a third switched sides to fuck a dragon. Of the three of us who were still around, Weiss got shipped off to a backwater in Ukraine, Mara got thrown at another dragon up in Canada, and I got stationed here. All three of us were under suspicion. The rogue agent had been sentenced to die, and we'd let him get out alive. For all HQ knew, any one of us could still be working with him.

That lack of trust meant I was kept out of the loop on important details. All my information was given on a need-to-know basis, and as long as I obeyed my instructions and stayed outside the salt circle, I would never need to know what was inside this factory.

Further in was another circle made of solid silver. Beyond that, a ring of cold iron. You could still see the cracks and indentations where the cranes had come in to lay down the pieces before they'd been hammered into place. But that was before my time. By now, the silver was badly tarnished and barely visible through the weeds; the iron was so badly rusted that I could probably have broken the circle if I kicked the right place.

It was quiet here. On the factory grounds there were no trees for the wind to disturb, and only the distant echoes of crickets filtered through the darkness. Consequently, I had no trouble hearing the jangle of the chain link fence as it was pulled aside. It couldn't be my partner. We worked on alternating shifts, and he wouldn't even be awake for another five hours.

Which meant it was an intruder.

I stepped out of the beaten track and back onto the uneven pavement, keeping my flashlight low.

They were close enough that I could pick out four sets of footprints, and the frantic heavy breathing of a large dog straining on a leash. A girl's voice broke into giggles.

"Oh my God, I can't believe I'm doing this."

"That's the point, isn't it?" said another voice. The same age, if I had to guess. Male, late teens or early twenties. "If you go to the same places everybody goes, you're just gonna wind up with the same pictures everybody takes. The only way you're gonna get anything new is if you do something nobody else is gonna do."

God, not more teenagers. I was a seasoned detective, not a rent-a-cop.

Once a month or so, I'd get a bunch of urban explorers who wanted to take some creepy pictures of an abandoned factory for their blogs. Some called ahead to ask for permission, and I sent them away with warnings of crumbling infrastructure and contaminated soil. Anywhere else, I wouldn't have wasted my time stopping them. Anywhere else, the hobby was relatively harmless trespassing, the kind that didn't hurt anyone so long as they were careful and had all their shots.

Here and now, though, it was anything but harmless.

I waited until I had a good position, then swept my flashlight across the intruders, catching each one in the eyes.

"Holy shit!" one of the boys yelped. Another girl let out a scream that sounded closer to a squeak.

"Freeze!" I barked. "This is private property. The four of you are trespassing."

One of the girls stepped forward, trying to maintain control of an enormous German shepherd. She'd probably brought it for protection, but it was too busy whining and fidgeting to intimidate anyone. "I am so sorry, Officer. I had no idea. We were just here for a project, and—"

"I don't want to hear it," I said. "This place is dangerous. You all need to get out."

"But if you could just let us look around for like five minutes," said one of the boys.

"Did I stutter?" I flashed my light squarely into his eyes. "Either you kids turn right around and walk out through that damned fence, or you get in my car and I'm taking you all to the station. Is that clear?"

I got a mumbled chorus of "Yes, ma'am," and "oh, man," and "yeah, sure," from three of the voices. The fourth was more preoccupied.

"Rexie, heel!" The dog was pulling so hard she was at an angle to the pavement. The choke chain was pulled so tight that the poor mutt could barely rasp for air, but it wasn't letting up. Its belly scrubbed the ground as it dragged itself forward an inch at a time, its claws digging into the cracks of exposed dirt. "Come on, Rexie! Sit! Down! Come here!"

She gathered herself for one mighty tug, and promptly lost her grip on the chain. The dog took off running.

"Hey!" the girl shouted. "Rexie! Rexie, come back here!"

The dog made a break straight for the factory, and so did the girl.

"No, wait!" I sprinted after her. "Dammit, kid, it's dangerous!"

She was young, but after the freshman fifteen and a long semester of sitting at a desk, she was slow. I should've been able to catch her easily. But the beam of my flashlight was fixed on the girl's feet, not my own, so I didn't see the crack in the pavement before it caught my foot. I hit the ground hard enough that gravel and broken glass sliced into my leather gloves. In an instant I was on my feet and running again, not even bothering to brush off the debris, but I'd lost precious time in the fall. When my flashlight caught the girl's feet, she was well on the other side of the circle.

Meph

"Are you ready for this?" Arkay asked. I appreciated her erring on the side of caution, but all her double-checking was starting to make me anxious. Maybe that was the point.

"Yes, I'm ready."

She leaned close enough that I could smell the fabric softener on her clothes, and she fastened a coarse blindfold over my eyes. "And you remember your safewords?"

"Red for stop, yellow to slow down, green for go." It was getting to be a ritual between us. We'd done this plenty of times on the bed, until that had grown— if not comfortable, then at least familiar. But this wasn't supposed to be familiar.

"That's good." She was on my side now. I heard her bare feet moving across the carpet before she took my hands and feet and fastened them, one at a time, into steel handcuffs.

Familiarity didn't stop the surge of adrenaline that hit as soon as the cuffs locked into place. My pulse rose. Sweat moistened my palms.

"How are you doing?"

"I'm green," I said, and I meant it. The anxiety was a wake-up call, but it didn't overwhelm me anymore.

"Good." Now her voice came from somewhere above me. She'd stood up. It had been easy to follow her movements when we did this on the creaking mattress, but under the cushion of carpet, her floor was solid stone, and her footsteps were light and careful. I held my breath and listened for the soft rustle of fabric and the nearly inaudible sound of a pin falling to the floor.

The crawling fear in my gut left me hyper-vigilant. I focused that fear, let it hone my senses and drive my movements. Keeping track of the pin required focus and attention. I shuffled toward it on my knees, keeping the chains of my shackles taut so they wouldn't rattle and give me away. I had to be quiet. If I made a noise— if she heard me— she'd be angry with me. She'd lock me away.

I heard footsteps overhead. Oh God, she'd heard me. She was here. She—

"Meph?" Arkay asked.

Arkay. Not the Contessa. *Arkay.*

I was in her apartment. I was safe.

I let out the breath I'd been holding. "I'm… green."

"You sure about that? We can take a break if you need one."

"I'm sure."

"Okay." She stepped back and again became the guard in our simulation. I waited for her footsteps to move away, and I resumed my crawl to the pin.

I must have miscalculated somewhat. When I did find it, it was because the pin stabbed me in the ankle. It took a good deal of fidgeting and shuffling to get it into my hands and poke the slender bit of metal through the keyhole of the cuffs. Once there, though, the rest was muscle memory. A few twists, some awkward fumbling, and a bit of pressure, and the handcuffs slid first off one wrist and then the other. The shackles on my legs came away almost as an afterthought. I pulled off the blindfold and blinked at the sudden brightness.

"Good job, Meph." Arkay stood over me, just within arm's reach, and she smoothed my hair with a gentle hand. "That's your fastest time yet."

I leaned into her touch and tried to take my mind off my still-racing heart rate. "It's easier to move quietly without the mattress."

"Yeah, I noticed. But hey, now you've got practice moving on a super noisy surface." Her hands kept moving down my neck, my shoulders, my back. My forehead slid against her chest and found a resting place between her breasts. Her knees migrated to straddle my thighs, and my alertness took on an entirely different focus. Arkay called it aftercare. She said it was essential to the process of working my way out of these goddamned phobias. Usually by this time, I couldn't care less what she called it, so long as she kept touching me. "It looked like things were getting a bit rough for a second."

"Yeah." Coherent thought? What was that? "It's… fine, though. Getting better." I repositioned to take the pressure off my knees and pulled her closer against me, my thumbs catching the waistline of her jeans. "I think I'm ready to go through with it."

"A few more trial runs wouldn't hurt." Her words were more a sensation against my neck than they were a series of sounds. When she put it like that, I had a hard time arguing with her. I would put up with a thousand of these sessions if she kept ending them this way.

But I didn't have time for a thousand sessions. A cold weight washed over me, and my fingers dug into her hips. It probably would have hurt her, if she were human. Instead, her expression softened into concern.

"Meph, you don't have to go if you're not ready."

"Ready's got nothing to do with it," I said. "If I don't accept the Order's offer now, they aren't going to give me a chance to reconsider."

"Then you don't have to go back at all." She said it like it was a matter of fact, not like she was offering absolution free of charge. But absolution had to be earned. After all the wrong I'd done, all the people I'd hurt, all the evil I'd contributed to, I couldn't just accept her forgiveness. I had to do something to make it right, and that meant going back to the Order.

"I'll be careful," I said softly.

"Damn right you will." She smoothed my hair again, her gesture as protective as it was affectionate. "I can still get you that GPS tracker if you want it. Anything happens, and we can be there in minutes."

"They'll be looking for one."

"They're not nearly as creative as I am about hiding these things." She flashed a wide, toothy smile. A dragon's smile. It faltered when I felt something buzz against my leg. "Shit."

She didn't bother taking the phone out of her back pocket, so I pulled it out for her. The screen lit up with an alarm.

"Got somewhere to be?" I asked.

She plucked it from my hands and tossed it at the couch. "Whoops. Sorry, guys. I had an alarm and everything, and I totally slept through it. You know how these things are. My bad."

I could go along with the lie. Even if I couldn't keep her from having to attend these godawful conferences, I could give her a pleasant reason to be late. I would certainly enjoy helping her procrastinate.

But like I said, absolution had to be earned.

"You should probably go," I said reluctantly.

"I don't want to."

"I don't want you to, either. But it's important." I pushed lightly at her hips, and she climbed out of my lap, extending a hand to help me up.

"Tell you what," she said. "I'll make sure these windbags wrap it up quickly, and when I get back, I'll make it up to you."

I grinned. "I'll be looking forward to that."

She pursed her lips into an exaggerated kiss, and slipped from the room. As soon as the door shut behind her, the grin slipped from my face.

As pleasant as that offer sounded, I wouldn't hold her to it. On her best days, these conferences dragged on for hours, and she always came back gray-faced and bone-weary. I hated how much it took out of her. I hated how little I could do to help. But it wasn't like I knew anything about the politics of non-humans, or their customs, or their psychology, or anything at all that didn't involve murdering them. At this point, all I could do was stay with her at night and help her get at least a little bit of sleep before she went back for another round.

Maybe that was another reason I had to go back. So I wouldn't feel so goddamn useless.

Arkay

I took a deep breath and plastered on a professional smile before I opened the door to the conference room. On one side of the table sat a stern middle-aged man in a business suit, whose intense brows hid large, expressive eyes. His name was Ren Matsumoto, the head of a syndicate of youkai in Japan. Beside him sat a muscular woman in a brilliant golden sari— Shreya Kumar, the general of an alliance of rakshasa in Uttar Pradesh. Nadia had recommended I include a tea service, so between them sat a pitcher of Southern sweet tea, loaded with enough sugar to crystallize into rock candy when it hit your teeth. Three glasses had been filled. None of them had been touched.

"Mr. Matsumoto, Madam Kumar, I hope you haven't been waiting on me."

They had and I knew it, but neither said as much as I took my chair at the head of the table.

"Not at all, Arkay," Matsumoto said with a bow of his head. I noted the distinct lack of 'sama' at the end of my name. Apparently that was expected when addressing dragons where he was from.

At least Kumar was generous enough to hide the edge in her tone. "I'm sure your affairs take precedence."

Really? This again?

I took a swig from my own glass. "My affairs aren't what we're here to discuss, Madam. Let's get right to it, shall we?"

"The Matsumoto Syndicate wishes to offer its most heartfelt condolences to the Hoarde and its newest members in this time of strife," the youkai said.

"And we greatly appreciate the sentiment. Just like we appreciate the doctors and supplies you sent to help us with the transition. That both of you sent." I offered a smile and a nod to Kumar and tried not to look impatient. Which part of 'let's get right to it' didn't come across when I said it?

Kumar leaned forward. "Matsumoto and I have been corresponding on the matter, and we would like to expand our support of the Hoarde in future endeavors." Matsumoto looked like he was starting to reconsider. "When last we convened as a whole, you raised concerns that the factory you found wasn't the only one of its kind."

"Concerns would be putting it mildly." If I had any doubt, I would have tried harder to keep Meph from going back to the Order. "We just have to find them."

"And to that end, we believe a direct approach would be most expedient." She smiled the way a boxer would throw a punch. "Naturally, as the first factory was found in your territory, we will leave the workings under your command, but the Alliance would like to pledge its full support. What weapons and soldiers you might need will be gladly supplied. And tactical expertise, should you require advice on how to proceed."

"The Matsumoto Syndicate, of course, would be remiss to withhold our services. I'm afraid our martial contributions can't be quite as generous as the Alliance, but we can offer monetary support to help bolster your forces."

Okay, now I definitely knew something was up. If they actually wanted to support me, they'd do it in a larger conference where they could encourage their other allies to do the same, instead of asking to talk in private. The last time I'd been subject to this kind of hard sell, I'd wound up with the weight of the Hoarde on my shoulders.

But I couldn't just tell them to go fuck themselves.

"Thank you both for your generosity," I said carefully. "I will take your offers under consideration and speak with my councilors about how to proceed." If I said the wrong thing— or even the right thing in the wrong way— then we'd be down two allies. And sure, Nadia might be able to figure out a way to cope, but that usually took twice as much work and four times as much stress as she already had on her plate. Besides, I had my own agenda. "But while I give that matter my attention, I'd like to bring another matter to yours."

There was something predatory about the way their eyes followed me.

"I'm aware that the Matsumoto Syndicate owns controlling interests in several major publishing houses and news channels. Madam Kumar, your own family is instrumental in the production of several popular serials."

"We are." Her mouth twitched. "Why? Are you craving the spotlight?"

"I'd like to plan for a time when it can't be avoided," I said carefully, because I couldn't give the straight answer.

I hated hiding. I hated that most people who looked at me automatically assumed I was frail and weak and human. I hated that people who called me what I actually was got declared delusional. I hated the knowledge that my passing for human was the only reason I could even set foot outside this miserable cave without causing a riots. I hated that people like Meph and Rosa and even me could be duped so easily by genocidal butchers like the Order, because we couldn't do a simple Google search and find out whether they were legit.

The entire system was broken. And of all the people in the world, I was one of the few who could challenge that system and live to talk about it.

Whether I would fuck it up was another matter entirely.

"I think the world needs to know about us," I continued. "About all non-humans. Sooner, rather than later. And I think when that does happen, it'll go a hell of a lot smoother if the media response is in our favor."

"That would be unwise," Matsumoto said. "Secrecy protects us from the Order."

"Does it?" I asked. "Or does it just make it easier for them to pick us off? Our people can't just run to the police and say 'help, the bad men are gonna kill me because I occasionally have scales and a tail', because they're just going to be written off as crazy. I've seen it happen plenty of times."

"That's why we have dragons," Kumar said stiffly.

"There aren't enough dragons out in the world to keep this from happening," I said. "But humans outnumber the rest of us ten to one, and if they find out about this, they can stop it."

"And if they turn on us, they can erase us entirely."

"Maybe they can," I admitted, sitting back. "But then why wouldn't the Order be printing this stuff on the front page of the news? Why hide what they're doing? They're the ones keeping up the masquerade, not us."

"Even if you could win over the majority," Matsumoto said. "You won't persuade everyone. And the repercussions will be dire. I understand Russia's politics are uncomfortable for lesbians; how do you think they will react to poludnica? Would your Fext ever again be welcome in her home country?" I bristled. That was a low blow. "Secrecy did not begin with the Order. It began because we were being hunted by humans across the globe. Because we had a very long history of being hated and hunted. They lull their children to sleep at night with stories about how to kill us."

"And yet there are entire genres about how much they want to have sex with us," I said. "Stories change. And right now, we have the power to change them."

Kumar let out a puff of air that might have passed for a laugh. "We will take it under consideration," she said, throwing my words back at me. "I hope you extend our offer the same courtesy."

Meph

I wasn't very popular in the Hoarde. I probably never would be. But the Felldeep's bazaar was crowded enough that most people didn't recognize me, so long as I kept a hood over my head and didn't draw attention to myself. Most of the people who worked there were too focused on buying and selling to care much about who shared their marketplace. I sidled up to the flower cart from the side, grabbed my selection, and pushed a handful of crumpled bills into the florist's clawed hands before she could get a good look at me. I took pride in my technique. I was smooth. Stealthy. Unnoticed.

Hopefully my exit would be just as quick. Abrupt, like setting a broken bone. One minute I'd be here, and the next I'd be gone, and then I could focus on my job and Arkay could focus on hers. There'd be no need to waste time on goodbyes if she wasn't there to see me off.

Except when I got back to Arkay's apartment, she was already pulling her key from the door. She wasn't kidding about cutting her meeting short.

Her eyes fell on me, and I froze. "Arkay. You're back. How was the meeting?"

"Meph?" She frowned, puzzled. "Are those flowers?"

I felt the ridiculous urge to hide them behind my back. Instead I pushed my bouquet of blue alstroemeria toward her. "I know you're not interested in anything... romantic. But I saw these in the bazaar, and they're the same color as your scales. And they're supposed to last a long time in water. And they smell nice. And I noticed that you tend to gravitate toward pleasant smells when you're upset. Or familiar, anyway, but I'm assuming a link between familiar odors and pleasant ones, which can honestly be two completely distinct categories—" God, I was rambling.

But Arkay took the bouquet from me and buried her face among the blossoms with a fond smile. "Have I told you lately that you're a total nerd?"

Just like that, the tension drained from my spine. "You know, I think I can live with that."

"Good. Because I like you that way." She bounced up on her toes and kissed me. "Come back safe."

Monica

We had protocol for this.

If somebody crossed the circle, they weren't coming back. I was supposed to escort the rest of the kids off the premises and report the loss back to HQ. The Order had entire departments set aside for cover-ups. They'd come up with a convenient story to tell her family so nobody ever came looking for her.

But she was still alive. I could see her right now. And that meant I could still save her.

I was on thin ice with the Order already. There was no telling what would happen if they found out about more insubordination.

And maybe if an innocent kid's life wasn't on the line, that might have mattered.

"Goddammit, kid." Salt, silver and steel passed under my feet as I crossed one circle after another, and then I crossed onto broken glass and peeling linoleum.

The factory was dark. There were no windows at all past the lobby. Inside, everything was pitch black, lit only by my flashlight. From down the hall came the scrabbling of clawed feet against the crumbling tile floors and the echoes of human footsteps.

"Come back here!" I took off after the sound, emerging from the hallway into an open chamber with multiple doors in every direction and enormous vats sunk into the ground. The sounds echoed hauntingly off the metal walls, distorting and reverberating until it seemed like the entire room was full of struggling bodies. I shuddered and listened harder, straining to pick out the direction of the sound, but they seemed to come from everywhere at once. I stepped over a rusted hatch door and continued on my way.

I moved further, up one hallway and down another, until I came to a magnetic refrigerator door from what must have been a kitchen, its rubber seal cracked and stiff from age. Through the cracks came the horrific stench of rotting meat, so thick that vomit crawled up my throat. But I could hear something from inside. A grotesque, inhuman howling.

Maybe her dog had gotten in to sniff at the rotting meat and gotten caught on something. Maybe it could lead me to the girl. Maybe it was beyond saving, but I'd rather shoot the poor thing than let it suffer.

I sucked in a breath of relatively clean air and opened the door.

The stench hit me like a freight train. But more than that was the *noise*. Thousands of voices were joined in a wall of sound, a single endless shriek of agony. I clapped my hands over my ears and felt blood wet against my palms. My flashlight fell to the ground. Its beam rolled across the enormous space, illuminating enough lumpy, misshapen bodies to fill an auditorium. Some were in pieces. Some were flayed. All of them were impaled on meat hooks that hung from the ceiling. Their iron chains swung as they writhed. Those that still had mouths and vocal cords screamed, their jaws distended, their gums bloodless and rotting.

I grabbed my flashlight off the ground and hauled ass out of there. I slammed the door shut behind me, but the screams and the stench filtered through, following me until I put half a dozen rooms between me and that freak show. I don't know how long I kept running, but I never wanted to stop, and I had enough adrenaline to keep going forever. Traction gave out before my body did. The brittle remains of loose papers covered the floor of what had once been an office. One of the pages skidded underfoot, and I fell. The edge of a rusted filing cabinet scraped my head on the way down and carved into the side of my forehead.

"Shit," I hissed, touching the wound. It was bleeding hard, but head wounds always do. I might need stitches when I got out of there. But not yet. First I needed to find the girl. There was still a chance she was alive in there.

I pressed my hand to the side of my head to stifle the bleeding and tried to collect myself, but a sound caught my attention.

The light of my flashlight whipped across the walls, but I couldn't find any organic shapes. Nothing that could have caused the noise.

It came again, louder this time: the long, rasping drag of a body over the rough floor.

"Kid?" I lowered my flashlight and swept the area again, searching the floor. "Kid, I know this place is freaky, but I'm here to help. Let me see you and we can get you out of here and back to your family."

My only response was another scraping drag, and a long, low rattle of breath. The echoes were too loud and hollow for me to pinpoint a location, but one thing was clear:

It was getting closer.

"Kid?"

My eyes strained as I searched through the darkness. I whirled around a second time and then a third, trying to catch some clue as to where the sound was coming from.

"Who's there?" I demanded, unholstering my gun. "This is the police. Identify yourself and come out with your hands up."

I didn't actually expect the thing to obey me, but it didn't hurt to try.

"Kid, is that you? Come out, or I will shoot you. I repeat, I *will* shoot you. I am armed."

Still no reply. But it kept coming.

I swung my flashlight around, and this time I caught movement. The light reflected off what looked like a length of chain, blood-stained and stretched across the floor. It had been moving toward me.

Slowly I panned the light along its length. My hands shook on the gun.

"Freeze! Put your hands on your head and don't move!"

Finally my flashlight passed over… I couldn't even give it a name anymore. It looked like it might have been quadrupedal once. The useless stumps of mangled hind limbs trailed behind it, tangling in the chain as it dragged itself forward, a few inches at a time, with the remains of its clawed hands. Its flesh was stiff and hard, like roadkill left too long on hot pavement. Long hair fell in matted strings around its head. No, its *skull*. It was more bone than anything else, covered in places by a few fraying strings of flesh.

Bile rose in my throat. I'd seen this before.

Without another moment of hesitation, I opened fire and sent a bullet through the zombie's head.

The dry skull shattered like a clay pigeon.

I picked up my flashlight again and started running. That was the thing about zombies— they were slow, but there were usually a lot of them. I still remembered the last time I'd seen something like this, back when I'd been pinned inside a garage while they swarmed outside, throwing themselves at the doors to get in. These weren't the brain-hungry zombies of Hollywood tradition, but they'd still rip me apart if their necromancer gave the order.

That was the key to this mess.

I needed to stop wasting bullets on the sons of bitches and find whoever was in charge of this hellhole. Kill the necromancer, and all the zombies would drop like the corpses they were.

I just had to stay alive long enough to do it.

Meph

It turned out to be for the best that I didn't take Arkay up on her offer for a tracking beacon. As soon as I got into the Order van, I was searched, patted down, swept with a metal detector, and then searched again. One of the guards even instructed me to squat down and cough.

It was undignified, but I expected as much. I'd spent six months fraternizing with a dragon, three months after that as another dragon's prisoner, and another two years after that blowing in the wind, with only sporadic contact with the Order and its agents. Never mind that I'd been actively fighting against Arkay for most of that time; as far as they were concerned, I was still very much in bed with the enemy.

But now that had taken on a new significance to them.

Just like before, my trial was held in the Chicago headquarters. There was a sense of *deja vu* as I crossed the elaborate mosaic of the lobby and read scripture off the trim of the elevators. But this time, I was escorted by armed guards. This time, when I passed endless placards of fallen soldiers, I wondered how all of those people had died. How many of them had actually saved lives with their sacrifice, and how many had been butchers? How many were mowed down by grieving lovers, or parents protecting their children?

How many of them had no idea what they were really fighting for?

I kept my expression neutral as I was led into the council chamber and my guards took their places in the corners of the room. Another pair stood on either side of the door, in case I tried to make a break for it.

I had no intention of running.

I squinted at the Synod. The sun was behind them and cast them into harsh silhouette, but I recognized a few of the shapes from my last trial. Archduchess Stavros and Grandmaster Burns sat on opposite ends of the long table. Closer to the middle, Gage watched me with careful eyes. If this went well, he stood a chance of regaining his position as a Grandmaster. What would happen if I failed him again?

"State your name," said a voice from among the shadowed figures.

I hesitated. "I don't have one. It was officially rescinded, along with my rank and standing within the Order."

I could feel a glare more than see one. "State *a* name, then," the voice corrected, sounding annoyed. "For the record."

That shouldn't have amused me as much as it did. I'd been sentenced to *damnatio memoriae.* Usually that carried with it a death sentence, followed by a complete purge of that person's records, both in the Order and in the outside world. As far as I knew, I was the first person in recent history, if ever, to have that sentence reversed. Which meant that they had no protocols for how to handle me.

"For the past three years, I've been referred to as Mephistopheles. Before then, my name was Adam Preston. What your records will call me is up to the wisdom of the Synod."

"Preston, then." I recognized the voice of Archduchess Stavros, and gave her my full attention. She looked even more frail than the last time I'd seen her, but it was the brittleness of old steel. "Let us see if you've earned the right to take back that name." She regarded me in silence for several long moments. "You've made it quite difficult to judge you. You have operated as an outlaw and a traitor to our Order, yet Gage reports that you have been working in…" She glanced at him skeptically. "Deep cover, was it? We have evidence of you fighting against our enemies, and some say that puts you on our side. But we have many enemies, and some of them hate each other as vehemently as they hate mankind. So we leave it to you, then. Whose side are you on?"

"I am, as I have always been, on the side of the Order. On the side of God."

"Then what do you call this prolonged absence? An apostasy?"

"It's exactly as Gage said." My gaze flitted at him as I tried to remember weeks of memorized instructions. "During my work conducting surveillance on Rosario Hernandez, I developed a theory about the workings of Potnia Theron. I hypothesized that what we perceived to be supernatural abilities were not in fact innate, but patterns of behavior that could be learned and replicated. I was confident enough in my hypothesis that I allowed myself to be placed into compromising positions for the sake of continuing my study."

The hairs on my neck stood on end. Someone was watching me. Not the collective of the Synod, either. I expected their scrutiny. This was another feeling entirely. Something familiar.

"Gage asked me that day how much faith I had in my hypothesis. How far I was willing to go to test it. I hope my work has answered that question."

Grandmaster Burns spoke up. "Are you seriously proposing that you did all of this *for science?*"

"With all due respect, Grandmaster, I did it to save lives. Hunting dragons is by far the most dangerous act a member of our Order can undertake, and I believe it's because we've been approaching the entire pursuit from the wrong angle. If my research can save even one life—"

"Yes, yes, that's very noble of you," said the Archduchess. "Save us the pretty speeches and get to the point. What did your research find?"

"That our taxonomy of dragons is flawed. For centuries, we've classified dragons according to their place of origin, their preferred habitat, their regular diet. But according to my research," Doctor Magbantay's research, actually, "the single most telling detail is whether or not they use human speech."

"You're joking," said a voice from the shadows, and I nearly jumped. It was a female voice, but not *her* voice. *She* wasn't here. *She* couldn't possibly be here.

"All dragons are capable of it, but they don't have a language of their own. They don't need one, because they'll kill each other on sight, and in their unGodly arrogance, they don't see other creatures as worthy of communication. And yet some dragons still adopt human speech. Not to speak with people, but to speak to *one* person. One single person who dramatically alters the way they interact with the rest of the world. For centuries, we have operated under the premise that dragons are inherently chaotic and unpredictable, but I've found that if you take into account the nature of a dragon's relationship with that person, you can accurately map out their every action with acute precision."

The Archduchess raised an eyebrow. "Is that so?"

"It's the only reason why I'm still alive. Based on my observations of her interactions with Hernandez, I was able to successfully navigate the dragon Arkay's moods and habits. Observation of other dragons has fallen in line exactly with the same hypothesis."

For nearly an hour they grilled me, challenging assumptions and cross-examining my facts. I'd spent weeks memorizing the pages of Doctor Magbantay's Index of the Inhuman. I was prepared, but every question elevated my heart rate. Sweat moistened my palms and beaded down my neck. My throat constricted and I stumbled over my words, but I forced myself to keep talking. The air was getting thick. I could feel her nearby. I could practically smell her perfume, the notes of rushfoil and belladonna so subtle I might have imagined them.

I had to keep it together. If I lost it now, they'd suspect me of being tainted by something. The lingering aftereffects of a succubus, or a poludnica, or any of a hundred other creatures that could get inside my head and twist me around. Everything I said would be discredited. This whole affair would be a waste of time. There would be no way I would get enough clearance to be useful to Arkay.

I focused my thoughts on her. On the exercises we'd done together. On the memory of her face. The way she moved. The sound of her voice.

And you remember your safewords?

Because she cared about me. She didn't want me to go through with this if I wasn't ready. But I was. I could do this.

Red for stop, yellow to slow down, green for go.

Dragons always—

Green for go.

I told her I could do this, and I would, dammit.

"Preston, answer the question."

I'm green. I'm green.

They were going to find me out. They were going to kill me. If the Contessa didn't beat them to it.

My lungs weren't taking in enough air. I couldn't breathe. All the air smelled like her. She was here. She was coming.

"Preston!"

Somebody rose from the table.

"Dammit, I told you to search him!" I couldn't identify the voice. Female. The Archduchess? The Contessa?

Spots danced across my vision.

Dammit, Meph, now is not the time to pass out.

I held up a finger. My hands trembled. "One moment. Just… just one…"

Just ride it out. Let it happen, and then move past it.

I took deep breaths through my mouth. The air was stale, but it kept me from smelling the Contessa's perfume. I needed to ground myself, so I focused my attention on the Archduchess. Her silver hair was covered in black silk, the veil embroidered with red poppies. The ruby on her finger caught the last sparks of sunlight. Her hands were long-fingered and heavily scarred, unnaturally smooth where she'd been burned.

The guards were at my sides. Members of the Synod were on their feet and raising their voices. But she remained perfectly still, her eyes on me, watching my collapse with a look of… of empathy?

Of recognition.

My breaths started to feel like they were filling my lungs again. The shaking subsided enough that I no longer felt like I was rattling apart.

"I— I apologize," I rasped. "I… the last time I was in this room, I wound up with a death sentence. I hope you can understand that I'm feeling some anxiety right now." I forced my face to relax and tried to inject some lightheartedness into my tone.

The Archduchess raised a hand, and the guards stepped back. "Continue to answer honestly, and we won't need to carry out that sentence."

"Yes, Ma'am. I intend to."

Monica

I crouched low behind the desk, trying not to breathe. The mummified corpse of a minotaur stomped past me, its dry hooves pounding on the tile floor with an earthshaking rattle. As soon as its footfalls echoed from around the corner, I let out a rattling breath and turned on my flashlight again. There was no danger of the light reaching the minotaur; the bulb barely glowed bright enough to show me my own feet anymore.

Insects swarmed across the walls and floor, no longer fleeing from the beam of my flashlight. I crawled over them, and they crunched under my hands and knees. Not squished, but *crunched*. When I moved my hand away, I found not the gooey wetness of bug guts, but the dry crack of empty chitin ground into powder.

Even the goddamned bugs were zombies in this hellhole.

My flashlight flickered and died. I gave it a smack in hopes of reconnecting the wires inside. Stupid cheap piece of shit.

I crawled out from under the desk, grateful for the gloves on my hands. God only knew how many insects were swarming on the surfaces under my fingertips. I restrained a shudder and climbed to my feet, keeping my hand out to feel for obstacles, another to help me follow the wall.

It had to be morning by now, but that was only a guess. The factory had no windows to let in the light or indicate how long I'd been walking. I tried to check my phone, but the battery died not long after I got lost in here. I was moving at a snail's pace already to avoid attracting attention with unnecessary noise. Now that my light cut out, I went even slower.

I listened for any sign of the girl. Barking from the dog, or crying, or attempts to call for help. The fact that I didn't hear anything didn't mean anything. Maybe she had the presence of mind to stay quiet. Maybe she'd lost consciousness.

Or maybe she was dead.

Another set of footsteps headed my way. They were lighter than the minotaur's had been, softer, with what sounded like soggy shoes between its feet and the tile floor. I stumbled backwards and ducked into the opening that I'd walked past a few moments before. It didn't seem like these things could see in the dark any better than I could, but I still crouched low and flattened myself against the wall, holding my breath.

Could they see me, though? Could they smell me?

It wasn't the kind of thing you learned about in the police academy, and years of experience on the police force hadn't done shit to prepare me for the supernatural. Otherwise, maybe I'd have recognized a cooler full of organs as the components of a necromantic ritual. Maybe I would have recognized an angry dragon when I saw her, and known better than to separate her from the Potnia Theron that kept her from going postal.

Instead, I'd assumed that she was just drugged and delusional. I'd assumed that handcuffs would restrain her, and that cinderblock walls could keep her contained. But I was naive. I was ignorant.

I saw her rip apart a grown man like he was a stack of junk mail, and I actually thought pointing a gun at her would do anything more than make her mad.

I saw fist-sized craters in our interrogation room and dozens of recently de-animated zombies, and I was stupid enough to think that counted as evidence of magic. That my years of service to the force and the city meant I would be listened to when I gave my statement. Instead I was thrown off the force. Gently, of course, given leniency because the higher-ups said I'd had a mental break. They said all those bodies had left me deluded.

Even after I completed my psych evals and earned back my side-arm, things changed. People looked at me different after I'd cried 'dragon'. People stopped trusting my word. My instincts.

The only person who believed me was Green, and only him because he knew exactly what dragons were. Only unlike me, he knew enough to keep his mouth shut and not draw attention to himself. He was smart. I wasn't.

But he taught me to get smarter. And when there was nothing left he could teach me, he sent me to an Order compound out in New Mexico.

I would have called it a cult or a paramilitary group, but what they were doing was real. I'd seen it with my own eyes. And now I was a part of it.

The footsteps passed, and I got back up, patting myself down to get the zombie bugs off my face and clothes. I needed to find the girl and get out of here.

It was too dangerous to confront these monsters in the open, the Order told me. There were dragons out there who had entire governments in their thrall. Syndicates of oni and youkai controlled enough wealth across Asia to send the world economy into a tailspin. And even if they didn't, there would be riots in the streets if word got out. Mass suicides. Witch hunts. Nobody would feel safe if they found out that their worst nightmares were actually real.

So the Order worked from the shadows, and I was left in the dark.

Meph

After four hours of grueling interviews, they finally let me out.

The Order gave me a room to bunk in while I underwent my trial, one of the apartment suites on the higher floors usually reserved for agents who were passing through on assignment. I couldn't tell anymore if it was meant as a courtesy or as a way of keeping an eye on me until I passed the scrutiny of the Synod.

There was a time when I would have admired the superior security of the accommodations. Now it made my skin crawl. At a moment's notice, the electronic locks could be changed to render my keycard useless and leave me trapped behind a triple-bolted steel door. With enough effort, a dragon might have been able to smash her way through the bullet-proof windows, but there was no way I could manage it, let alone survive the thirty-story drop to the street below.

Protective wards were cast in iron and set into the walls. I could identify the artistry of their shapes and swirls, but it wouldn't be the first time I'd seen artistic bars on a cage.

I avoided spending time there.

What I needed right now was Arkay and her particular brand of aftercare. Lacking that, I would have settled for fifty bucks' worth of cheap vodka from the nearest bar. But my keycard wouldn't let me out onto the ground floor. Most of the building was barred to me, thanks to my probationary status. The elevator would only take me to my apartment, to the interrogation chamber, and to the mess hall.

I went with the third option. It occurred to me that I might be able to duck into the elevator the next time somebody was going down and hitch a ride with them— but even if I didn't get stopped by the armed receptionist, that kind of disappearance would shatter all illusions that I was still loyal to the Order. If I wanted this to work, I'd have to remain obediently inside the cage.

I loaded up a tray and sat down in the far corner of the cafeteria, close to the window. Natural sunlight felt disorienting after I'd spent the last few weeks underground. Still, the bulletproof glass was a solid wall at my back, and unlike the interior walls of the mess hall, it wasn't hiding security cameras.

My back was still clammy with sweat when I picked up my sandwich. I had grabbed it without looking at its label. Now I parted the bread, staring nonplussed at the meat inside. It was just lunch meat. Maybe bologna or ham —

Or long pork.

My scalp prickled as the intrusive thought crawled through my mind. And that was all it was. An irrational, unrealistic idea that slipped into my head without provocation. It had nothing to do with rows of people hanging like swine from meat hooks in what looked like an industrial butcher shop, or the nagging question of what the hell anybody would do with that many bodies—

Vomit burned my throat, but I swallowed it down and tried to wash the taste out of my mouth with a bite of apple. No torture and mutilations involved in produce, right?

Right?

Damn, I needed a drink.

Within a few bites I reduced the apple to a browning core. I was contemplating the origin of cyanide when I heard the familiar rhythm of a cane on the bar floor, and my old handler lowered herself into the seat beside mine.

Mara gave a low whistle. "Damn, Adam. You alright?"

"Any chance you brought me vodka?" I asked.

"No. But I hear they keep some bottles of wine for the higher-ups in the back. Show them that kicked puppy face of yours and we might be able to convince them to spare a couple."

I shuddered. Just the word made my tongue curl in anticipation of dry bitterness. "No. No thanks. No wine." I hadn't touched the stuff since the Contessa.

"Adam, I'm serious. You look like shit. Maybe you should go lie down or something."

"That's really not going to help me right now." I abandoned the apple core beside the sandwich. "Stay. I could use the company."

She sat back with a nod. "Do they have anything on you?"

"Hard to say. Most of today's interview was just them asking me questions. Nothing exactly pointed."

"You sure about that?" She flicked a bit of lint off her sleeve.

Oh. She meant whether they had me bugged. "No, I'm clean."

"The more important question is whether it matters. You having second thoughts now that they're letting you back in?"

"By now the Contessa will have heard about me coming back," I said. "She'll be watching me."

"Is that a yes?"

"It means I'll need to fly under the radar for a while. But there's nothing stopping me from keeping my eyes open." It wouldn't be that far from our original agreement, back when I'd been barred from the Order's systems. I would find leads about the Contessa's spies in the Order, and Mara would spread the word to investigate them. Enough people owed her favors to make her formidable, but it wasn't just that. Mara had stuck with me, even after I was thrown out of the Order. She was loyal— not to the organization as a whole, but to the people in it. And they repaid that loyalty in kind.

I hoped she would understand that that was what I was doing.

"Speaking of leads." I lowered my voice. "You said you saw the security footage from the factory."

"Some of it. I saw you duking it out with a dragon."

"Did you see both of them?"

She frowned. "There were two dragons in there?"

"The other one was already dead." I leaned in closer. "I didn't exactly have a chance to look at it up close. But the Contessa has been using the Order to kill off her rivals, and specifically spoon-feeding the people she wants promoted. We might be able to find her lackeys by looking at the list of repeat dragonslayers."

"Careful, Adam," she said. "There's a lot of important people on that list."

"I know. Maybe check out the other end, then. See if you can find the places where the dragons end up, see if you can find a list of injuries or cause of death anywhere. Look for anything unusual. Tactics that don't match up with regulation training. Injuries that don't match the report. That kind of thing."

"I'll see what I can find," she said. "Don't hold your breath, though. I didn't even know these factory things existed."

Thank God. I didn't know what I'd do if Mara was part of this abomination.

"Makes sense, though," she added after a thoughtful moment. "It would explain the Boneyard."

The name rang a distant bell. I'd heard the word spoken, but never explained. "What is it?"

"Purgatory." She wrinkled her nose. "A six-month stint doing the most mind-numbing drudgery you can think of. It's where they send people they don't want to deal with. Hotheads who need more discipline, rookies who can't handle regular fieldwork, fuck-ups who haven't pissed off enough people to get thrown at a dragon."

That didn't sound anything like the faith-shattering, soul-withering horror I'd experienced. "And this is a factory?"

"It used to be," she said. "Now it's just an old husk of a building with a shit-ton of wards around it."

Something still wasn't clicking. "Why would you ward an empty building?"

She flashed a grim smile. "I never said it was empty. Adam, do you remember Monica Sharp? She was on our team, right before you got the can."

"The detective, right?" That was years ago, and we hadn't exactly worked together for very long. "She wasn't exactly the talkative type."

"Converts never are," Mara said. "It's different for you, Adam. You were born into the life. Most of the people who join us, it's because they've seen some serious shit." She picked up my apple core and twisted the stem between her fingers, letting the core rotate slowly in the air. "You don't need to worry about making friends with her anymore, though. They found her tracks crossing the Boneyard's wards. Nobody who crosses that circle ever comes back."

Arkay

I checked the row of clocks on the far wall of the conference room. Every one of them said it was ten past the hour. The meeting should have started by now.

The Hoarde technically belonged to me, but no one person could cover all the minutia of running such a sprawling organization. It was like a giant clock, with hundreds of thousands of moving parts that needed perfect coordination just so they wouldn't run into each other. That was what these stupid weekly meetings were for: so we could coordinate between Nadia and her soldiers, Quinn and his medical staff, a water nymph named BeeGee and her IT department, and more than a dozen other executives and upper-tier managers who made sure the whole fucking Hoarde didn't explode.

Exploding felt a lot more likely these days, since our head of security organized a lynch mob and then resigned. I didn't exactly get the warm fuzzies about the remaining security staff; those who hadn't run off with him had been personally trained by him. So now we needed to weed out the most trustworthy candidate from a pool of potential traitors, and we needed to do it without pissing off another fifth of the Felldeep. And since my single strongest talent seemed to be pissing people off, it had to be a group decision, made by people the rest of the Hoarde actually liked and respected.

If only they would show up. It was fifteen past the hour now, and I was still the only one in the conference room.

What the hell? Had I gotten the day wrong or something? Did I do the math wrong on this stupid twenty-four hour clock?

I dug my phone out of my pocket. I meant to check my calendar, but I didn't need to. There was a message waiting for me. A group text. The meeting had been postponed by a half hour, thanks to an emergency in the hospital wing.

I glanced at the clock. It wasn't the kind of problem I could help with, except by keeping my nose out of it. I could go back to my apartment, but by the time I reached it, I would need to head back. I didn't even have time to stop by the Bazaar for something to eat.

Fantastic.

I swung my legs against the side of my chair. I had some vintage Flappy Bird I hadn't played in a while. That could probably keep me busy. But before I could find the right app, my screen lit up with a call from an unknown number.

Suspicious, I put the phone to my ear. "Hello?"

On the other side of the phone came a heavy breath. A sigh of relief. "Hey. I was scared you wouldn't pick up."

"Meph." I sat up abruptly. "Are you okay?"

"I'm sorry," he said. I could practically see his shoulders curling in on themselves as he shied away from— I didn't even know what. I couldn't hear any other voices in the background, no sounds at all except for his own agitated pacing. "I meant to call sooner."

"Never mind that. Are you alright?"

"Things got a little iffy during the interview," he admitted. "But it's okay. I think I've got it handled."

"Meph—"

He cut me off before I could finish. "And I'm making progress. My contact is investigating other factories; if I play this right, I'll be able to get you an itemized list before too long. She already got me one location."

"Meph, you're a miracle." I rose from my chair and grabbed a sharpie out of my pocket. "Where is it?"

"A small town in upstate New York, a few miles south of Albany. They're saying the place is abandoned, but they've got people guarding it. It might be worth your time to investigate. Also..." He hesitated. "Do you remember Monica Sharp? The ex-detective who was working with me, back when... before. She got brought in on that case because she said she knew you."

I stopped jotting down the details on my forearm and frowned. Why bring that up? "What about her?"

"That's the last place she was seen before she disappeared. If you do go investigating, can you…" His voice trailed off into uncertainty.

Monica Sharp, I wrote on the inside of my elbow. "I'll keep my eyes open."

"Thanks. Let me know if you decide to investigate," he said. "I'll ask around, see if I can find any more details. I'll let you know how it goes."

"Be safe," I said.

"I will." He took a breath, like he meant to say something else. But instead he said, "Goodbye," and the phone screen lit up beside my ear. The call was over.

I tried to distract myself with phone games, but I couldn't escape my anxious frustration. Meph didn't sound good, but he didn't want to give up on his mission yet. I'd have to make sure he didn't overestimate his abilities without making it look like I didn't trust him. I had to investigate the factory he'd found me, but not in such a way that would make them link our raid to our source. A delay might help, but that could potentially cost us innocent lives, and meanwhile—

"You're going to kick through the upholstery if you keep that up," Nadia said, stepping through the open door. "Did something happen?"

"What? No. Phone call from Meph." I sat up again and pulled my sleeve down to cover my elbow.

"That bad?"

"No. He's fine. He says he's fine, anyway. If everything goes well, he's hoping to get us a list of Order factories. I want us to have a plan in place for when that happens."

"Does he know how many there are?" she asked.

"It's mostly still hypothetical. Right now he's only got one, and he's not sure there's anything actually in it."

"One is enough to start."

It was also enough to get him killed.

I checked my phone one last time before it laid it on the table, face-down. The meeting was set to start in seven minutes, and I needed to focus. "I also got double-teamed by the Matsumoto Syndicate and the Rakshasa Alliance."

"I do hope you mean politically," she said.

I rolled my eyes. "If I meant otherwise, I wouldn't need your help. The Alliance is trying to bait us into starting an all-out war with the Order, and they're offering to give us soldiers to do it. Matsumoto's all up on that shit, and they're waving money under my nose to finance it."

"That's very generous of them."

"It sounds too good to be true."

"Good. You're learning." She sat down at my right hand, suddenly all business. "The Order Grandmaster in charge of the Kansai Prefecture just died, and his replacement is about as aggressive as they come. The Rakshasa Alliance is divided on political issues, and it's starting to crack their unified front. Add to that a generation that just came of age after a lifetime of hearing about their noble warrior legacy..." She kept going, but I got the gist of it. They had problems and they wanted to solve them by painting a bulls-eye on the Hoarde.

"So they're both using us." My tongue ghosted over my teeth. "We're a distraction for one and a diversion for the other."

"Don't take it personally. Matsumoto and Kumar's priorities are the good of their own people. Our needs don't belong on their agenda any more than theirs do on ours."

"Yeah, sure. So this is the point where I tell them to go fuck themselves?" Nadia narrowed her eyes, and I amended, "Politely, of course."

"If you haven't refused their offer yet, then don't. We could use money and soldiers right about now."

"Especially if we're gonna be the whole fucking world's meat shield," I muttered.

"They assume they can predict your every move just because you're a dragon. They think that the only reason you haven't rained hell down on the Order is because you don't have the resources to manage it— that all they need to give you is the freedom to act the way you really want to."

She wasn't wrong. I really, truly, sincerely wanted to run up to the nearest Order headquarters and rip its foundations out of the earth. I wanted blood and vengeance and fury. It throbbed in my chest like an old addiction.

I'd given into it once. I ripped my way through the scum of the earth and their minions. I tasted their blood and got drunk off their fear. I shrugged off their bullets like they were flies. I was all-powerful. I was unstoppable.

But at the end of that road stood Rosario. It didn't matter how much she loved me. She hated what I'd done. She'd looked at me with horror and despair. And even if she could forgive those pieces of shit for everything they'd done, she would never forgive me if I killed them. But there were other ways I could destroy the Order.

"Then they'd better be ready for one hell of a coming out party."

Meph

The next day came another three-hour cross-examination with Grandmaster Burns. The day after that, Grandmaster Adimari, then Chaplain Petric. Each interview was just as tedious and drawn-out as the last, and each one carried with it a constant threat. If I misspoke, if I used the wrong inflection or the wrong turn of phrase, I would die for my crimes. Somehow I managed to get through them without any more panic attacks, but they still took a lot out of me.

On my best nights, I only managed a few hours of sleep. I'd only been back with Arkay for a few weeks, but I couldn't get over how quickly I'd acclimated to sleeping in her company. I'd forgotten how much safer I felt in the shadow of a dragon, even when everything else around me was alien and new.

I was in a bizarre looking-glass world, stepping from one distorted reflection of reality into another. In the Felldeep, my gut instincts told me to run away screaming from the Hoarde, to grab the nearest sharp object and fight my way out of their subterranean labyrinth. Yet for all of that reflexive disgust, it felt right. My soul was at peace despite the rest of me being in a constant state of alertness.

Now I was back in the Order, where every inch of the compound felt familiar. I recognized every symbol and every snatch of scripture. I knew the angles of the architecture and the motifs of the art, and they resonated with those same parts of me that had admired their shapes without understanding when I was a child. It called out to me. It was my home. And there was a part of me that wanted to stay here, to spend the rest of my life surrounded by humans just like me who believed the same things I did. I wanted to crawl into a confessional and have my sins absolved.

But the things I'd done couldn't be absolved by the words of men. Especially not these men.

Everything about this place was wrong, no matter how much I wanted it to be right. I wanted to go back to feeling at home. I wanted to go back to being so sure about the world and my place in it. And at night I lay awake, haunted by the knowledge that I would never feel that way again.

Most days, I dealt with the stress in the mess hall, a notebook on my lap, drawing relentlessly to ground myself. Muscle memory invited me to sketch Arkay again— if anything, I had more experience with the lines of her face than any other— but instead I tried to force myself to depict the people around me.

How many of them knew about the factories? How many of them had done things they would regret for the rest of their lives?

How many of them would find out and be perfectly fine with what they'd learned?

While I drew, I listened in on other people's conversations, jotting down notes alongside the pictures. Even if I didn't have names, I had a record of their faces. Soon I had an idea of their schedules and timelines, which ones were gossips and which ones were tightlipped, which ones had important jobs and which ones were good at getting information out of others.

It didn't take long before strangers noticed my drawing, and not much longer before people started asking me to draw them. Vanity might have been a sin, but so was gossip, and I indulged both impulses.

Those fancy swords the top-ranking officials have, the ones supposedly made of dragon bone— where do you think they come from? What happens to monsters' bodies when they're disposed of? How do we even know the things we know about monsters?

My questions earned me mostly theories and speculation, but in increments I learned more.

"A friend of mine got transferred to a factory thing in Ukraine a while back. She still keeps in touch, but they don't exactly have reliable internet up in the mountains."

"I know a guy whose old handler used to work on making ghoul-bile poisons down in Colombia. Yeah, I remember his name."

I contacted them through the email in my burner phone, and as often as I could, I snuck into a hidden alcove, accessed the pinprick holes in the Order's security that Mara mapped out for me, and gave Arkay what information I had distilled.

I didn't know how long I could keep this up without getting caught. I didn't want it to be for nothing. But I couldn't deny a more selfish reason for calling her. Hearing her voice in my ear gave me the illusion that she was still beside me. She worried about me, asked me how I was feeling and whether I was eating enough. She let me ramble myself into incoherence when my anxiety ran too high, and talked me down into some semblance of calmness with soft, soothing tones that meant more than the words they contained. It was a fragile, thin lifeline, but I clung to it desperately. This was what I was coming back to. This was who I would please with my success. This was what I would lose if I failed.

This was why I could never really come back to the Order. Because I couldn't stand the thought of losing Arkay again.

Arkay

"Medical Team, do you copy?"

"Er… yes, we're ready," Quinn said into my earpiece.

"Bravo Team?"

"We copy, boss," Yash said.

"And the Alpha Team is ready, too," I said. "All right, everybody, listen up." The four people inside the van leaned in closer, and the voice in my ear went silent.

"The Medical Team will be waiting in the wings until you're called. Bravo Team, your targets are the two Orderlings assigned to guard this factory. Recon tells us that they're on alternating shifts, so one should already be asleep. We've found no evidence of backup guards or sniper nests, but that doesn't mean they don't have some kind of failsafe on hand. The Alpha Team will take the factory itself.

"The fact that the wards around the factory require daily reinforcement tells us that there's still something inside, and either they don't want it found, they don't want it out, or they don't want anyone in. We may be dealing with an artifact, or we may be dealing with a person. As of yet, my agent in the Order hasn't been able to find anything more specific than that, so I want all of you prepared for anything. Anticipate the worst, but don't use aggressive force unless there are no alternatives."

I nodded to Tomasi, our team's expert in spells and wards, and he took himself off mute to talk to the entire group. "So far we've got evidence of silver, steel, brick dust, black salt, and some pretty intricate networks of charged crystals. Those barriers won't do much to impede a physical force, but they will wreak havoc on more metaphysical entities. As of yet, we can't rule out demons or fae, or something else altogether. Keep in mind that most of these wards are meant to deal specifically with evil spirits."

"That isn't saying much," muttered Yash. "They think all of us are evil."

"Take it to mean aggressive," I said. "There's no signs of them delivering food or other supplies to the Boneyard. Whatever's in there, there's a good chance it hasn't been fed in twenty years or so. Anything that's scared and hungry is going to be dangerous. Doctor Magbantay?"

Quinn cleared his throat. "Right. There are a number of creatures that can survive multiple decades without feeding, which suggests an extended lifespan and slow metabolism. This facility is too small to house anything as massive as a living island, but it's also been here for more than a century. Therefore it's not unreasonable to believe that we may be dealing with a member of a race previously believed to be extinct. As there is a very real possibility of this creature being a vampire, it is of utmost importance that you avoid cuts or abrasions to the skin, as the smell of blood may be enough to drive them into a frenzy. Report everything you notice. I will be listening to your broadcasts and attempting to make an identification and extrapolate how to best subdue it without unnecessary violence..."

He continued talking, and I checked my phone. Three in the morning. Why did everything in my life happen at three in the freaking morning? And why did meetings keep getting scheduled at seven? It was shitty planning, if you asked me.

Quinn stopped talking. The voices in my earpiece went silent, and all the eyes in the van turned back to me.

"All right, people," I said. "Let's get started."

We unloaded from the van and moved quickly toward the factory. It wasn't long before we hit the first part of the barrier. Salt and brick dust made up the outermost ring, just basic circles to stop evil spirits from crossing from one side of the circle to the other. Since none of us qualified as spirits, we left those intact. The next ring in was made of silver, badly tarnished and bent at odd angles where the ground had shifted.

So how was it still here? I'd slept in plenty of abandoned houses that had been stripped of copper wire so someone could make a quick buck. Who in their right mind would leave thousands of dollars' worth of silver just lying on the ground like that?

Deeper in, so close it nearly touched the factory's walls, lay a circle of cold iron. Endless inscriptions and symbols had been stamped into the metal, barely visible under the thick rust.

"Looks like most of these are seals of some kind," Tomasi said, kneeling low over the circle. "I don't recommend breaking it— we don't know what kind of backlash it could have."

I frowned and reached a hand over the circle. It didn't repel me or anything. I half expected to feel something like a force field, but no dice. "Is it safe to cross?"

"I'm not seeing any signs yet that it isn't, but we can't know for sure."

That was good enough for me to step over it. It didn't explode or anything, but I could feel magic surging like electricity on my skin and dancing metallic on my tongue.

"Tomasi, I want you to stay here and figure out what's going on with these markings. Sandro, stay with him. Anything turns sour, I want you two to get the hell outta Dodge." I gestured to the remaining soldiers. "You two are with me."

One was a rakshasa with dental implants where his tusks used to be. The other was a cucuy with careful eyes and long, slender hands. Both were newbies, fast-tracked to active duty because we were too short-staffed to train them properly. In all the chaos of organizing the mission, I hadn't even gotten their names.

I led the march into the darkened building. The ground around the lobby was covered with broken glass and detritus.

The inside was dark, illuminated mostly by flickering flashlights and the more steady light of tactical glow sticks. Short-pile carpet rotted on the floor, covered in overturned furniture and the mashed-pulp remains of old papers.

I peered more closely at the peeling strips of wallpaper that hung from the ceiling. "Huh. That's weird."

"What is it?" Quinn's voice crackled in my ear. We were barely ten feet into the building and already it felt like I was going through a tunnel. "Did you find something already? Someone?"

"It's what I'm *not* finding," I said. "There's no graffiti. Like, anywhere"

"Oh." He sounded disappointed. "Well, it *is* an Order facility. There are guards."

"Guards never stopped me from tagging a wall," I said. "And we're talking two people on alternating shifts. It wouldn't be all that hard to sneak past them with a few cans of spray paint. But there's nothing here."

"Somebody broke the windows," the rakshasa pointed out.

"With what, though?" the cucuy asked. "You could probably throw a rock a pretty fair distance. Or maybe a pellet gun…" As she moved to get a better look at the broken glass, something snapped under her foot. She stepped away, revealing the bones of a dead bird.

It wasn't the only one, either. More than a dozen piles of beak and bone lay scattered across the floor. The ground was covered in feathers.

"Bones are a good source of calcium," I mused. "You'd think something would have eaten these by now." Bits of flesh still held the skeletons together, dried into leather by sunlight and time and conspicuously ignored by scavengers. Not a good sign. "Must have been one hell of a lazy cat."

We moved deeper into the lobby, our lights scouring the hallway for signs of life. The place definitely looked like it had been abandoned for a while.

Something skittered nearby, and I whirled to the source of the sound.

"You hear something, boss?" asked the cucuy, shining her light over my shoulder.

"Yeah," I said. "Didn't you?"

She shook her head.

I breathed in deep, my nostrils flared. The air smelled like mildew, like mold and bad meat and decay, and everywhere, the thick chemical tang of industry, full of ammonia and sulfur, copper and iron. It was gross, but it wasn't an animal smell. In fact, I didn't smell any living thing at all, except for the soldiers who'd followed me inside.

That couldn't be right.

"Let's keep moving," I said.

We plunged deeper inside, leaving the last vestiges of starlight far behind. The only light came from the devices in our hands and the tactical glow sticks hanging from our necks.

"Wait," said the rakshasa. "Did you hear it?"

"Yeah. I hear it." Only it wasn't the same sound before. This wasn't the skittering of something tiny. It was more like a clatter. There was mass behind this sound. Weight. "Neither of you happened to open a broom closet just now, did you? There was no comical avalanche of cleaning supplies?"

"No?"

So much for the simple explanation. I paused, sweeping my flashlight across the floor deeper down the hall. In the distance, the light lost too much focus to be any use. It only illuminated empty shadows, and beyond them, a square of inky blackness where the hallway opened into a larger chamber. It smelled like bone dust and metal polish and roadkill that had been left in the sun so long that it hardened and dried.

"Olly olly oxen free," I called, stepping out of the shelter of the hall.

The rakshasa fidgeted. "Do you really need to do that?"

I gave him a look. "We literally have neon green lights announcing our presence. We couldn't get any less subtle if we tried. And the fucking echo really isn't helping anything." The clatter was louder now, closer, but I couldn't pinpoint its direction. It seemed to be coming from all around us.

My soldiers exchanged glances.

"What echo?" the cucuy asked.

"It's these fucking walls," I said. "It sounds like somebody dropped a cutlery drawer down an escalator in here."

"Then why aren't our voices echoing, too?"

I blinked.

Oh.

Shit.

Slowly I turned around, dragging my light up the wall. This time there was no mistaking the source of the sound: yellowed metatarsal bones, loosely bound to the lumpy tarsals with strips of unfinished leather. In place of proper leg bones were— that couldn't be right— *swords*. Two swords, the same shade of stained-tooth-yellow as the bones, and they were expertly crafted aside from the missing hand guards. Further up the skeleton, knives and scythe-blades had been arranged on a long, reptilian ribcage. My light glinted along the carved surface of a femur that was halfway to becoming a broadsword, still porous and unpolished. The bones shifted with a light clatter, tilting to better catch the light.

If there'd been any doubt in my mind that it was a dragon, it evaporated.

It was wrapped dramatically around the entrance we'd come through, waiting for my flashlight to strike its skull, posing like this was a goddamn photo shoot instead of an ambush.

Look at my bones. Aren't they pretty? Aren't they grand? Don't I impress you? Gaze upon me and tremble, puny mortals.

"It couldn't just be a giant-ass skeleton," I muttered. "Oh, no. It had to be a diva."

I don't know if it understood enough English to recognize the insult, or if just got tired of waiting for my flashlight to move on from its leg. My soldiers turned around just in time to see its skull lurch into the beam of light and snap open wider than skin and ligaments would have allowed, roaring with a sound of shrieking wind and clattering bones.

I did the only sensible thing I could think of, and I roared right back.

The dragon swerved, its empty sockets fixated on me. If it had any flesh around its teeth, it would have been snarling. And, being the generous soul that I am, I demonstrated what the gesture should have looked like with a snarl of my own.

It seemed like a good idea at the time.

The bone dragon hurled itself off the wall and straight at us. My soldiers dodged left and I rolled to the right. Before all two-hundred-odd bones had left the wall, the skeleton changed direction and kept going after me, its tail lashing the floor where the rakshasa scrambled to his feet. The other dragon's focus was entirely on me.

"Get out of here!" I shouted to them. I didn't stay to see if they obeyed. Instead I took off running down a narrow corridor. The bone dragon chased after me with all the deadly momentum of a speeding freight train. The blades of its ribs sent up a fountain of sparks as they ground against the floor behind me.

I burst through the hallway into another huge chamber, the bone dragon close behind. My flashlight danced wildly across the far wall, but it didn't show me an opening. Before I had a chance to look properly, sixty feet of calcified territorial rage bore down on me. A fleshless claw caught me by the thigh and hurled me into the air. I hit the wall hard, hissing in pain.

But I knew pain.

I landed with my legs under me and rolled to one side before its claws could rake through my flesh. In the green light of the glow stick around my neck, I glimpsed one of the leather strips that held its bones together. The flesh was discolored and stretched, but not enough to obscure the tattoo of a crucifix.

Again the dragon lunged, and I twisted out of the way like a matador, catching it by the vertebrae of its neck. I should have been safe there, protected by its own limited range of motion.

But of course, a body is only actually limited by its own ligaments and tendons. Which this thing didn't have.

Its leg rotated in its socket and caught me in the chest. Talons as long as my forearm embedded themselves in my body armor and tried to throw me again. But this time, I wrapped my arms and legs around the limb. The dragon roared again and slammed me into the floor. It probably meant to crush me, but its bones didn't have enough weight behind them. Instead, the carved blade of a metatarsal sliced into my arm. I pulled back with a hiss and grabbed at the hilt to push it away.

One solid wrenching pull, and the blade came free of its restraints. The other bones of its foot rattled against each other, loosed by the unexpected slack in their bindings.

The dragon gave another reedy howl and descended on me, its teeth glinting eerie green as its jaws stretched wide. Its teeth were wickedly long and sharp enough to carve right through me. I didn't stick around to find out for sure. I let go of its foot and gathered my feet underneath me just in time to swan dive straight into its open mouth. Vicious fangs snagged my clothes as the jaws snapped shut, but I kept moving. There was no tongue or throat to impede my fall. Only the knotted tangle of leather that wrapped around the base of the skull. A snap of my claws, another pull, and its bottom jaw dropped to the floor. The rest of its skull followed a moment later.

Decapitated, the dragon thrashed wildly on the floor, but its attempts to claw me off its neck only dislodged more vertebrae. I crawled along its spine and sliced through the leather joints that connected its limbs, and then made my way down its spine. Finally satisfied, I jumped off and dragged myself into the corner, safe to dose myself with *Styx* while the dragon's desperate flailing finished my work. Within minutes, it had rattled itself apart, and I was alone in the dark with a pile of harmless, shuddering bones.

By the light of my glow stick, I found my flashlight and looked around. I hadn't really been paying attention when I was running for my life through the pitch black abandoned factory, and now I had no way to get my bearings. There were three hallways that branched off the way that I'd come, all of them gouged beyond recognition by the bone dragon's passing. None of them showed any sign of light. I tried to follow the trail of my own scent, but my senses were overwhelmed by the fresh blood clotting under my clothes. That wouldn't be any help, then.

"Hellooo!" I shouted down the nearest hall.

The only reply was the rattle of the dragon's bones.

"Shut up. Nobody asked you."

The bones rattled louder out of spite.

"Okay, then. We'll do this the old-fashioned way." I turned back to the three tunnels. "Eenie, meanie, miney, moe."

The hallway on the far left looked right, more or less. I even got to a room that looked sort of like the one where I'd left my soldiers, but it was empty.

I turned on my radio.

"Hey, guys? Where'd you go?"

A garbled, staticky signal assaulted my ears. "Boss? —ou okay, boss?"

"I'm fine," I said. "You guys?"

"We're—" The cucuy's words got lost in the endless crackle. "—a way out."

Fuck. Trying to find our way back to each other was going to be fun. "Keep looking for a way out," I said. "I'm going to try going deeper."

"Arkay?" Quinn's voice cut in on our frequency, though slightly less garbled than my soldier's had been. "Oh, thank God, are you alright?"

"A couple scrapes and bruises. Nothing I can't handle. Did you know there was a zombie dragon in here?"

"A —ht? I can't hear you, you're breaking up." He spoke more slowly. "Did you hit your head? Are you experiencing heavy bleeding? Do we need to send in backup?"

"I told you, I'm fine. Seriously, did you not hear the part about the zombie dragon?"

"We heard," Tomasi interrupted, joining us on the frequency. "Doctor Magbantay is just concerned. We've had nothing but dead air for the last forty minutes."

"What are you talking about?" I asked. "I haven't even been in here that long. It's been… what, ten minutes? Twenty, tops."

"What are *you* talking about?" Tomasi asked. "Arkay, you've been in there for an hour and a half."

I looked up at the blackened halls.

"Well, fuck."

Monica

I huddled behind a piece of industrial equipment while the thunder of combat echoed through the halls. Every instinct told me to run for it, keep running and never stop, but I remained still.

That's what you were supposed to do in situations like this. Stay perfectly still. Don't attract attention to yourself. Most monsters can act human for a while, but as soon as you run, you've triggered a predatory instinct and marked yourself as prey. If you can't stand your ground, you're as good as dead.

At least, that's how the Order taught it. It was one of the few details I'd managed to hold onto.

When I joined, I'd assumed there were only dragons and necromancers, and maybe some vampires and werewolves duking it out like in the movies.

Turns out vamps got wiped out at the turn of the century, and werewolves disappeared at least a hundred years before that. Even with all of them gone, there were still hundreds of species and subspecies of monster, all of them hiding in plain sight.

I spent ten months learning all of this at the Order compound in New Mexico, but there had been too much information to go over for me to get in-depth on any of it. Some of the other cadets training with me had grown up in the Order, and it showed. Without a second thought they could rattle off the taxonomy of poludnica, their relation to other pseudo-fae in the Slavic countries, their periods of peak power, and their traditional dances. Meanwhile I could barely pronounce the word, let alone remember they could do that weird eye thing.

But at least I knew not to run.

My hands felt clammy inside my gloves, but I clung to the metal pipes. Down the hall, the sounds of combat finally subsided, leaving a distant clatter in its wake. It was hard to tell from over here, but it sounded to me like whoever had won the fight was leaving.

I pried myself out of my hiding spot and continued moving.

It had to be morning by now, and I was all too aware that I hadn't had anything to eat or drink since before sundown. After a night spent soaked in adrenaline, my tongue felt dry and brittle in my mouth, and my head still ached from when I'd hit it earlier. The pounding of my skull was loud enough that it almost sounded like footsteps.

Wait. No.

Those were *real* footsteps, echoing my own and coming this way. Something else moved up ahead: a long shadow swaying slowly against the darkness. I froze, and the shadow did too, without delay or hesitation.

It was my shadow, I realized, barely visible against the pitch black. But if it was my shadow, then that meant the source of light had to be behind me.

I whirled to face it. After so long in darkness, the glow seemed almost blinding, and I threw my hand in front of my eyes to block it out. After a few seconds of squinting, I could make out the source of the light: a green glow stick hanging around a human's neck.

At least, she looked human.

"Yeah, a whole lot of bones. Bones. I said *bones*. As in spooky skeletons and stuff. Yeah. Dismembering them doesn't seem to hurt them much, but it definitely slows them down." The voice was familiar, though I'd only heard it a few times. That voice had changed my life. Ruined my life. "Shit. Did I lose you? Quinn?" She looked up. "Wait. Who's there?"

I unholstered my gun and aimed at the light. Firing would bring a swarm of undead monsters down on me, but it would bring them down on her, too.

"Hey, calm down," she said. "It's just me."

"I know who you are." My voice was hoarse from breathing in all this stale air. It got the point across well enough, though. "Get on your knees."

"Buy me a drink first." She said it reflexively, entirely unconcerned as she stepped closer.

The glow stick was impossibly bright; it burned at my retinas even when I closed my eyes. After a few moments of pain, I no longer had to squint to see her: a skinny Japanese girl in a shaggy pixie cut and military-grade body armor. She must have recognized me, too, because her face fell.

"Oh," she said. "It's you. I know you."

I pulled back the slide of my Deagle as a warning. The click was especially loud, thanks to a thick layer of grit on the metal. "I said get on your knees."

"Are you going to shoot me?" She knelt without taking her eyes off me. "We knew each other, didn't we? Or we met, anyway. You arrested me. You let me take off the handcuffs because they were hurting me."

"I let you go without wearing them because you were going to kill my entire precinct otherwise," I snarled. "I should have put a bullet in you."

"You probably could've." She nodded, somber. "You were a good person, Detective Sharp. What happened?"

My old rank felt like a slap in the face. "It's not *Detective* anymore, thanks to you." I advanced, the muzzle of my gun still leveled on her. "You got me kicked off the force. You got me assigned out here in the middle of nowhere. You ruined my life."

She frowned. "But I didn't do any of that stuff."

I could shoot her right now. They'd probably let me come back to someplace that mattered, if I could find the way out and drag her goddamned body with me.

"I mean it," she said. "I mean, yeah, you let me walk out without handcuffs. But it's not like I attacked anybody after that. Nobody even noticed until way later. But even then, that was you, not me. I've got absolutely nothing to do with the police, and I sure as fuck can't get you transferred anywhere. So why is it my fault?"

"You dragged me into this bullshit!"

"How?" she asked. "You're the one who arrested me, remember?"

"I was just doing my job!" I was shouting now, and my voice echoed off rust and rot and bounced back to me deformed beyond recognition. "Nobody ever told me about dragons or zombies or necromancers. Nobody asked me if I was prepared to deal with any of this shit. Nobody ever trained me. I was just trying to do the right thing, and I lost everything!"

My chest heaved with my hoarse gasps. I didn't even want to blow her head off so much as I wanted to keep shouting, but another sound filled my moment of silence. Bones clattered on the linoleum floor.

"Shit."

Arkay glanced over her shoulder into the dark. "That wasn't the dragon, was it?"

"There's a dragon in here, too?" I demanded. She shot me a look. "There's *another* one?"

"There is, but they just went all to pieces on me. Total drama queen."

Was that supposed to be some kind of joke?

The rattle of bones came closer.

"Put away the light before it sees us!" I hissed.

"Hm?" She glanced at her glow stick. "I'm sorry, weren't you about to shoot me?"

The thing was getting closer. It sounded big, but it sounded like there was only one. If I shot her now, I'd be bringing an entire crowd down on our heads. "Hurry!"

"I'll take that as a no." She tucked the glow stick into her collar, and the world was plunged into impenetrable darkness. Only a few sparks of light showed between the layers of her body armor, but they vanished as she turned away from me. As the bony feet approached, she disappeared entirely. There was a sudden crash, a rattle, and the meaty sounds of bone colliding with flesh. When the glow stick came out again, the skeleton lay in pieces on the floor.

"Really?" Arkay demanded of the skeleton. "Really? That's just immature." She glanced up at me. "Can you believe this guy tried to punch me in the boob?" She shook her head and turned away. In an instant she was eclipsed behind the wall, and I was surrounded once again by darkness, interrupted only by the faint gray of the doorway.

Maybe the dark was getting to me, but I didn't like the idea of spending another hour alone in this goddamned factory.

"Wait!" I hurried after her. "Where are you going?"

"Well, Bonejangles over there was coming from this direction. I figure there must be something important that way. Worth checking out, anyway."

"You can't just run off and leave me here in the dark."

I could practically hear her rolling her eyes. "Then quit dragging your feet and come with me."

It was a bad move. I knew it the moment I made it, just like I knew she was a dragon. But she had light, and she had equipment, and she had the brute force to fight off these monsters. I could fight her again later. Right now, I needed to focus on getting out of here alive. "Shouldn't we be focusing on finding an exit?"

"What, don't you know how to get out?"

I shook my head. "This place is practically a labyrinth. I've been going in circles for... Jesus, I don't even know how long."

"The place isn't all that big. I've seen high schools with more square footage. Either you have the world's shittiest sense of direction, or—" She paused, frowning. "Oh. Okay, never mind. Thanks, Tomasi." She glanced back at me. "It's magic."

"What?"

"All those spell circles outside? One of them's outfitted with like a... what the fuck was it, Tomasi? It messes with your spatial reasoning, your memory, all that jazz. Gets you all turned around so you get lost when you really shouldn't. Tomasi's working on disabling that particular feature. It'll take some time, though, if we want to avoid any particularly nasty backlash."

"There's someone else in here, too," I said. "A girl. A college student, maybe. I came in here looking for her. She might still be alive."

Arkay looked at me strangely. "We can take a look if you want. When did that happen?"

"She ran in here only a few seconds before me. That was... I don't even know. A few hours ago, I think. It's easy to lose track of time in here."

"I can believe it." She peered around at the endless black. "There's a chance she's not around anymore."

"I know that. But I still have to look."

"Okay," she said. Calmly, softly. "Okay. Are you okay to walk?"

"What makes you think I'm not?"

"Then come on," she said. "Let's look for that girl."

Arkay

I'd always assumed that navigating a maze would be easier if you did it in a group. Turns out that only works if one of the members of the group had any idea where they were going. Too often we hit dead ends, and when we doubled back, the halls behind us looked weird and unfamiliar.

It took an embarrassing number of wrong turns before I went back to Labyrinth 101 and pulled a sharpie out of my gear. It was supposed to be for emergencies, to write down last-minute memos in case I risked overdosing on Styx, but it worked just as well for marking our path.

I used my old tag, a stylized RK, along with an arrow to show which way we'd gone. Sharp glared at me when I scrawled the first one on a doorway.

"Really?" she asked.

"What?"

"Somebody carved that into the bodies of good cops. That symbol belongs to a serial killer."

"It was mine first," I said. "Not my fault the fucker stole it."

I left another mark every time we went through a door or made a turn, but it didn't make much of a difference. More than once, we passed through a door, only to find an arrow pointing back the way we came.

Several times Sharp pointed out a tear in my clothes or a cut on my face that hadn't been there a moment before. My glow sticks dimmed and died without warning, and I had to replace them, and then replace them again. When I took inventory of my supplies, I noticed three syringes of Styx were empty. I only remembered using one.

After way too long of walking, we stopped in a room that didn't already have a mark.

It was a laboratory, the walls lined with candles, the floor painted black and smeared with chalk. The shelves were covered with crystals and silver bowls and bones. The walls and counters were covered with photographs of chalk circles.

I knew those circles.

I'd been in a place like this before.

"This is a necromancer's lab." I crushed a beetle under my shoe, and pulled back to look at its empty carapace. "Well, that explains all the bugs."

"Attracted to all the corpses?"

"Any building's gonna have a shitload of bugs. Normally they eat each other or get eaten by spiders or some shit like that, so you don't really see them. But around here, nothing lives long enough to become a predator. They don't need to eat, so they're just kind of sticking around. And eventually that adds up to a lot of little creepy crawlies."

"Did your friend tell you that?" Monica asked.

"Hm?"

She pantomimed the earpiece I was wearing.

"Oh, Tomasi? Nah, I haven't been able to hear him for the last four hallways or so. This room is probably a cause of that."

Sharp crouched to examine a long femur, deliberately arranged at the corner of a nine-pointed star. At another point of the star lay an unmistakable skull. "Those bones aren't human, are they?"

Getting oddly specific there, don't you think? "They belonged to people," I said.

"But were they humans?"

I glowered at her through the dim light. "No, they probably weren't human. I'm guessing ghoul or succubus or something. But they were still people. They still had goals and friends and families. They didn't deserve to wind up here any more than anybody else did."

"Says you."

"Yes, says me."

You know, nobody's making me keep you around. I could just kick out your knee cap and leave your rank ass in the dark.

I could.

But I wouldn't. I may not have single-handedly ruined her life, but she was still part of my collateral damage. I had a responsibility to her. But that didn't mean I had to listen to her racist bullshit.

I looked over the photographed circles and changed the subject. "Looks like they were experimenting. Like, full-on scientific method kind of experimenting. You can see where they washed the chalk off the floor when they made their alterations. Most of these circles are only slightly different—probably a lot of refining and perfecting going on."

"So these are all necromancy?" she asked.

Dammit, I'm trying to read.

"Not all of it," I said after a heavy breath. "The symbols here are all wrong for that. That circle over there is meant for warding. Protection. See these over here, the Arabic? This set of circles wards against djinn. The runes over here are for fucking with the reflexes of people who enter the circle uninvited, kind of like what's around this building." I'd picked up the auxiliary information mostly by watching Tomasi work during raids. I recognized their general purpose, but I couldn't pick out any one from the set.

"But I thought you said it was necromancy."

"For spells like this to have any real power behind them, they have to cost something," I said. "Blood. Sacrifices—preferably ritualistic ones. And you'd have to do a shit-ton of different rituals if you're gonna be stapling together this many different types of magic into one spell."

Deeper inside the core of the circle were symbols that were meant initially for key processes in alchemy. In necromancy, those same processes had taken on another purpose.

Mortification. Extraction. Inhumation. Rarefaction.

I frowned. That couldn't be right. But it was right there in front of me.

Revivification.

I looked more closely at the circle, the perfect arrangement of intent and meaning.

"What the hell are they teaching in that Hoarde of yours?"

"I didn't learn it from them," I said quietly. "I learned it from Matheson. You know, Mr. Reanimator from back in Indy. You guys apparently never found his evil lair."

Monica raised an eyebrow. "You did?"

"He brought me and Rosa there when he was trying to kill us. Turns out the guy had one hell of a library. And then Rosa got hurt, and you guys burned down my house, and it was fucking cold outside. So I hid out in the old lab for a while."

For two weeks, I camped out in that basement, and I only left to eat and shit. Every other waking moment, I pored over the books. I read them cover to cover, memorized every symbol, every formula, every spell. If Rosa was going to die, then she wouldn't be dead for long.

"You wanted to bring her back," Monica said.

"Wouldn't you?"

It wasn't that easy. The spells in the books showed how to raise the dead, but they wouldn't be revived. The corpses would be inanimate puppets, without mind or memory or a will of their own. Another spell outlined a different procedure. You could suck the life out of one person and transfer it to someone else to keep them alive. To heal them. To make them okay.

"You said magic like this had to cost something." Monica stared at me, her face hidden by shadows. "What was it going to cost?"

"Not as much as I was ready to pay."

As far gone as Rosario was, I'd have to kill someone. Not just one person, either. Dozens.

But it wasn't like I'd take innocent people. I'd go after the ones who deserved it—rapists and child molesters. Scum of the earth whose lives meant nothing compared to hers.

But Rosa wouldn't see it that way.

And the fact that I was willing kill all those people for her? To save her?

She would never forgive me.

That's why I torched the house and everything inside it. That's why I went looking for Meph.

But how was I supposed to explain that to Sharp when she was staring at me like I was dog shit on the bottom of her shoe? I didn't even know if it was because she still blamed me for everything bad that ever happened to her, or because I'd dared to think about necromancy, or just because I wasn't human.

I tilted my head and flashed a cheerful rictus. "But hey, they wouldn't be dragons, so that makes it okay, right? Because killing off dozens of innocent people is only a bad thing if they're just like you, right? After all, who cares if some person's skull is just lying on the ground like that, as long as it isn't human?"

Sharp bristled. "That's not what I meant."

"You sure about that? Because that's definitely the message I've been getting. Or is it not even about protecting your own anymore? Is it just about humans being the master race and to hell with everybody else?"

"I said it's not like that!" Sharp stormed forward. "Stop twisting my words around."

I let out a hoarse, ugly laugh and rose to my feet. "Look around you, Sharp. We're standing in a death camp, on top of a laboratory full of experiments powered by so many blood sacrifices that the fucking radio doesn't work anymore, and you're arguing semantics?" I leaned in. "You personally hunted down and murdered mourners at a candlelight vigil. Not soldiers. Not criminals. Nurses and mechanics and preschool teachers. So don't you fucking *dare* judge me."

"Then why are you here, if I'm the antichrist?" she demanded. "Why not just kill me already?"

She looked ready to punch me, and I wanted her to. I could snap her like a twig and call it self-defense. I wanted to. I was so fucking tired of playing nice with people who hated me. But I couldn't.

"Because it wouldn't be right."

Monica

We stepped through the door into another huge chamber. Strip lights swayed overhead, suspended from the ceiling by long chains. The light of the glow stick showed the faint outline of figures all over the floor. Most of them looked human, or mostly so, sitting and standing and curled on their sides. When we entered, almost every head turned to face us. A few of them turned away with a shudder. The floor before us was strewn with bones, most of them broken into pieces, some shattered so profoundly that they'd been reduced nearly to dust.

I searched the entrance to the room, but there was no sharpie tag near here. Wherever we were, we hadn't come this way yet. Arkay wasn't the one who caused all this damage.

So who was?

"Get out," said a low, slow, reedy voice. "Turn back while you still can."

Another wheezing voice echoed the first. And another followed it, all in a haunting chorus. "Get out, get out, get out."

"We're working on it," Arkay said, walking through the undead crowd like they were holiday shoppers. A few cringed away from her.

But one of them caught my attention.

A large dog, or the remains of one. Its bony tail was wrapped in dusty fabric and tucked tight against its leg, but it still curled protectively around the corpse of a young woman.

She stroked at a bald patch on the dog's leathery shoulders. "It's okay, Rexie."

I'd only heard her speak once, and now her voice was cracked and hoarse, but I recognized her instantly. She'd only been here for a few hours. Days at most. Barely longer than me. But her skin had dried into leather, and in places it receded entirely to expose yellowed bone. Her eyes were shrunken and shriveled and and rheumy white.

This wasn't supposed to happen. I was supposed to save her.

She looked me in the eye. "You need to get out of here. Hurry, while there's still time."

"Time for what?" I asked.

"Just go!" she hissed. Her voice rose. "Hurry, before he—" Another zombie's hand clapped over her mouth, its skin covered in flaking scales that would have looked more at home on a fish.

"Quiet," the other zombie hissed. "You'll wake him."

When the other creature released her, the dehydrated muscles of the girl's face twisted into an unmistakable expression of fear.

I crouched beside her and lowered my voice to a whisper. "Who is he?"

The girl shook her head, her mouth clamped tightly shut.

"Please," I said. "I want to help you, but I need to know what's going on."

"There's no time," she breathed. "Please, just run—" The word broke halfway through the syllable. Her mouth hung open, stretching into a silent scream.

The entire room had gone quiet.

"Uh… Sharp?" Arkay said. "I think something just happened."

Keep your voice down, I hissed. Or I tried to, but my mouth wouldn't open.

Around me, dozens of figures uncurled and climbed to their feet. The ones already upright moved toward us, their motions stiff and unnatural.

"Okay, you made your point," Arkay said. "We're leaving. Hear that, Sharp? We're leaving."

What's happening? I wanted to demand, but I couldn't. My mouth wouldn't move. Only my legs did.

"Guys, I'm down for self-defense, but I don't want to hurt you." Arkay retreated further. "Can we just calm down?"

More zombies shuffled toward her, blocking off her exit. Mine too, if I could figure out how to make my legs obey me.

"Monica, can you hear me?" she asked.

Yes, I can hear you!

"Say something, Monica. Do something. Give me a sign."

I strained. There had to be some way to get through to her, but I couldn't even blink on command.

"Dammit!" she hissed.

I was closest to her, and so I was one of the first to lunge her way. But my movements weren't the ones I'd practiced in endless hours of training and sparring. These were stiff. Jagged. Arkay ducked under my lunge easily and dove between the legs of the nearest zombies.

"You guys aren't in control of yourselves," she said. "This isn't you. Try to fight it."

I was trying. Goddamn, I was trying, but I had nothing to show for it. My body wouldn't obey me, and the crowd descended on her. Dragon or not, a mob this huge was going to rip her to shreds.

Arkay

The zombies surged, and Monica vanished into the crowd. No time to enact a dramatic rescue. I tucked and rolled through a barricade of the undead and scrambled up a ladder.

"Tomasi, can you hear me?" I said into my earpiece. "Come in, Tomasi. I really need you right now."

The undead followed me up, but they were bottlenecking at the ladder. At least that would buy me some time.

A voice crackled through my earpiece. "…'rkay?"

"Tomasi, there's freakin' zombies, and they're swarming. Please tell me you know anything that can help with this."

"I can— what you need— do— s—"

Dammit, this wasn't helping.

Most of these zombies had been hanging around for decades. By now they were barely more than mummies, held together with scraps of fabric and leather. It wouldn't take much to rip right through them, especially if I got big and scaly first.

But they were victims here, conscious and unconsenting. I wasn't going to just mutilate them, not if I could help it.

Whoever was controlling them wasn't going to wait for me to come up with a plan. I had to avoid dying first. And that meant I had to get higher.

I found handholds in the rusted wall and scrambled up to the ceiling. I clung upside-down to an I-beam, but already the zombies were following after me, and more were coming up the opposite wall. The beam rattled to the beat of dozens of new hands clattering toward me. A metallic groaning joined the chorus of undead moans. Pieces of metal fell loose from the weathered ceiling, loosened screws and flakes of rusted iron and chittering bugs.

Suspended fluorescent lights crashed to the floor, along with the iron chains that had anchored them to the ceiling. It would have been a safety hazard, if almost everyone in this room wasn't already dead.

I looked to the beams on either side of me for escape, but they were too far away for me to jump, and already they were crowding with more bodies.

Only two directions left to go: up or down.

I anchored my thighs against the beam and punched straight into the ceiling. Jagged iron tore through my armor and bit into my skin, but it was old enough to crumble under the blow. When I pulled my fist back, it was bloody and illuminated by a blinding light.

Sunlight streamed through the hole I'd made, so shrouded in dust that it seemed almost solid. My eyes stung, but I squeezed them shut and took another punch at the ceiling, and another, and another. When the hole was wide enough, I squeezed through, wincing when the jagged metal sliced into my chest. But that didn't matter.

I was out.

Sunlight poured down around me. The corrugated metal of the roof stretched out in every direction, offering an unimpeded view of the city around me. A Hoarde van was parked in the distant weedy parking lot, and beside it lounged the weary figures of my strike teams. I could walk right to them. It didn't matter what effect the spell circle had on my mind; it couldn't get me turned around when the way out was directly in my line of sight. The zombies clamored below, struggling to make it through the narrow hole. A few of them might get through, but they wouldn't be able to follow me past the edge of the circle. A little more running, and I could leave them behind. I could leave all of this behind.

Sharp was already lost. Besides, Meph had only ever asked me to find out what happened to her. Now I knew. Mission accomplished. I had no obligation to stay. Not for him. Not for her. Not for anyone.

But it wasn't about obligation.

I turned around, moving forward until I felt the stability of an I-beam under my feet, and I stomped another hole through the corrugated iron beside it. A few feet further, I did the same thing, and then I did it again. Every puncture in in the roof let in another shaft of light that stabbed through to the floor, until the inky blackness lifted into a murky dark.

Vague shadows became defined shapes, and even the figures still on the floor became clearly identifiable. There were dozens of zombies, most of them frantically dragging themselves up to my level.

All but seven.

Six of them stood perfectly still, posed like soldiers at attention in a circle around the seventh, who sat in a cracked leather office chair. The seat didn't have nearly as much style as the one I had in the Felldeep, but I recognized a throne when I saw one.

One of the zombies managed to squeeze through the largest of the holes and started across the roof toward me. More followed after it. Too bad; it looked like it took a lot of work to get all the way up here.

I peeled open the newest hole and slipped through, leaving them behind. I found my way to a suspended light and climbed down, letting myself hang a good fifteen feet over the zombies' heads.

The six guards were arranged on the edges of a circular iron gutter that had been set into the floor. Geometric patterns spiraled inside it, drawn in rusty brown beneath a layer of dust. The man in the chair squinted up at me with yellowed, bloodshot eyes. His hair was thin and wiry, his skin sallow and unnaturally pale. I couldn't guess at his race— his features were sunken and sagging, like the bones of his face had started to dissolve under his flesh. He looked more like a corpse than anyone else here, but his chest rose and fell in the rhythm of his ragged breathing. I recognized his uniform, even under endless layers of dirt. I'd seen people wearing jumpsuits just like it in the last factory.

"Our necromancer, I presume."

"At your service," he rasped. The corners of his mouth lifted and warped into a savage grin. "I hope you enjoyed my work? I'm very proud of it."

I bet you are.

I shifted my weight, and the chain squealed as I started to swing.

"What am I saying? Of course you don't understand. They never do." He laughed. It was a rasping, harsh sound. "You thought you could just come in here and catch me, didn't you? Oh, but you're just their pawn, aren't you? They sent you here to do their dirty work, just like they sent all the others. Just like they sent me. But that's not enough. You know why? Because I'm smart. I'm brilliant. And you—you're nothing but a dim bulb. Burnt out. Useless."

He was trying to bait me. Make me attack so I'd leave the safety of my perch.

I tilted my head. "So that's how you're doing it."

The necromancer hesitated, squinting against the light.

"People come looking around, you drag them into the circle, and then you suck the life out of them. In the literal sense." I definitely had his attention. "Normally something like this shouldn't completely substitute food and water, but I'm guessing those were your modifications, weren't they?

The necromancer straightened slightly. "Not entirely dim, perhaps."

"You're definitely meticulous. I saw those circles in the other room." It was a trick I'd learned as a stripper. Most people liked to be the center of attention more than they liked lap dances. Keep the conversation focused on them, and they'd tell you anything.

"The product of years of research." God, was he seriously preening? "They were idiots to throw me away."

"Same old story," I said. "Heard it a hundred times. They love the results you give them, but…"

"But nobody likes the mess that comes with it. Nobody ever wants to pay the price. But you did, didn't you? That's how you know about all of this, isn't it?" He looked me in the eye. "Do tell me about her. It's always a woman, isn't it? What was she? Your mother? Your sister? Your girlfriend?" His grin turned obscene. "Oh, what did you say her name was? Rosa?"

My knuckles tightened around the chain. Static crackled in the air around me. The fluorescent light under my feet sputtered and glowed.

One well-aimed leap. That was all it would take, and I could rip the bastard's head from his shoulders. I could do it. Fuck, I wanted to do it.

I forced my fangs to revert back into ordinary teeth, but sparks still fell from my fingertips. "You heard that, did you?"

"You'll find that sound carries so very well in this place."

"Yes, her name was Rosa." I hooked a knee around the chain and leaned lower. "You would have liked her. Most people did."

"Come closer, dear. It's hard to hear you."

I leaned further. "She would've felt sorry for you, being locked up in the dark for so long."

He laughed. "Not locked up. I'm the king of this domain."

"The king of corpses," I said flatly. "The Order put so many sealing spells on this place that I'm surprised the basic laws of physics still work. They've kept a constant guard over this place for decades. It's not even considered a good gig, either. It's a shit job, where they send the people they don't like. It's meant to bore people to death."

He sneered. "They were frightened of me. Jealous of my powers."

"Let me whistle you a tune, Mister Scientist, and you can tell me if I'm off key." A slight shift in my weight, and I started swinging from the long chain. The fluorescent light blazed under my feet, and somehow the necromancer looked even more lifeless and pathetic. "They hire you for your brilliant work on spells or circles or whatever. Maybe you've heard about necromancy and its corrupting influences, but you tell yourself that couldn't *possibly* happen to you. You're *moral*. You're *righteous*. You're doing it for truth and justice and God and kittens and all that bullshit. You're above it all. And your bosses, they tell you they trust you. That you won't let them down like the last guy did. They tell you how he was arrogant and self-absorbed and weak, like this was all just his own flawed character instead of his neurons literally *melting* inside his skull. And you told yourself that it couldn't *possibly* happen to you. But then it did, didn't it? You started getting paranoid. Forgetting things. Maybe you started feeling bugs crawling on you when you couldn't see them. Maybe you started seeing things that weren't there. Maybe you called it stress and overwork, because you were so dedicated to your job. But it wasn't stress, was it? And your bosses started to notice. So one day you come to work and you're the one scheduled for the chopping block."

"They were going to kill me!" he shrieked. "After all the things I'd done for them! After all my hard work and loyalty, they were just going to throw me away!"

"And there's the refrain," I said. "You'd be surprised how many times I hear this same song. And you know what? Most of the time, I'm on the side that says people don't deserve that. But you—you're a special brand of shitty."

"I am a martyr!"

"You butchered and enslaved hundreds of innocent people to save your own skin. That's about as far from 'martyr' as you can possibly—" I leaned too far, and put too much weight on the single chain.

The straining links stretched and snapped. For a delirious instant, I felt weightless, grabbing at the swinging chain to save me, but I plunged to the ground.

I didn't have time to gasp in pain before six bodies descended on me, pulling me prostrate into the center of the circle. The necromancer stood over me, a bronze knife in his hand. "I was doing God's work."

"You sure about that?" I pushed myself up just enough to look him in the eye. "This looks an awful lot like hell to me."

He brought down the knife.

I brought down the lightning.

Monica

The necromancer went rigid, twitching and jerking like he'd been tased. His hold over me tightened, strangling me in its grip. Then it fell away entirely.

I was free.

I acted on instinct. In an instant, my sidearm was out of its holster and in my hands, aimed at the bastard's head.

"Wait, don't—"

With three short squeezes of the trigger, I emptied the rest of the magazine into what should have been his skull.

Instead my shots went wide. The necromancer fell to the side, dropping just underneath the line of fire.

I released the magazine and rammed another in its place. Meanwhile, Arkay threw the dogpile of zombies aside and lunged to her feet.

"What the fuck was that?" she demanded.

I stormed forward. "He needs to die."

"No, he fucking doesn't!" She stepped into my path. I tried to shove her aside, but she wouldn't budge. "Sharp, think for one second—"

"I am thinking!" I snapped. "Take a look around you. He has to be stopped. He has to pay for what he's done."

"And you're gonna make that happen by shooting him while he's unconscious?" She jumped in front of me again. "You were a cop, Sharp. What the fuck happened to justice and due process of law and all that shit?"

"There are no laws for people like him." I took aim, but she grabbed my arm and forced it to point at the ceiling. I tried to wrench out of her grip, but her hand was like iron around mine. "Dammit, let go of me!"

More hands were reaching out and grabbing at me, pulling me back and away. I thrashed, but I couldn't get leverage against anything except for Arkay's hold of my arm. He was regaining control of the zombies. I had to kill him before he started after us again.

Arkay forced the gun away from me, and the mass of hands yanked me back, pulling me away from the circle.

Of course. She knew about necromancy.

"This is you!" I shouted. "*You're* controlling them!" I writhed so hard that my joints threatened to give way. "Dammit, why are you siding with this piece of shit?"

Her expression stilled. Her light cast long shadows across her face. "I'm not." She raised her voice. "Sharp, think.

216

You've seen what happens when you kill a necromancer. All their spells break. Everyone they raised goes back to being dead. *Everyone.*"

The static in the air thickened, and the lights above her head started to glow. The surrounding lights joined in, casting a dim, murky light on the room, but for the first time, I could see clearly. Living corpses, their desiccated faces contorted in determination and fear as they held me down. Other bodies twisting away from me, their faces hidden behind their arms, like they were bracing for an explosion. The skeletal figure of a minotaur clutching a calf protectively against its chest.

"These aren't mindless brain-munchers," Arkay said. "They're sapient, self-motivated people, when he's not controlling them. If you kill him, you're gonna kill them all."

Another figure stepped close behind Arkay. A teenage girl with her hand on a whimpering dog. She'd been human once. She'd had her whole life ahead of her, and she could have been incredible, if only I'd saved her.

The strength drained out of me. I stopped resisting my restraints.

"He has to be stopped," I said weakly.

"I know. And he will be. One phone call and I can get him to a nice dingy jail cell. My guys have read up on this stuff. They'll figure out a way to hold him so he can't hurt anyone else."

She held out her hand in command. The hands that held me started to loosen, and I slid to my knees.

Arkay gave directions to the zombies and called whatever contacts were waiting on the other side of her earpiece. I didn't move. I didn't even look up until she dropped the necromancer in front of me and perched beside him.

"You okay?" she asked.

No. Not by any stretch of the imagination.

"Tomasi's almost done getting that directional spell down. As soon as he does, they can send someone in to come get us."

"How long has he been working on it?" I asked. I didn't really want to know. Or maybe I knew, and I didn't want to find out if I was right.

It was like Schrodinger's Cat, stuffed inside that box. As long as you didn't open it, it could have anything inside. If I didn't ask, then everything was exactly as it had always been. No more or less than what I expected.

"Forty-four hours," she said. "Between him and a few other specialists they brought in. The poor guy had to sleep eventually."

Almost two days. "You haven't had anything to drink since then," I said.

Schrodinger's cat wasn't an actual thought experiment, but a parody of one.

I raised my head to look her in the eye. "How long was I in there before you came to get me?"

She held my gaze. "Three years."

Just because you weren't looking at the damn cat didn't make it any less dead.

"Meph— Adam— he asked me to look for you as soon as he found out what happened, but he was asking about your body. I don't think he expected you to still be around."

"It doesn't seem like that long." I looked around at the other zombies. The other victims. The girl who vanished inside this hellhole seconds before me. "Do I look like that?"

Arkay pulled out her phone, heavy in its rubber casing and already most of the way through a reboot. "Would you like to see?"

She turned on the front facing camera, and gingerly I took it. The light of the screen and her glow stick weren't enough for a glamor shot, but that didn't matter. No amount of lighting would make that picture seem flattering. The face on the screen was shriveled and leathery, the eyes glazed white, the cheeks perforated. Strips of flesh hung loose around a gash on the side of my head, close to the temple. My hair hung loose and matted around my face.

I pushed the phone away with a shudder. "You said you read up on this stuff. Can you fix this?"

"There's no harm in asking. I'm sure there's somebody somewhere who knows for sure."

It was a gentle way of saying no.

I turned my stare to the unconscious necromancer. "All the people in here— they didn't all wander in after the circles were up, did they?"

"I think I tried explaining it to you once," Arkay said. "But I don't know if you remember. It's easy to forget stuff in here. This facility was a death camp. Every time the Order captured someone alive, they were brought to a place like this. They've caught a lot of people over the years."

"I thought we were doing the right thing." My voice was small. Frail. "I thought we were saving people."

"Yeah." Arkay turned her head to the inky ceiling. "I hear that a lot."

Meph

It was almost two weeks before I got a call back from Mara.

"Adam, we need to talk. Now."

The mess hall was crowded that day. Not a good time for a conversation. "Not now. I'll call you back as soon as I'm in my room."

"Now." Her voice was like iron.

I lowered mine. "Did something happen?"

"Like you don't know. You knew what was in those files, didn't you? This was all some kind of sick setup, wasn't it?"

"I only know what I saw," I said carefully.

"This is entrapment. You're— you're tainting me. You're making out like everything I do is for— for this.

You're making me out to be some kind of— of genocidal monster."

"I never said that."

"I'm doing the right thing!" she snarled. "I'm saving lives! I'm protecting innocent people from having to live through what I did. They took my leg, dammit!"

I braced myself against the table. "One of them did, yes. And that one deserved to die. I'm not arguing against that. I will never argue against that." I lowered my voice until it was less than a whispers. "But Mara, there were *children* in there."

"If we let them live, then they'll grow up into killers! If you spare the children, they'll remember who turned them into orphans, and they'll come after us! They'll be a thousand times worse than their parents ever could have been! So we have to kill them. We have to stop them from becoming real monsters. We have to stop them from becoming— from becoming—"

"From becoming just like us?"

She was breathing hard. "Don't do this to me, Adam. Don't drag me into this with you."

"You did the research, Mara. You saw those files, not me. Tell me it was staged. Tell me it was all an elaborate plot to turn us against them."

"I believe in our Order. I believe we're doing God's will." She said it with the rigidity of recited prayer. "We have to be. Everything we dedicated our lives to can't be wrong."

"And maybe it isn't. Maybe this isn't the Order at work. Maybe it's the Contessa. We know she's been manipulating the Order to kill her rivals for her. Maybe this is how she gets rid of the monsters who won't pledge their loyalty to her. God knows what she tried to do to me."

"This would be just like a dragon." Mara's voice dripped disgust, but underneath that veneer was a gleam of hope.

"It would, Mara. I know it would. We know she's got agents all the way at the top. My money says they're the ones behind all this. They're the ones twisting us around into something vile and evil. But that that's why we have to be careful, Mara. If we can't trust them, then we have to think for ourselves. Use our own judgment to figure out if the orders they're giving us are right or wrong. We can't keep blindly following them anymore."

"I'm not going against the Order," she said.

Dammit, dammit, dammit. If she turned on me now, I was fucked. She'd turn me in, and I'd be locked up and—Stop. No. If I went down that road, I would wind up in the throes of another panic attack. Think rationally.

"I'm not asking you to. I'm not asking you to leave or to try to sabotage them. I'm just asking you to stand up against the parts that have been led astray."

"And who's the one to decide who's been led astray, Adam? You? Or one of your dragons? How many are you working for these days? I've lost count."

"Not me," I said. "And not anybody else. You, Mara. I want you to look at everything you've seen, everything you know, and I want you to think. I want you to make a decision based on what you believe is right."

"And what if I don't want to make a decision?" she asked.

"That's still a choice." I lowered my voice. "Mara, you're the smartest person I know. You've been more places and done more things than most people can imagine. If there's one person on this goddamn planet who I believe can make an informed decision, it's you."

"You're asking me to commit insubordination."

"I know," I said. "But I'd rather sin against my superior officers than against God."

It was a dangerous line of thinking for someone who'd grown up in the Order, especially to another member. But what really cemented me as the single most imbecilic person in the whole human race was the fact that I'd chosen to make my statement in the middle of the crowded mess hall.

I looked up. Heads were turned in my direction. A pair of armed guards were striding across the room toward me.

"Make your choice, Mara," I said quietly. "I've made mine."

The call ended just as the guards arrived at my table. "The Archduchess will see you now."

Arkay

I was prepared for things to get complicated when we came back with two hundred and fourteen zombies, and the Hoarde didn't disappoint. Our doctors worried about them carrying weird undead diseases. Pragmatists suggested letting them wander in the Forest as an added security measure, and bleeding hearts argued against forcing them back into the dark. Only the ones in Order uniforms were dealt with decisively, all of them squeezed into holding cells and interrogated as quickly and thoroughly as possible.

We didn't have much time. For decades, the necromancer had subsisted entirely off the life force he'd stolen from the people who wandered into the factory. It had kept him going, but just barely, and without more sacrifices, his organs were on the fast track to failing completely. It wasn't a certain thing, though. With generous applications of Styx, we could save him, but it was getting scarce. Besides, he was a war criminal. A lot of people skipped past asking if we should save him, and went straight to debating whether we should execute him outright or let him die slowly.

But if he died, so did two hundred and fourteen other people.

Yash and Doctor Magbantay were organizing volunteers to talk to them all and find out what they wanted, asking about their families and religious needs and last requests. They'd already collected more than a hundred letters to be distributed to loved ones.

But that brought with it its own set of problems. Though most of the victims were like us, plenty of them were human, and so were the intended recipients of their last statements. And too many of their final goodbyes came with an explanation of what had happened to them, including the Order's war on our people. We could send them anyway, and just hope that their loved ones disregarded a last goodbye as some kind of deranged joke. Or we could send somebody with the letters to explain properly what had happened—and in doing so, out the world of nonhumans to dozens, maybe hundreds, of muggles.

Our allies wouldn't like that. So it was my job to persuade them.

"Matsumoto, I'm asking you to listen to reason." I managed to keep my voice relatively calm. Hopefully he couldn't tell by my heavy breathing that I was pacing circles around the Felldeep's conference room. "What happened with Meph is not an isolated incident anymore. The captured

Order members are defecting in droves. The ones who weren't working at the factory to begin with are outraged that this was going on under their noses. That's why the Order has to keep them ignorant. That's why they have to keep the *world* ignorant. Because if people realized what was actually going on, the Order would fall apart."

"You're basing your predictions on incidental evidence and wishful thinking," he said. "The backlash could result in a total genocide."

"We're already dealing with genocide, don't you—" Maybe I'd gotten too excited, because the call cut out. "Fuck."

There were limits on how much a rubber case could protect against my ambient electricity. I pulled the phone away from my ear and hurried it into a reset cycle.

I needed to switch tactics. Stay calm. I already knew that passion wouldn't persuade him.

The phone had barely switched back on before the screen lit up with an incoming call, and I put it to my ear without another glance. I wanted to say my piece before he had a chance to change the subject. "Listen, Matsumoto. If you don't want me to expose the youkai, that's fine. I only intend to out myself. Show the world what a dragon really looks like. I'm tired of living in the dark."

But the voice on the other end didn't belong to Matsumoto.

"Then you will burn."

Meph

The Archduchess stood over me. I was confined to my chair, unable to stand, shackled at the wrist and ankle to the table before me.

"Mephistopheles," the Archduchess tested my name on her tongue. "An apt name. Satan was the first traitor against God, and he sits in the lowest circle of Hell for his crimes. Fitting that you'd name yourself after *their* ilk."

Actually, the circles of hell originated from the Divine Comedy. Biblical fanfiction, Rosario once affectionately called it. I forced myself to focus on the memory, on the soothing presence Rosario always exuded, even when she herself was tense. It didn't have quite the same effect within the confines of memory. My pulse thundered in my ears. Despite my attempts to control my breathing, my breaths came shallow and harsh, and none of them seemed to fill my lungs. I had to tell myself that I wasn't really dying, that this was just the beginnings of another panic attack.

That the Contessa wasn't really in this room with me, so close she was practically breathing down my neck, ready to crush my throat with one perfectly manicured hand.

Oh God. Oh God.

"I've already told you," I said breathlessly. "I'm not a traitor. I've been—" *Oh God.* "I've been working undercover—"

"You were caught in the act of sedition and espionage," the Archduchess snapped.

"Not against the Order," I said. "Please, you have to believe me."

"I have to believe nothing you say. You are a liar and a disciple of liars. A disciple of *dragons*."

"Archduchess, that's who I'm trying to fight."

She leaned close. "You're lying."

"If I've been less than forthcoming, it's only because I don't know who to trust. There are dragons who have their claws in the Order. Who have spies of their own in this organization, and who are manipulating its members to do their dirty work." I was rambling without stopping for breath. Every time I sucked air into my lungs, it tasted like the air in the Contessa's house, in her study, beside her. I could smell—

I could smell her perfume.

I looked at the Archduchess. Her brows were knit in judgement. Not surprise. Not disbelief. She was still standing close enough that I could inhale the perfume off her skin.

"But you already knew that, didn't you?" I asked faintly. Her eyes narrowed. There, finally, was the first inkling of surprise. She knew. Of course she knew. "You're—"

From her side holster she drew a small-caliber gun. An elegant weapon, easy on arthritic joints. It wouldn't be enough to pierce a dragon's skull, but then, she was more than just a dragon slayer, wasn't she?

"It's you, isn't it? You're the one the Contessa was talking about. You've had the whole Order under her thumb for— oh God, for years." I giggled. My fears confirmed, the panic attack rebounded into giddy energy. "She's been handing you dragons on a silver platter for years now! You made your career as a dragon slayer. Did you ever actually kill any of them, or did she do that for you, too?"

How long would it take Mara to notice the patterns in the dragons the Archduchess had killed? How long before she realized they were all the Contessa's rivals?

"All you're doing is ensuring your damnation," she said.

I grinned, manic and hysterical. "Then I'll see you in hell."

Between us, a phone rang.

Arkay

I yanked the phone away from my ear. The number came without a name and an unusual number of digits. But I would recognize that voice anywhere.

"Contessa," I said. "Why the fuck are you calling me?"

"Language, *Schlängelchen*. I would like to make you a proposition."

I choked out a laugh. "You're kidding, right? You broke my fucking neck. You tortured Meph. No, I'm not making any deals with you."

"I recommend you—"

I hung up.

The phone rang again, and I answered. "Which part of fuck off don't you—"

The screen at the far end of the conference room lit up. It showed a video feed of two figures, seen from above. The camera had a bad angle and shitty resolution, but I could still make out the faces.

Meph, chained to an interrogation table, his eyes wide with panic as he stared down the barrel of a handgun.

The Contessa's voice returned. "Do I have your attention?"

My mouth was dry. "Yes."

"Are you absolutely certain?" she asked. "I would be happy to help you focus."

The screen split in half. Meph, much smaller but still at gunpoint, took up the left half of the screen. The right was an outside view of a kitchen window. Rosario leaned against the counter, chatting cheerfully on the phone while she stirred a pot.

"What do you want?" I demanded.

"That is the question of the hour, isn't it?" The Contessa laughed, and I got the sudden urge to claw the skin off her neck and pull out her vocal cords. "What if I told you to scoop out your eyes with a teaspoon? One for each of your little pets. Would you do that?"

My lips peeled back from my teeth. *Like hell I would, you twisted motherfucker.* But my voice was frozen in my throat.

I remembered the fights I used to have with Rosario, back when we were living on the streets. I remembered how much I hated when she'd drag us back to the Valley, where drunken men would demand to cop a feel in exchange for a night in a warm tent. In the shelters, where she'd make me wait outside for a half hour so the people who ran the place didn't realize we were together, and every minute apart was a minute she was unguarded against predators disguised as saints. Even when I was right there, ready and willing and desperate to protect her, she told me to stay back, to sit there and take it with a smile, because at least we wouldn't be freezing.

I fought her on it every single time, because nothing was worth compromising our dignity. Nothing was worth sacrificing our pride.

I was young, then.

I knew better now.

I unclenched my jaw. "Is… is that what you want me to do?" The words tasted like ash in my mouth.

She laughed again, and it felt like a cheese grater over my raw nerves. "You would do it, wouldn't you? And then you'd simply take your medicine and be good as new. I've snapped that scrawny neck of yours, and yet here you are, alive and walking like it doesn't even matter. Because nothing really matters to you anymore, *Schlängelchen*. Nothing but these two. So let me remind you what it's like to have something to lose."

The woman who stood over Meph pulled back the slide, took aim—

"Don't!"

"Very well." I could hear the smile in her voice, and it dripped like slime down my neck. "Turn to face the camera. I want to see your face."

Utterly numb, I inched to the side, staring down at the camera at the end of the room.

"The last time we spoke, you asked me why I didn't act against death camps in my territory. I would like to tell you what a certain commandant told me, once upon a time."

I didn't have to see her face to recognize a cold predator's smile.

"I own you."

Interlude:

A Lesson in History

This section was originally the prologue of Book 9. Part of the intention of the Urban Dragon series was to emphasize the complexity of people as a whole, and the Contessa was no exception.

—JWT

Monica

Nothing lasts forever. Not even the undead.

The necromancer who raised me was dying. When his heart stopped beating, there'd be nothing left to tie me to the mortal world. I would die, and this time, nobody would bring me back.

There was a time when that probably would have bothered me a lot more than it did now. My friends and family all assumed I was dead, my sins were atoned for, and I had no affairs to put into order. After all that, the worst part was the waiting, left alone with fermenting dread and a growing sense of impatience.

I needed something to do with myself. Something to leave my mark on before I left. So in my last months, I threw myself into one final investigation. The same dragon who had the Order under her thumb now had Arkay on a leash. At first glance it seemed like straightforward behavior for any crime lord, draconic or otherwise, but this was different. She wasn't using them to keep herself in power, but to attack each other while she lurked in the shadows.

And the worst part was that she'd pulled me into her machinations, not just once but over and over again. For years I thought I was saving people while she used me as her personal attack dog, and she didn't even give me the dignity of knowing I was dirty. But all of this had to make sense to her. She had a reason for what she was doing. Once we found it, we could negotiate with her, threaten her or bribe her or appeal to whatever twisted perversion made up her sense of justice.

Problem is, the Contessa never seemed to act directly—or if she did, she never left any evidence behind. She was intelligent, methodical, careful. I'd put away dozens of people just like her, back when I was on the force, people who thought they were too clever to leave a trail behind. Too smart to get caught.

So I looked into history. Not just her recent history, but the expanse of it, starting in the eighteen-hundreds and working my way to the present. From more than a century of arrest records and receipts., I sifted a scattered handful of coincidences and inconsistencies. They were barely worth noting by themselves, but connecting the disparate pieces was a cohesive narrative, one that had been obscured, but never quite erased.

Nazi Germany, 1938. Three servants working for a wealthy eccentric arrived in a small village in the heart of the

Black Forest with the intention of shopping at the village market. One of the three was a known lesbian; another was identified as Roma. A small argument between the three and a local vendor quickly escalated, and soon the police arrived on the scene. Reports of the event detailed that a local commissar began brutally beating the three with a cudgel— a beating which abruptly ended when the officer was lit on fire. He burned to death in the town square, less than ten feet from a public fountain.

None of the witness reports mentioned a dragon or a tall woman dressed in red. According to official reports, the event was a tragic accident. Completely natural and totally unpreventable.

After the death of the commissar, statistical analysis showed a dip in the number of locals who were deported to concentration camps as compared to those living in the surrounding area. Nazi officials were sent to investigate the discrepancy, but they were reported missing while going on hunting trips in the Black Forest. The few who survived reported no anomalies whatsoever.

It was easy enough to piece together. The political climate of the time put the Contessa's servants in danger, so she singled out one of their attackers and made an example out of him. The show of force worked, at least for a time. Vulnerable populations probably started flocking to her, showing off their best and brightest in hopes that she would take them under her wing. But even if nobody believed stories of fire-breathing dragons, that kind of notoriety didn't go unnoticed.

1940. Commandant Hermann Durer took up command of a nearby concentration camp. He had little authority in the greater region, and was never credited for making any changes in policy or command, but within three months of his transfer, the number of deportations within the village more closely reflected the rest in the region. Over the next several months, resistance strongholds in the nearby Rhineland went up in flames, always in the dead of night. Their leaders vanished, only to be identified in a mass grave inside Durer's camp.

1941. Durer requisitioned materials and equipment to rebuild his labor camp after the facilities were damaged in a fire. According to his report, more than a hundred of his camp's prisoners died in the flames, but that number was inconsistent with the number of bodies found in surrounding mass graves. Evidence suggests that they escaped.

Later that year, the Order of Saint Michael of the Sun sent Gianna Stavros to investigate reports of dragon attacks in the east of France. Her investigation led her first to Durer and then to a young green-scaled mountain dragon that had recently arrived in the Black Forest. She killed both with a brutal efficiency that soon marked her as the most ruthless dragonslayer of the twentieth century.

The rest of the details were more muddled, but current events helped bring a degree of clarity.

The Contessa had a secure prison facility in her home, but she insisted on keeping Meph far away from her, she moved him almost constantly, and she was obsessive about giving Arkay proof of life. It wasn't just gloating. It was paranoia. She worked with enough confidence in her process to suggest intimate experience with taking a hostage from a dragon, but the sloppiness of her technique suggested that she had no previous infrastructure in place for the act. She wasn't a past perpetrator, then, but a victim.

It fit with the narrative. Commandant Durer stole someone from her, someone important enough to her that she'd give up the rest of her region to save them. She allowed herself to be made into a common attack dog and obeyed without resistance. When she finally attacked the concentration camp, her attack was abrupt and overwhelming and surprisingly short.

That was the puzzle. It lacked the precision of a rescue or the drama of a distraction. If anything, it seemed like the raw destructive force of a rampage, awe-inspiring but prematurely aborted. She razed four buildings, but stopped there. Durer was present, but he didn't die. Her attack had to mean that he'd lost his leverage over her. And after everything he'd done, she could have ripped him to shreds. Instead she went back to her forest and let a human steal her revenge. It didn't make sense. At least, not until the last piece fell into place.

The Holocaust wasn't the only thing going on during World War Two. At the same time, airplanes were raining down fire and munitions on population centers, guided ballistics missiles were blowing up targets over the horizon, submarines were ripping up ships from below, and top scientists were racing to unlock the secret of nuclear missiles. The Contessa was at least forty by this point. She went from living in a world where humans fought on horseback to one full of dirty bombs and unmanned drones. Even for a dragon, fighting back against the Nazi regime was little more than a noble death sentence. In a world where anyone could be a spy for the SS, the only hope of survival was total secrecy. She'd learned it the hard way, and she enforced that silence with merciless efficiency.

Because unlike the Contessa, the nonhuman world continued to move forward. They echoed humanity's every cry for revolution: for civil rights, for sexual equality, for secularization, for peace, for pride. Every time humans took to the streets in protest, nonhumans talked about doing the same for their own cause.

And every time, those movements were crushed before they could take root. No matter where they hid, the Order always found them. Their organizations were scattered. Their leaders were butchered. Every time, the movement was crushed. And the person who uncovered key information leading to each raid was none other than Gianna Stavros.

The Contessa was willing to work with the Order to preserve her secrecy. And when Arkay started talking about going public, the Contessa silenced her with all the hostile desperation of a cornered animal. But if going public scared her enough to make her attack, then maybe it would be enough to force her surrender.

Book 9:

Beloved of the Dragon

Rosario

It's not that I don't know the story. It's just that I don't know it very well.

I heard it from my girlfriend, and Kindra only heard it once. At three in the morning. In the parking lot of a bar after a double shift waitressing. While she'd been pretty hungover on grief.

All of that can make it hard to remember just about anything clearly.

For what it's worth, she heard it from Arkay herself, but that's really not saying much. Arkay was sick to the point of dying when the story happened, and she'd gone weeks without decent food or sleep when the story was told.

Nobody else knows what happened. Nobody else was there. So I guess it's only natural that it sounds a little bit like a fairytale. Maybe every story does, when the details have faded and all you've got left is saturated with nostalgia.

At the start of the story, I was homeless. I don't know where I came from before that happened, or who my family was, or exactly why they threw me out. I don't know if they were just awful people, or if there was some kind of fight that started it all, or if I did something wrong. That part of the story is gone, condensed into a catch-all "once upon a time".

So here goes:

Once upon a time, there was a homeless woman named Rosario Hernandez. She was me, but she's also so remote that she could have been anyone. She was one of more than seven hundred women in the United States who shared her name, and one of five hundred thousand people who shared her living situation. And really, there was nothing that set her apart from any of them, except for one little thing.

They didn't see the dragon under the Washington Street bridge.

Or maybe some of them did, and they wrote it off as a weird art installation for the college down the street, or some kind of viral ad for the zoo, or a hallucination. Maybe they had the good sense to walk away and pretend they didn't see it. Nobody knows, because nobody ever bothered to ask them.

Rosario ran away, too, at first. The dragon was forty feet long, all fangs and claws and scales, and she could tell just by looking at the thing that she was in over her head. She was smart enough that she wanted nothing to do with it. But when she walked away, she started questioning if she ever really saw it at all, or if she'd just imagined the whole thing.

So a few hours later she came back, feeling a little bit braver and a little more grounded in reality. She got up close enough to see it was real, to hear its wheezing breaths, and to poke its nose with a stick.

It was a dragon.

It was real.

And it was dying.

I don't know how she felt when she looked at it, this enormous predator that was too weak to lift its head when she got close. I don't know if she was moved by curiosity or compassion or pity. I do know that she left it lying there under the bridge.

She went to a fast food joint up the street, one that was in such a godawful location that the building changed franchises once a year or so, but it was the closest place she could think of. She spent every dollar she had managed to save, money that should have gone toward sleeping indoors for the night, and she came back with a bag of fried chicken.

Did the dragon perk up at all when it smelled its next meal, or was it still too weak to reach the offering when it was put on the ground between them? Did she have to feed it by hand?

She must have realized how huge the dragon was, and how quickly it went through the fast food. Did she wonder what it would do when it finished the last bag and realized her hands still smelled like fried chicken?

But the dragon didn't eat her. Instead it grew smaller and smaller until it looked like a young woman, barely Rosario's age at the time, dressed in torn and bloody clothes. She scarfed down the rest of the chicken like she hadn't eaten in weeks, and then curled up, shivering, in the homeless woman's lap. I'm guessing they sat there for a while. It probably took some time to come to grips with the fact that dragons existed at all, let alone that they could do that. Eventually Rosario gathered her up and brought her to a safer place, where there were blankets and tents and people who might know a language the dragon could understand, and she nursed her back to health.

Nobody told me how long Arkay stuck around before she went back to the Hoarde. Arkay said it wasn't very long at all, but that time must have meant something to her.

After that, she—I—the person I used to be—she didn't live on the streets anymore. She—I—lived in a house for a while. Had a nice job. Met Kindra.

When I was in the hospital, Arkay made sure I had the best medical treatment and the best bodyguards. Afterward, she got me an apartment. She got me an education. She got Kindra and Danielle jobs in the area so I wouldn't be alone with strangers. She treated me like I was some kind of princess. And maybe that's supposed to be flattering. Maybe I should have felt grateful.

But I'd looked up stories of dragons who keep princesses. One of them always winds up dead.

Arkay

The Forest was burning.

Dry trees went up in flames. Acrid smoke pooled like water on the cavern's ceiling. Living shadows darted through the smoke like fish, snapping up the sparks as they floated overhead.

I watched them dance, too dazed to make sense of my surroundings.

Voices were shouting. Somewhere, somebody screamed in agony, but those noises barely filtered through the ringing in my ears. Blood and charred flesh joined the scent of smoke and fire. Burning pine needles. Burning hair. Everything was burning.

I tried to sit up, but the attempt to move my arm sent a pulse of white-hot agony through my shoulder. I looked down. Shrapnel was embedded in my body armor, and my collarbone jutted through the fabric. Other arm, then. Now that I realized I was supposed to hurt, the pain washed over me like a wave, fierce and wrenching, almost unbearable. But it was the pain that woke me out of my stupor. People were hurt. The Forest was burning. If the fire wasn't contained, it could spread to the whole Felldeep. I had a job to do. I dragged myself upright, not bothering with my damaged arm.

The dead trees blazed like torches, their trunks cracking and splintering in the intense heat. Beyond them, rectangles of light marked open doors where volunteers rushed through with fire extinguishers and buckets of water to douse the flames. There was a conspicuous dark space directly in front of me where one of those doors had been a few minutes before. Now it was nothing but shattered wood and scarred stone clinging to the edge of a crater.

Terry flapped through the burning trees, carried by the heat they gave off. The eldritch abomination's mass was redistributed into something vast and thin, almost like a tarp that wrapped around the detritus and smothered the flames with its bulk.

"Sorry about the wait, boss," they called. "Just had to tie down Comet."

"Good call." We learned the hard way that our resident yggdradeer did not like fire. If somebody didn't restrain her, she was in danger of either hurting herself or trampling the people trying to put out the flames. "Work on putting out the fires, and keep an eye out for casualties. You're our eye in the… sky, so to speak." Okay, so it was the ceiling of a cave, but it was a very *high* ceiling.

Anyway, Terry got the idea. "Aye-aye," they said, and fluttered off to extinguish another tree.

I pressed on, in the direction of the nearest voice that cut through the chaos.

"I told you to check her for explosives!" an incubus shouted. He was a member of the retrieval team that had just come back. His name started with a… D? My brain was too scrambled to hold onto the detail.

"I did!" replied another member of the team, a menehune, their voice raised to be heard above the roaring flames. "She was clean!"

"You call this clean?" the incubus shrieked.

Retrieval team. I'd been heading out to meet the retrieval team after they acquired a new asset. A woman who defected from the Order. She said she wanted to help us. She said she had information. The names of Order leaders and where they'd be in the next few weeks. The locations of factories full of refugees who needed saving.

"We even made her take off her fucking shoes!" the menehune shouted. "We patted her down! I don't know where she could have put it!"

The team already fought off the obligatory ambush. Our informant even helped. She killed three Orderlings while our team made a break for the door. You'd think someone who was ready to kill for you would be on your side.

Now there was a crater where she had been standing.

"You two," I croaked. "Quit yelling and go help the wounded. That's an order." The two of them looked up as one, and their expressions twisted into horror. They were dirty and singed, but their burns were mild, blocked by closer bodies.

The bomb hadn't gone off until I got close. One second I was stepping forward to shake hands with our new informant, and the next, she was a fireball.

My team didn't find the bomb because it wasn't on her. It was *inside* her. And once again, I was the target.

Meph

I spent the last four years or so of my life being held prisoner by one organization or another. Turns out, you can learn a lot about someone by the kind of prison they keep.

When I was a captive of the Order, I was stuffed in a locked apartment, where every decoration was an unspoken assurance that even though I wasn't free to leave and could die at any moment, everything was perfectly normal. The Contessa had kept me behind glass like a museum piece, and then dressed me up pretty so I could sit at her side like a loyal pet. Arkay's dungeon had been bare-walled and barely used, outfitted more like a hospital room than a holding cell.

And then there was *this* sideshow.

I spent three days freezing my ass off in the back of a transport unit lifted from a state penitentiary. Before that, two weeks in an underground bunker somewhere near the Appalachians. Before that, an armored truck. Before that, a storage container inside an ocean liner, and so forth, *ad nauseum*. This week I was locked up inside a drafty storage unit, and not one that had been thoroughly cleaned in the recent past. The concrete floor was dusty and coated with a tacky grime. Somebody must have laid a shitty foundation, because a long, jagged crack split the space in half.

I was starting to feel like a connoisseur of confinement.

Take my guards, for example. There were always two, working four-week shifts. Every two weeks, one of my guards was replaced with someone new. They didn't speak to me beyond a few growled instructions and occasional barked abuse, but I heard them talking to each other, and over time I started getting a feel for them.

These weren't the Contessa's personal staff—*those* were immaculate in dress and positively dripping professionalism. These guys were trained well enough to pass inspection, but they lacked dedication. After a week of constant surveillance, they were bored and irritable. By the end of the second week, they got sloppy. By the fourth week, they were so ready to be out of there that they could barely bother to glance my direction.

It wasn't just indifference, though. The work was wearing on them. Constantly trying to cover their tracks and block out surveillance was a ceaseless source of stress. Lately, we were assaulted by sudden cold snaps and unforgiving blizzards that left my guards hoarse and sneezing. And all the time we were moving faster, more frequently, in more directions. I wasn't sleeping much, but at least I wasn't on high alert for most of my transit. At least I had the chance to sleep. They didn't, and it showed.

So when they picked out my cell and swept it for debris, they didn't scour the grit from the crack in the floor. When they passed my storage unit on their irregular rounds, they didn't take off their shoes to muffle their footsteps on the cold concrete. I knew when they were watching me, and when they were walking through the cell. And while they were in transit, I ran my fingers through the dusty grit of the seam.

This wasn't the first time they'd made this mistake. Like I said, exhaustion left them sloppy.

But this was the first time I came up with anything.

A paperclip had gotten lodged in the crack. It was small and thin, decorated with bright colors and stripes. Probably from a kid's school supplies, put in storage or something. Or maybe it belonged to someone like Arkay, who wasn't herself when she wasn't loud.

Footsteps headed my way. I rubbed the grit off the paperclip as best I could popped it into my mouth. It was completely hidden on the inside of my cheek before the door rattled open.

Arkay

As soon as Doctor Magbantay gave me the all clear, I retreated back to my apartment. I'd need to come back for another round of Styx later, but not until the first dose had worked its way out of my system. Until then, I got to deal with all the pleasantries of my body forcibly trying to piece itself back together in the most painful ways possible.

The process left me with time to kill and some potent fury to dispel, so I stashed my phones in a well-used Faraday cage and proceeded to EMP the fuck out of my bedroom with a few blasts of not-so-controlled lightning. The process left scorch marks on my walls and ceiling, but it was worth it to know that the Contessa didn't have anyone listening in on my phone calls. Just to be sure, though, I cracked open the phone case and searched it one more time for unsavory hardware. Still nothing.

Secure in my privacy, I texted my contact in the Order. A few minutes later, she called me back.

"Hello—"

"You said you vetted her," I snapped. "You told me this woman was legit."

"She was," Mara protested.

"Bullshit. The fucker swallowed enough explosives to bring down a building. Two of my people are dead." I raked a hand down my scalp and hissed as something sharp jabbed my fingers. When I pulled it back, I swore again. "I just found her incisor in my *hair*!"

"Jesus Christ."

"Mara, I want to know why this keeps happening."

"I'm doing everything I can, dammit. But it's not like I can check these people out in person."

I took a sharp breath, but she cut me off before I could use it.

"Don't you fucking dare, dragon. I'm putting my life on the line here."

"Yeah, and so is every one of my people who walks into a death trap because of your bad information."

"It's called war," she said. "If you can't handle the risk, get out of the business. I'm doing the best I can with what I've got, but I'm pulling at a hundred leads with almost no resources. This is as good as you're going to get."

Meanwhile, my strike teams were getting ambushed and the Felldeep was getting bombed on a regular basis. There were so many craters in the Forest of the Damned that Terry couldn't keep up with patching them all. We'd started putting buckets of water at most of our doors so people could wash their shoes after they stepped into wet cement.

And yet we managed to contain the worst of the damage. Enemy soldiers got in, but they never managed to get deep enough into the Felldeep to do more than superficial harm. For every person we lost, we saved a hundred more during our raids on Order factories. I felt like some kind of twisted actuary, comparing our losses to our potential gains and trying to calculate the magic number that made all of our work stop being worth it. Like if we lost that many people, we'd be forced to seal the doors and hide in the dark while we licked our wounds.

Except that wasn't an option.

My operatives were working under the assumption that their leaders were wisely measuring the risks and rewards of every command we gave, and that we would never intentionally send them into danger. And I wouldn't. Their loyalty mattered to me. *They* mattered to me.

But as long as I was in the Contessa's power, so were they. She didn't give two shits what happened to them, because her own precious followers were out of harm's way. And if I raised a finger to stop her, if I defied her even slightly, then Meph and Rosa would pay for it.

She still had them hostage. And until I got them out of harm's way, my hands were tied.

I dragged my attention back to the phone call. Mara was still on the line. I lowered my voice and tried not to sound as tired as I felt. "Any chance of good news, at least? Have you found Meph?"

"No." One word, heavy as a lead weight.

"You said you picked up his trail in Kolkata."

"And then they ditched their truck and used another vehicle. They're gone."

"Again?" I picked another tooth out of my hair.

"They know we're watching them," she said. "Is there any chance they're listening in on you?"

"None." This was my fourth burner phone in a month, and my room got EMP'd so frequently it was going to start glowing. "What about on your end? Could they be tracking you through the system? A keylogger or something?"

"If they knew I was involved, I would already be dead." The Contessa's agent— agents?—in the Order wouldn't hesitate to string Mara up for working with me. Unless this was a game, and I was already playing into her hands. I wouldn't put it past the Contessa to toy with us like that.

But that line of thinking led to second-guessing and paranoia and snapping at shadows. I shoved it aside.

"I do have some good news," Mara said. "I've got another defector for you, and he'll need a pickup. Everything I've found on the guy checks out. He's a convert, recently transferred to factory work, multiple warnings for sympathizing with the enemy."

"That's what you said about the last one," I said grimly.

"Like I said, risk is part of the business. He says he's willing to give you information in exchange for protection. Do you want him or not?"

I massaged my temples.

If he worked at a factory, he'd be able to lead us back to it. We could save hundreds of lives. Or he could be another ticking time bomb and potentially murder another handful of loyal soldiers.

I sighed. "I'll put a team together and call you back with the details. One hour."

"Got it."

The phone went silent.

I stared at it for a few long minutes, then tucked it into the inner pocket of my jacket. There was still a chance Mara was working for the Order. She'd contacted me, after all—nine months ago, right after Meph disappeared. She said she'd had a change of heart. Of course, two of my people had just been blown up by another woman who said she had a change of heart, too. But unlike her, Mara's information was good more often than it was bad, so I would have to trust her. Right now, I needed people I could trust.

I pulled my other phone out of the faraday cage. First I sent a text to Nadia.

Rally the troops. We've got another pickup.

Then I dialed a number that I had by now memorized.

I waited seven long rings before the Contessa picked up. "Ah, *Schlängelchen*. I've been waiting to hear from you."

Anticipation prickled under my skin. Just what did she know? Why was she expecting me?

The answer was nothing. I knew it was just another mind game, and I hated that it was working.

I kept my voice flippant. "Oh, good. If you already know, then I don't need to waste your time repeating old news. So sorry for taking up your time."

I didn't even bother lowering the phone.

"That is very funny," she said. "You have such a strange sense of humor."

"That's what I'm told," I said grimly.

"Give me your report."

We've got some breaking news that you're an ash-guzzling windbag with a brain so twisted even Jeffrey Dahmer wouldn't want to take a bite out of you.

I didn't say it, though. The last time I'd directly insulted the Contessa, I'd found one of Meph's fingers in a gift box outside my apartment door.

"My contact got me a lead on another possible factory. I'll be gathering a team to pick them up shortly."

"Very useful, this contact of yours," the Contessa mused. "A pity I can't congratulate your friend myself."

"If I had a name to give you, I would have done it already, but I don't. They aren't exactly forthcoming with personal information. Probably because they suspect I'll pass it on to you."

"However did they draw that conclusion, I wonder?"

"What, you think I told them? You think I'm going to brag about this situation?" I kept my voice controlled. The Contessa tolerated a certain amount of animosity— but only ever anger, never outright defiance. She got off on watching me squirm. "Now what about Meph?"

"Not so fast. You'll get your treat once I'm convinced you've earned it."

"I've given you my report," I said icily.

"Yes, you've demonstrated that you're capable of speaking. Now try to follow simple instructions. I know it must be difficult for you."

I seethed. "I'm listening."

"You've found quite a little treasure with Styx. The results so far have been impressive."

The miracle drug had been one of her first demands when she started blackmailing me. Our hospital faced dangerous shortages and our wounded were left in pain because so much of our supply went to her. Worse, we had no idea what she was actually doing with the stuff. Normally our supply was divided among hundreds of refugees and soldiers who were engaged in active combat. Even counting her recent converts, the Contessa didn't have nearly as many followers, and she made a point of having them avoid direct confrontation with anyone. She couldn't be using it all on herself, or she'd have gone Tabula Rasa a dozen times over by now.

So was she stockpiling it? Or was she using it on someone else?

That was the question that kept me up at night.

There was a silence on the phone. She wanted me to play her game.

"Glad you like it," I muttered.

"I do." If there was anything coy or friendly in her voice, it was the playfulness of a cat right before it eviscerates a mouse. "So much, in fact, that I'd like to try making some of my own. You simply must teach me how."

No.

No no fucking no.

"I... I don't know how," I said faintly. "I'm not the one who makes it."

"Obviously. Which is why you are going to find that very intelligent little pet, and you will bring them to me. Do you understand?"

Go fuck yourself with a rusty chainsaw.

"Yes, Contessa."

"You will find the identity of that troublesome little contact of yours, and you will give it to me."

"Yes, Contessa."

"To whom do you belong?"

My teeth grew sharp. I'd rather bite off my own tongue than submit to the likes of her. But lives were on the line.

"To you, Contessa."

"Very good, *Schlängelchen.* I look forward to hearing from you."

The call ended, and I wrestled with the impulse to smash the phone against the wall. I almost lost the fight when my screen lit up with a text. Meph stood in front of a white curtain, the fabric patched and stained from overuse. His hair hung in dirty tendrils around his face. His skin was bruised and blotchy, and he stood at a painful angle, like he couldn't force himself upright. His eyes drooped away from the camera, but his four-fingered hand clutched a copy of today's *Daily Mail.*

Still alive.

Immediately I forwarded the photo to Mara. I'd thrown the photos at freelancers I'd found on the darknet, but that gave me no results. The metadata on the files was scrubbed a few times over, and sent through too many proxies to trace back a starting point. Besides, every time I reached out, I risked the Contessa finding out about my investigation.

Or finding out more than she already knew.

She had somebody working for her inside the Hoarde. Somebody who made her deliveries, who kept tabs on me, who ratted me out when I so much as blinked without telling her first. It would be bad enough if it were just one spy, but I wasn't dumb enough to believe that. She got her information from Ivan, our old head of security. He'd been in ThreeClaw's inner circle, and afterward he joined Nadia and Quinn as the Hoarde's triumvirate of leaders. When he left to work for the Contessa, he took a fifth of our staff with him, but there were plenty of people living here who were still loyal to him, especially if I was the alternative. Any of them could be his spies. All of them, maybe.

It was enough to make a person paranoid.

If I had a single point of solace in all of this, it was that the Contessa hadn't laid a finger on Rosario.

Ivan's bodyguards were still on Rosa twenty-four/seven, but the photos they sent me were a lot less Tarantino than the ones I got of Meph. She'd be getting groceries, or decorating her apartment for Christmas, or going to class. Simple stuff. Normal stuff.

Nadia thought it was insurance. I might pull some risky stunts to save Meph; even if he got hurt in the struggle, it wouldn't be much worse than what he was already going through. But if my saving Meph got Rosa hurt? Or killed? I couldn't risk that. And if I tried to get Rosa to safety, the Contessa would execute Meph. I was tied down in two different directions with nowhere to go, and the Contessa kept making her demands.

But so far, her demands had been tolerable. The constant reports were a barb to my pride, but they didn't actually hurt anyone. Our raids against the Order were launched too quickly, with too little time for decent planning or exit strategies, but they needed to happen anyway. Our regular tribute of Styx left us short-supplied, but we still had enough to scrape by.

But now she was asking me to turn over Quinn. To render our supply of Styx null, and hers infinite.

Why?

She could immortalize an army with the supply she already had at her disposal. Who else did she want to hand it to? Other allies? How many of them would be as careful with it as we had been? How long would it take before somebody else started reverse-engineering Styx? Before it wound up in the hands of the Vladmir Putins and the Kim Jeong Uns and the Muammar Gaddafis of the world?

And what if it wasn't just used on the people in power? What would happen if human trafficking rings got their hands on this? How easy would it be for a cult leader to manufacture a flock of devoted followers with no memory of anything better? How many abusers would love the chance to force their victims into total dependence?

It was too powerful. Too dangerous. Too easily exploited.

So I picked up my burner phone and made one last call.

It took several rings before it picked up. "Hello?" Doctor Magbantay asked warily. "Who is this?"

I didn't bother naming myself. He knew me well enough to recognize my voice. "Quinn, how many batches of Styx can you make in twenty-four hours?"

"What?"

"How many?"

"I… I think two or three batches altogether. Five, if I don't sleep. Why?"

Five batches. Maybe a hundred doses altogether. And we had no knowing how many factory victims would be needing it after we went to Colombia.

"Make as many as you can, and then pack your things. Take all the money you have and withdraw it in cash. And then go. Don't tell anybody where you're going. Destroy your phone. I want you to disappear."

"You can't be serious," he said. "I have patients!"

"You'll find more patients elsewhere." My voice carried no inflection. "The Contessa won't give you the same opportunity."

"Mother of God," he whispered. "But—but my notes—"

"Destroy them. Every memo and annotation. Burn the paperwork and flush the ashes. Scrub the files and then wipe the drives. Leave nothing behind. You have twenty-four hours."

I didn't offer an explanation, and he didn't ask for one. He didn't fight me at all, beyond a single token effort.

How long he had been expecting this phone call to happen?

How long had he been waiting for all of this to come crashing down around him?

I began to ask him, but I was interrupted by the sound of my ringtone. My call to Quinn must have already ended.

I couldn't tell if the two calls came back to back or several minutes apart. I couldn't even look at the phone.

I stared straight ahead.

Twenty-four hours.

It was maybe enough time to keep Quinn from getting caught by whatever spies were lurking in the Felldeep. Maybe. But after that? If I didn't give the Contessa what she wanted, she would send me a visceral reminder. Meph had nine remaining fingers. Two ears. Two eyes.

How long did I have before she started carving off pieces of him?

How long would she drag out his suffering before she realized I was never going to pay?

How long could I bide my time before we were ready to fight back?

Meph

The garage-style door rose with a clatter, and then slammed down again after one of my guards slipped through. He had a pair of cuffs at the ready.

"Hands."

Obediently I thrust out my arms.

He had a taser, too, but it was cumbersome to hold onto it and manage the handcuffs at the same time. If I behaved for long enough, most of my guards eventually got lazy and stowed it at their side while they restrained me. The act put us in close contact. It wouldn't be hard to overpower him while he was caught up in routine. Stun him with a headbutt, grab the taser, and light him up like a Christmas tree.

The other guard was still outside the door, but four weeks without resistance meant he'd lapsed in his vigilance. He wouldn't have locked the door, and he wouldn't get a chance to do so before I hurled it open.

I'd tried that particular routine a half dozen times by now. The hallway was as far as I ever got, because the second guard was always armed. No matter my determination, I couldn't outrun a bullet, and I couldn't tase him before he pulled the trigger. And damn it all, I wanted to live.

So this time I didn't try to make a break for it. I didn't fight. I kept my hands forward and my eyes down. I let him cuff me without resistance.

"On your knees," he said, and then raised his voice. "He's ready. Come on in."

The door opened again and the second guard entered, carrying a thick white drop cloth and the day's edition of the *Daily Mail*. Yesterday it was the *New York Times*. Before that, *Der Spiegel*. They changed the paper every day, but the publications were always among the most widely read on the planet. It made it impossible for me to guess exactly where I was. He pushed the paper into my hands and unrolled the drop cloth, holding it like a backdrop behind me while the other guard pulled out his phone. It was abrupt, just a few seconds of carefully rehearsed movement, and then the phone was stowed in a pocket and the tarp was rolled up again. There wasn't enough time for me to make any signs or find some telling word to point to. Not that I hadn't tried.

I cast a furtive glance at the paper.

"You wanna read?" my guard asked.

"Hold up," said the other. "He can have it on the drive. I've got dibs on the sports pages. The Lakers played last night."

The first guard rolled his eyes. "For God's sake, you have a phone. Look it up."

"I'm a traditionalist."

"No, you're a fucking Luddite."

We were moving again? But we'd only just gotten here a few days ago.

I looked from one to the other, still silent.

"Keep him cuffed until he's in the truck."

The guards had already started moving. Before the sentence ended, they were in the hallway, and the door was rattling shut behind them.

That was an opportunity. They'd be too busy making arrangements to watch my security feed. I turned my back to the camera anyway before I fished the paperclip out of my cheek. A bit of effort straightened the clip and then doubled it into a hook. These weren't the single lock handcuffs that could be easily shimmed open. They required a bit more fidgeting, but I knew how to do this. Hell, I could do it blindfolded with my hands behind my back. I'd done it plenty of times.

A little maneuvering, and one of the cuffs slid open, and then the other.

My hands were free, but I wasn't. Not yet. I eased the cuffs shut around my wrists again, careful not to engage the locking mechanism. So long as my guards didn't look closely, they wouldn't be able to tell that I wasn't actually restrained.

The guards returned almost an hour later, and they escorted me down the long hallways. The motion-sensitive lights flickered and flared to life as we approached. Normally I found the sudden leap from dark to light ominous. Now it felt like anticipation.

A door was pushed open, and sunlight swept through the cracks between the loading bay and the back of the truck. I kept my head down.

One of my guards turned away to open the back of the truck. The other watched him, restless and eager to get this over with. He didn't glance my way until he heard the clatter of unhinging handcuffs, but by then it was too late. I had one arm around his neck and one hand at his side, pulling the handgun out of his belt. I didn't get the chance to use it before three gunshots went off, echoing like thunder through the loading bay. One went wide. The other two lodged in the guard's chest.

The man in my arms went limp and dropped away, taking my cover with him. I didn't need him anymore.

There was a split second of silence as the remaining guard adjusted his aim.

That was all the time I needed.

Arkay

My soldiers filed out of the truck first, securing the doorway against possible ambush. Our contact's information wasn't just good, it came with detailed schematics pulled from the foreman's office. We'd been able to take down the pill boxes and bring down the main staff with surgical precision. The offices had been scoured for anything of tactical value, the workers had been captured alive, and the building had been blown into rubble by a dedicated explosives team. In a few weeks, the jungle would start to reclaim the land. There would be no evidence of the horrors that had happened on that spot.

Almost no evidence.

Most of my soldiers trudged off to the showers, but a few stayed behind to direct the long line of refugees through the dark Forest and into the hospital wing. As the stream of people slowed to a trickle, Yash sidled up beside me, barely a shape in the shadows, and pressed a bundle into my hand.

"How much did you get?" I asked under my breath.

"Four hours of my own footage, plus some good stills. I did a sweep of the premises before it went down. Got some good shots of the butcher shop. And I managed to snag a couple of the security tapes. Some instructional videos, too. Nothing that'll be missed."

"You're the man, Yash."

He offered me a wan smile, then melted back into the dark while I followed the line of people. Deeper into the Forest, the enormous figure of a cave troll emerged from the shadows, barely illuminated by the dim glow of her lantern.

"Not this way," Dagny said to the refugees who tried to walk toward her. "There's wet cement over here. You want to go that way. See the nymph over there with the glow stick? It's blue? Yeah, you want to go to her."

Beside Dagny stood a smaller figure, equally bald but decisively human. His eyes bulged with horror, and he swayed so hard he probably would have fallen down if not for Dagny's enormous hand across the span of his back. He was one of a small army of academics I corresponded with back when Rosa was in the hospital. For the past nine months, I'd been smuggling them into the Felldeep. Only ever one or two at a time, and only ever with people I knew I could trust. It was always the same gambit: they got to see the Felldeep, meet the people, fall in love with our world.

And then they got a front row seat as refugees were marched out of death camps.

The tactic was as brutal as it was effective.

I settled beside him. "So how was the tour?"

Dagny blushed a faint shade of rose quartz. "Um… I think it went pretty well for the most part. Professor Hughes looked like he was having a nice time right up till the end, anyway. He said he liked my nails."

"That's because they're hella cute," I said. Dagny's fingernails were easily as large as playing cards, and today they were painted to look like Monet's waterlilies. It was part of what made her such an effective guide for our human visitors: for all her obvious monstrosity, there was a softness and sweetness to her that you couldn't ignore.

She blushed deeper. "Um. Thank you. But I don't think he's having a very good time anymore. I'm really sorry about that."

"It's not your fault, Dagny. You did a great job tonight."

Another refugee staggered our way, and Dagny stopped to point them to a safer path. Meanwhile, I turned my attention to Professor Hughes.

"Do you still think I'm making it up?" I asked quietly.

"I don't know what to say," Hughes whispered. The lantern light glinted off tear streaks on his face. "All these people…"

The refugees trudged, exhausted, through the darkened woods. Some, too mangled to walk, had to be carried by oni and other trolls. Around them, the air was thick with the scent of imprisonment— rank sweat, rancid meat, vomit, refuse, infection.

"Our doctors will do what they can for them." Never mind that our head doctor was suddenly missing in action. "After this, we hold a meeting with our allies about placing the survivors in new homes elsewhere. And then we work on finding the next factory, and we start the process over again."

"How many of these are there?" Hughes croaked.

"This is the eighth factory we've been able to find. The fifth with survivors."

"Jesus Christ." He swayed again, but Dagny caught him and kept him upright. "How could this happen?"

"The same way it always happens," I said quietly. "People don't know. The ones who know don't care. The ones who care are past the point of exhaustion. If we keep going at this pace, it'll kill us. If we don't…" I nodded at the line of defeated bodies trudging through the dark. "So we keep going."

"There's got to be something I can do," he said. "There's got to—"

An emaciated sayona stumbled and fell, curling into a ball. Hughes gave a low cry and rushed to her side. Others among the refugees shrank away from the sudden movement, eyeing the human cautiously.

"Are you all right?" Hughes extended his hands and helped the sayona to her feet. "Do you think you can make it the rest of the way? Here. Lean on me."

I cast an approving glance at Dagny, and then I fell into line beside Hughes as he started walking. "Do you really want to help?"

He stared at me, incredulous. Like he couldn't grasp how anyone could see this kind of suffering and want anything else. It would be nice if the people who'd hurt this poor woman felt the same way.

I slipped the bundle Yash had given me into his hand. "That's footage of our raid on the factory. Footage of what was done to these people. I want you to make copies."

"I'll send them to everyone," he said. "I'll go to the press."

"Not yet," I said. "There's a time and a place, but it's not now."

"What are you waiting for?" he asked.

"Wait," I said. "You'll know when it's time."

Meph

Four stolen cars and two state lines later, I pulled over on the shoulder of the highway, beside which had once been a rest stop.

Now the ramp to enter the stop's parking lot was barred and padlocked, and the space beyond was closed off with a chain link fence covered in bright orange signs. *Warning. Danger. Do not cross. Geologically unstable.* On the other side of the fence, the charred remains of the rest stop were barely visible from inside a sunken crater. A fissure shot away from the wreckage like an arrow, a depression in the earth that vanished into the mountain forests, following the collapsed tunnel that led into the Felldeep.

I didn't stick around.

At the next town, I stopped at a library and looked up every Hoarde doorway I knew of. The Chinese restaurant in Madison had exploded in a gas leak. The bakery in Toronto had an electrical malfunction and went up in flames. The laundromat in Long Island had been blamed on arson.

I called Arkay's number. No reply. I tried her email, but her away message said she'd be back by last July. I tried every way I could possibly think of to contact her, but I came away with nothing. Absolutely nothing. And I hadn't been close enough with anyone else in the Hoarde to get a phone number, let alone bother memorizing it.

What the hell happened? Was the Hoarde even around anymore?

I was a wanted man driving stolen vehicles. I couldn't just go to the nearest city and ask around for a secret monster organization.

I looked up Rosario Hernandez, on the off chance she hadn't changed her name. I was met with three thousand results on Facebook alone.

There had to be somebody I could contact. Anyone who might still be on the grid.

Sweet Jesus, *anyone*.

I sat up.

Father Gabriel.

He wasn't hard to find. He was too set in his ways to go to ground or quit his profession, and that made him one of only a couple dozen deaf Catholic priests in the world. A quick Google search told me he was still preaching ASL and

LSE sermons up in Fort Wayne, not far from where he'd watched over Rosario.

It would have been an eight hour trip if I made it a straight shot, but I was a wreck. I managed clean clothes and a shower in a truck stop, and then ditched the car in a town called Pomeroy while I ate and slept. I still looked like shit, but at least I wasn't immediately identifiable by smell alone.

Not to human noses, anyway.

I wondered how long it would take Arkay to pick up my scent if she crossed my path now. She was still alive. She had to be. Otherwise they wouldn't keep taking my picture every few days. Proof of life meant somebody still cared if I lived or died. And there was only one person in the world who still fit that description.

I took a circuitous route to Fort Wayne, going wide out of my way and changing cars often to make sure I wasn't being followed. Father Gabriel was my best chance, but he was still a civilian, and the last thing he needed was this mess on his shoulders.

I arrived in the city early, and took a pew in the back row of his Saturday morning sermon. Father Gabriel spoke while he signed, and his beatific face was projected onto the screen behind him to better show the movement of his hands. My own hands were covered by gloves, mostly to hide the missing finger.

It was strange to sit in on his service. It had been years since I'd been to church, and those had always been fiery sermons on the importance of holding your ground against sin and being righteous warriors for God. Father Gabriel preached something else entirely. I listened in a near doze, lulled by his droning voice and the quiet peace of the room.

As the sermon ended, I lingered at the corners, watching as the rest of his flock lingered and exchanged fluttering words with him. He was a warm man, well loved by his congregation, and it took the better part of an hour before the chapel emptied and we had any semblance of privacy.

I stepped forward tentatively. The last time I saw this man up close, he had a broken leg and I had a gun trained on him.

He looked up as I approached, and his brow furrowed. Did he remember me? Did he remember what I'd done?

"Father Gabriel?" I said softly. "Listen, I'm sorry I'm coming here like this. I know I shouldn't. But I need to talk to you. I need your help."

He frowned, not looking at my eyes. "I'm very sorry, but I haven't entirely mastered lip reading yet."

Wait. "You can't hear me?"

He laughed softly, but his gaze was still fixed on my mouth. "That's one phrase I do know fairly well, actually. No. I'm afraid not. Do you sign? I can call for my interpreter, if you'd like."

But that didn't make sense. He wasn't naturally deaf—it was something he'd done to himself. The kind of physical injury Styx was made for. I assumed he would keep up the pretense of his deafness after being healed, just because that kind of miracle would have attracted unnecessary attention. But after all this time?

I don't understand, I wrote, when he offered me a pad of paper and a pen. *Arkay should have fixed this.*

He smiled gently. "She did offer to return my hearing. But I've found that I'm no less without it. And as I am now, I am better able help the people I serve. That's all I require."

I glanced back down at the paper and scribbled another note.

I'm sorry. That was rude of me.

"Hardly the worst I've encountered, I assure you. But tell me, how can I help you?"

I hesitated. *Do you remember who I am?*

He raised his eyes from the paper and looked directly into mine. My knuckles tightened on the back of the pew as I braced myself for his judgment.

"You're a young man who has lost your way and found it again more than a few times," he said quietly. "But unless I've been misled, you've never once stopped trying to do what's right."

I swallowed.

"Arkay told me about your situation," he said. "She said you might come to me for help."

"So you're in contact with her?" I asked aloud, and then scrambled to repeat the question on paper. *You know where she is? Can you get a message to her?*

He hesitated. "I can try. But I can't promise altogether satisfying results. She hasn't been returning my correspondences lately."

Dread pooled in my chest. *Outdated away messages?*

"You too?" he asked softly.

When did you last hear from her?

"June. You?"

April. Something happened to her. I don't know what. But I need to find her. If she's in danger, I need to help her.

"I'm sorry," the priest said. "I don't know how to help you."

I looked up. Maybe he did.

What about Rosario?

He blinked at the name. "What?"

The last I heard, Rosario was living outside the Felldeep. *If there's one person who can get into contact with Arkay, it's—*

I swore under my breath as another realization dawned on me.

When's the last time you heard from Rosario?

"A few weeks ago," he said. "Why?"

They came after me and Arkay. If they haven't come after her, they will.

"Who? The—" He lowered his voice. "The Order?"

Them and another dragon. I don't know what they want from Arkay, but they're trying to hurt her. That's why they did this to me.

"I don't understand," Father Gabriel said. "What did they— *Dios mio!*"

I ripped the glove off my mangled hand. My trigger finger was gone, the first knuckle mangled by a messy cauterization and puckered from infection.

I lowered my hand again to grip the paper. The pen shook as I wrote. *What do you think they'll do to Rosario?*

He stared, wide-eyed and unbelieving. It took him several long seconds to tear his eyes away from my hand and back to the paper.

If something's happened to Arkay, then Rosa might be in danger.

Do you know how to find her?

Please.

Slowly he shut his mouth and swallowed. "Rosario isn't a part of all this anymore."

I know. But that doesn't mean they won't come after her anyway.

Please, I wrote again.

"I..." He swallowed. "I'll let her know you're on your way."

Arkay

Visiting the Valley was my oldest tradition. Even when we lived on the streets, Rosario insisted we bring food and supplies to the homeless camp whenever we had enough to spare, usually after I'd robbed some asshole and had to spend all his money before he cancelled his credit cards. She gave me a million reasons why it was worth my while to help out the Valley—that it was a sign of solidarity, that they'd help us when we were in need, that it would be better to have them on our side than against us—but in the end, only one reason mattered. They needed help, so Rosa wanted to help them. Because Rosa wanted it, I obliged. I kept going even after she got hurt, because that's what she would have wanted me to do. Because it was the right thing to do.

Early on in my servitude, the Contessa had called me out on my monthly excursions to my native homeless camp. She accused me of using them as spies.

"I don't know how things are in Germany," I told her at the time, "but over here, government aid doesn't actually cover things like diapers and tampons. Do you have any idea how awful it is to have a dragon's sense of smell in a place where nobody can afford to get diapers and tampons? When you can't afford your *own* tampons? And I'm not just talking smell, I'm talking as a vector for disease, especially because fresh water for hand-washing and showering is in short supply if you don't have a house or the money to buy something first, because store employees like to rub it in your face that restrooms are only for paying customers, so you have to choose between being a paying customer and buying a fucking stick of cotton to shove up your vagina because it's fucking *Niagara Falls down there*, and—"

That was about as far as I got before she hung up on me. She didn't ask again.

As the official dragon of the Hoarde, I wasn't limited to sending physical supplies. Now I had access to teams of doctors and therapists I could send in on a regular basis, and countless front businesses that needed human employees to man their registers. We took care of the residents of the Valley. And in return, they took care of us.

As soon as we arrived, I was greeted by the Mike Jones, the longtime mayor of the homeless camp. For a while we exchanged inane volleys of "how's it going?" and "how are you" and all those other rites of polite conversation, and then Mike allowed the pleasantries to fall aside and leaned in close.

"How's Rosa?" I asked quietly.

"She's alright," Mike said. "Still striking up conversations with folks waiting for the bus, still taking those long walks around town, that kind of thing. She started her new semester last week. We see her sometimes, heading to class. It gets dark early these days, but Sue always makes sure she gets home alright."

I let out a heavy breath. "I appreciate it, Mike."

He gave me a soft smile. "I know you didn't always believe it, Arkay, but we take care of our own. Even if they don't remember us."

The Contessa had arranged for Rosa to move out of Chicago back to Indianapolis. It was a tactical move: the apartment was downtown and required a key to get in and out of the main building, which made it easy for her agents to monitor anyone who came and went. The lack of a parking lot near the building meant Rosa's car was left with Kindra in Chicago, two hours away and unavailable in case of an emergency. Most importantly, moving her out here kept her isolated from the people who could possibly come to her rescue. Rosario was entirely vulnerable.

But more than a tactical move, bringing her to Indianapolis sent a message. This is where Rosa and I had been homeless together. This was where we'd measured our needs for food and warmth against basic dignity. We came from these streets, and this was where Rosa would die if I didn't keep up my end of the deal.

But the Contessa miscalculated.

Because to the Contessa and the bodyguards she hired, the homeless were invisible. She didn't see a community of people struggling to survive. People with voices. People with unlimited, untapped potential. People with internet access.

And, thanks to the flash drives hidden inside the supply crates every month, people with thousands of documents, photos, and videos that the Contessa wouldn't like being made public.

A cluster of small children had gathered around us, breaking up our conversation. The oldest of them was maybe twelve, the youngest still wearing the diapers I'd delivered on my last visit. They weren't all from the Valley. News of our supply runs travelled fast, and people tended to drop by when they heard we were coming, especially parents with little kids.

"Hey," one of the older kids said. "You Arkay?" His arm was around a younger boy, maybe his little brother, who was leaning out so far that he nearly fell over.

"Yeah, that's me." I tilted my head. "What's your name?"

"Devon." His voice lowered into a mutter. "I heard some people around here sayin' you're a dragon. Like, with wings and stuff."

I glanced at Mike and flashed a smile. "Sorry, kid. 'Fraid I don't have any wings."

"See?" he told his brother. "I told you ol' Sue was full of shit."

"I never said that." The last words slurred as my teeth sharpened. Blue scales rose and hardened across my skin, creeping down my face.

Devon's mouth fell open.

His little brother's eyes widened with glee. "See? She's real! I told you!" His voice came in gasps. "I heard you got horns! Do you got horns?"

"Nah. Just antlers." I grinned, toothy and wide. "Wanna see?"

It took effort and concentration to pull out a single aspect of my big-and-scaly form, rather than slipping into it entirely. Most of the time I did it in combat, armoring myself in scales or trading out flimsy human fingernails for claws. But I'd had more practice lately. The refugees we found tended to be skittish around new people, sure that every humanoid face was an Order soldier. Getting them out and to safety in a decent time frame was a balancing act: I had to look draconic enough to be trustworthy but still have a mouth that could handle basic speech. Turns out scales and such were pretty persuasive in that field. Also, giant-ass antlers added a solid foot and a half to my height, which made me a lot easier to see in a crowd.

And they were really freakin' impressive.

The kids pressed in close, and I knelt down to give them a better look.

"Omigosh, it's like a reindeer!" said one of the little kids.

I tilted my head from side to side, mostly just showing off. "Around Christmas, I have them out all the time and string them with the little blinking lights you put on a tree. Nadia over there hates it." I wiggled my fingers at her, but she didn't respond. She was frowning at her phone. I'd have assumed she was texting someone, but I recognized the statuesque grip of a person recording a video.

The kids giggled, and one of them reached a hand out to me. "Can I touch 'em?"

"Go right ahead." And the next thing I knew, I was being swamped by little hands, all of them petting and brushing at my antlers. It was weird—I didn't have any nerve endings inside the antlers themselves, but I could feel the pressure of hands on me. A few hands strayed lower to pet my hair and my shoulders. Probably the little kids who didn't know better. Maybe.

"All right, kids," Mike said after a few minutes. "Time to let Arkay get up. Be sure to say thank you."

There was a jumbled chorus of thanks from the kids, and slowly they dispersed, many of them back to parents who stood back and watched me with wary attention. Several people lowered their phones.

Rosario

It was too cold for a walk in the park. The sidewalks were an obstacle course of ice and puddled slush, and the morning wind left my fingers numb as I clutched my cell phone, but I was too freaked out to stay cooped up indoors. I needed to be moving. And more importantly, I needed to have this conversation someplace where the entire thing wouldn't be heard and recorded.

On the other end of the line, I could hear Kindra stomping through her house. Where I was anxious, she was pure righteous fury. I appreciated her anger. It was easier to try to be calm while she fumed on my behalf.

"Listen," she said. "I know Gabriel's a priest and all, but what the goddamn flying fuck? He just gave this guy your *address?*"

"His email said it was an emergency," I said. "That this was all a matter of life and death."

"Oh, it's *gonna* be," she muttered.

"I don't even know if this is the same Adam Smith," I said. "I tried looking him up, but there are like three thousand people with that name. For all I know he could be somebody else entirely."

"Or he could be the guy who shot you." On the other end of the line, a door slammed. "Have you tried emailing Father Gabriel back? Did you tell him how completely not okay this is?"

"That was the first thing I did." I pulled my phone away from my face and checked my inbox again. "He still hasn't written back."

"You don't have to let him into your apartment," Kindra said. "When he comes by, keep the door shut and don't let him in. That's what you've got bodyguards for, right? So they can kick his ass out of there."

I tugged at my braid. "But what if it really is important? What if it's not even the same Adam Smith? I mean, I wouldn't know. I've never seen the guy." At least, not since I woke up from my coma.

"No," she said. "But I have."

It had only happened once. The night before I got shot, he'd picked me up from the place where Kindra and I worked. The fact that he'd been that close to my girlfriend still haunted me. She could have died. And unlike me, she didn't have any supernatural kingpins waiting in the wings to wake her up.

That was one nice thing about being forced to move all the time: as long as Kindra was in Chicago and I was in Indy, she couldn't get caught in the line of fire. Unless, of course, she decided to swan dive right into the thick of it.

Which, from the sound of it, was exactly what she planned to do.

"Kindra, no."

"Too late, I'm already in the car," she said. "Give me three hours and I'll be there."

"Kindra!"

"If it's the same guy, then I want to be first in line in kicking his ass. Or second in line, if you want first. And if it's not him, then you and I can do dinner and a movie or something, and we can send angry emails to Father Gabriel for springing this shit on you. We'll even use nasty words like 'darn' and 'heck'. He'll be scandalized."

"Who needs bodyguards when I've got a knight in shining armor?" I asked dryly.

"I don't have a white horse, I do have a Mustang and a Colt .45. Do you think that'll work?"

"Kindra, really," I said, trying to be firm. "I don't want you getting involved in this. It's too dangerous."

"I know." Her voice became earnest. "But this is a genuinely freaky situation, and I really don't like the thought of sitting on my ass while you have to deal with it on your own. Let me help you. I can put on booty shorts and wave pompoms while you beat the shit out of this guy, if you want, or I can make popcorn while your bodyguards bust his balls for you, or I can just hold your hand and let you know whether or not this guy is really *the* guy, so you have five minutes less worrying to do. I don't care how I do it, Rosa, I just want to be there for you."

Despite the fact that I was standing in two inches of slush, I felt suddenly warm. "A movie does sound nice, actually."

"Then we can do a movie."

I let out a long, heavy breath. "Drive safe, okay?"

"You stay safe, too," she said. "I'll be there soon. I love you."

"I love you, too."

The call ended, and I lowered the phone. For a few seconds, Kindra's smiling face lingered on the screen before it was replaced by my inbox. Father Gabriel still hadn't emailed me back, but I could still see the timestamp on his message.

If she didn't run into traffic, Kindra would be here in three hours.

According to Father Gabriel, Adam Smith would be here in two.

Meph

It was unnervingly easy to get into Rosario's apartment building. There was no doorman, no heavy security at all beyond a locked front door. All I had to do was jog up and say "hold the door, I forgot my key" while another tenant was leaving to walk his dog, and I was inside the lobby. The Contessa's goons could have breached it in a heartbeat.

Rosario's apartment was on the fourth floor, high enough above the roof of the building next door to make climbing in through the window inconvenient, but not particularly difficult. At least the door had a deadbolt, though a few solid kicks could probably bring it down.

That's why you're here, I told myself. *Somebody has to protect her.*

I took a deep breath and knocked.

For several long seconds, there was silence. Then the muffled sounds of footsteps moving behind the door.

After nearly a minute, I knocked again. "Rosario?"

The floor creaked. She was probably watching me through the peephole.

"Listen, I'm sorry for coming here like this," I said. "I know you probably don't want to see me, and I wouldn't be bothering you if I could help it. And I promise, if you just hear me out you'll never have to see me again."

"And if I don't hear you out?" a muffled voice said from the other side of the door.

I shut my mouth. The natural answer was that I'd conduct surveillance from a discreet distance, but acting like a crazed stalker probably wasn't the best way to earn her trust.

"I... don't actually know," I said. "Coming here in person was kind of my last resort."

"As opposed to emailing me, you mean. Or calling me. Or sending me a postcard, or a snap, or a tweet. None of that occurred to you?"

"I don't have a phone." Now that I said it, I realized how stupid that sounded. "I... I'm sorry. I haven't slept in..." God, how long had it been since I escaped? "I'm not thinking clearly."

"You're not thinking clearly, and you want me to let you into my apartment?"

I pinched the bridge of my nose. Most of my thoughts for the past how-many-hours had been occupied with spiraling fears of the Contessa and her soldiers. Every car I passed on the highway might have been one of theirs. Every truck could have been transporting another prisoner. There hadn't been room in my head for any scenarios that didn't involve them finding me again.

"I'm sorry," I said again. "I didn't even think— would you rather talk someplace more public? The bar next door? Or the… I think that was a library up the street? I swear I'm not trying to make you uncomfortable."

"You sure about that?" The door opened. "Because you're doing one hell of a good job of it."

When I had known Rosario, she had been all softness and gentle warmth. Everything from the lines of her smile to the curve of her shoulders had been inherently disarming. But that had been almost four years ago, and something had changed. She still looked mostly the same, but for the first time, I was intimately aware of how much taller than me she really was. Her heavy frame seemed less pillowy and more solid, her stance less open and more guarded. She leaned against the door frame, watching me with careful eyes. Her baggy sweater bunched around the small of her back.

"I'm sorry," I said.

"You say that a lot."

"I have a lot to be sorry for."

For a moment she didn't reply. She studied me intently, her long lashes heavy over her clear brown eyes. Finally she spoke: "You're him, aren't you?"

I swallowed. "I'm—"

I'm sorry. I didn't mean to. I've changed. I've learned. I tried to help Arkay save you. I tried to make up for the things I did. I tried to be better. I tried, I tried, please believe me, I tried.

I cleared my throat, trying not to choke on the words. "I'm the one who shot you."

"That's one mystery solved." She stepped back from the door and jerked her head to one side. "Come in and tell me what the hell you're doing here."

"Are you sure?" I glanced nervously down the hall. "If you'd rather talk someplace else—"

"I've got three bodyguards and a pissed-off girlfriend drawing straws about who gets the first crack at you," she said. "If you try anything, they'll make you regret it. So there's no reason to get the police involved, too."

"Oh." I meekly followed her through the door, wincing as it shut behind me. But there were no vengeful combatants waiting on the other side. The apartment was innocent and mundane. A television took up the far wall, the screen paused on a pair of beautiful women gazing soulfully into each other's eyes. A stack of textbooks lay open on the coffee table, their pages marked with colorful post-its. I tore my gaze away from this exposed slice of her private life and back to her.

She stood over a secondhand couch, carefully angling her body so I wouldn't see the gun tucked into the waistband of her jeans.

"You came here for a reason," she said. "What is it?"

"I think you're in danger. Not from me," I added quickly, and the rest came out in a hopeless babble. "I swear I wouldn't— but there's a dragon. The Contessa. She's had me locked up for almost a year now, and I only got out yesterday, and now everything's wrong. I've tried contacting Arkay, and I can't get through to her. Nothing I've tried works. I don't know what's safe anymore. I don't know who to trust. But I know she hates Arkay, and if she's willing to use me to get to her, then she might not stop there. She might try to come after you. And maybe both of you know all of this already, but I had to warn you. And…" I faltered, ashamed. "And I need to talk to Arkay. I don't even… I just to hear her voice. Just…"

I looked helplessly back up at Rosario. She returned my gaze, but there was less of an edge in her stare. In its place was something like pity.

"Okay," she said. "We're going to try that again, but with complete sentences this time. Now start at the beginning and explain."

And I did. The words came out in a jumble of halting sentences and hopeless backtracking, but at least Rosario was listening. Unfortunately, I only got a few sentences in when I was interrupted by a sharp knock at the door.

"Miss Hernandez?" asked a curt, military voice. "Is everything alright in there?"

Rosario sighed. "Surprisingly, yeah." She didn't seem all that shocked by the interruption, or by the sound of a key in the door.

"We're coming inside," said the voice on the other side.

There was no reason to panic. She had mentioned bodyguards before, after all. "I take it that they finished drawing straws?"

"I guess so."

The door opened, and I suddenly wanted to hide behind something. Under something. Three burly rakshasa stepped inside, their winter coats bulging over weapons and armor. Instinctively I backed away from them, retreating into the relative safety of the living room.

This was fine. They were here to protect Rosario. Not to lynch me. Even though that was more or less what she'd threatened earlier. She could keep them from attacking me. Even though Arkay hadn't been able to do that, and she was a dragon.

The anxious sweat running down my neck probably didn't make me look any more innocent right about now.

"Are you alright?" asked the closest rakshasa, immediately looking Rosario up and down for injuries. The one behind him fixed me with a considering glare. All three looked like they could break me in half.

"I'm fine," Rosario said, though her posture didn't relax. "Adam, tell them what you told me."

I glanced at her and tried not to beg with my eyes. The last few times I had to plead my case to people who were deciding whether or not to kill me, I'd had time to prepare a statement beforehand. Anxiety attacks were easier to deal with when I wasn't preparing a speech extemporaneously.

"They're the ones who can help you, anyway." Her voice was firm, but there was some comfort in it. "I haven't had Arkay's number in my contacts since the last time I switched phones. If you want to talk to her, their boss is the one who's gonna be able to hook you up."

"Explanations aren't necessary," one of the rakshasa said. "We know who he is."

"Do you?" Rosario asked, sounding less than impressed.

"Miss Hernandez, your life is in danger. We're here to relocate you to a safer location."

Unimpressed became incredulous. "Again? For how long?"

"Until the danger has passed. I need both of you to come with me."

She stood straighter, her stance rooted into the floor. "I just started a new semester!"

"Miss Hernandez, this is a very serious matter."

"I know," she said, unmoving. "That's what you said when you relocated me here, and you said that would only be for a couple of weeks, and that was in *August*. Where are we going, and how long are we going to be there? Should I even bother writing this essay?"

The rakshasa advanced slowly, approaching her like she was a wild animal. "We're doing this to protect you. Arkay was very clear—"

"I don't want her protection," Rosario snapped. "I want to know what the hell is going on. I'm not going to let her yank me around unless I have all the information."

"We don't have the authority to make those kinds of demands," the second rakshasa said.

"Then have Ivan do it," she said.

My blood ran cold. "Ivan? The…" I swallowed against a rope that wasn't there. "The minotaur?"

"Yeah," she said. "He works for Arkay."

"No, he doesn't." My voice came out strangled and hoarse.

The nearest rakshasa turned to loom over me. "Ivan Pandev is the Head of Security under Arkay."

No, he wasn't. He resigned almost a year ago. Besides, he and Arkay hated each other. There was no way in hell she'd bring him back on. Especially not after he'd tried to murder me.

I straightened my own stance and tried to fake a confidence I didn't feel. "I'll believe that when I hear it from Arkay."

The bodyguard's lips peeled back, revealing a pair of golden teeth where his tusks used to be. "We don't take orders from you."

"But you take them from me," Rosario said, stepping close. "Whatever the hell's going on, your boss can explain it to me herself."

The other two rakshasa exchanged looks of exasperation.

"Miss Hernandez, this is an urgent matter—"

"Then she can do it over the phone," she said. "I want to talk to her."

"A dragon can't be bothered with every minute detail of every operation," he said. "She's too busy—"

They couldn't have told a more bald-faced lie.

"Too busy for me, maybe," I said. "Not for Rosario. Go ahead and call Arkay. See what she thinks about all of this."

"Sir?" asked one of the rakshasa covering the door. His voice betrayed a note of unease.

"Not much of a choice, is there?" asked the leader, and he reached into his pocket for his phone. He stepped back, watching us as his call went through, but his open contempt didn't seem to faze Rosario. "Sir? This is is Jay. Please extend our apologies to the Contessa. It seems they already know."

Arkay

I tapped at the earpiece connected to my phone.

"Er… boss?" I only vaguely recognized the voice of one of the secretaries working in administration, let alone her name. She was a… selkie, maybe? One of these days, I was going to make name tags a mandatory part of the uniform. "There's an emergency meeting. You're needed in the conference room right away."

"What kind of emergency?" I asked, but I got no answer. She'd already hung up.

I frowned at my phone. *What the hell?*

I headed toward the conference room, but I turned on my headset and sent another call before I got through the door. "Hey, Nadia. You hear anything about an emergency?"

"What? Where?" The quality of the call shifted as she put me on speaker to check her phone. "No, I haven't been sent anything. What happened?"

"That's what I'm trying to find out." That wasn't *at all* suspicious or anything. Of the two of us, Nadia was the most capable of defusing a bad situation. I only ever got called in first when the problem needed a dragon's stamp of approval, heavy lifting, or a quick substitute for a car battery.

"Tell me what you find," Nadia said.

"I'll do you one better. Stay on the line and you'll get a front row seat."

The Felldeep was a labyrinth of unmarked magic doors that jumped nonsensically from one end of the compound to the other. If you knew your way around, you could cross from any one room to any other in less than five minutes. If you *didn't* know your way, you could get lost for months. It was another line of defense to protect against the Order and their soldiers. If by some miracle they got past the Forest, they wouldn't get much farther.

But the Order wasn't our only enemy.

The scent hit me the second I opened the door: a combination of musk and tree sap and sickly sweet flowers that grated my nerves and boiled my blood. And coursing through it like a neon sign for the senses: the unmistakable smell of dragon.

In the bright pink armchair at the end of the conference table sat the Contessa, flanked by an eight-foot minotaur, both watching me with unfiltered contempt.

That explained how she'd gotten in here. Ivan had lived most of his life in the Felldeep, and half of that as our head of security. Nobody knew these halls like him.

"Ivan. And the Contessa." I forced my expression into something slightly more genial than a snarl. "You should have called ahead. I would have prepared refreshments."

Nadia hissed a Russian profanity into my earpiece. "They're here?"

Ahead of me, the Contessa flashed her teeth. "Come now, *Schlängelchen*. It's rude to give our names without introducing your friend. Who is that on the phone?"

Nadia swore again.

The Contessa's smile hardened. "Don't make me repeat myself."

This was a calculated move. The Contessa wouldn't come here except to make a power play. Defying her now would have consequences. But the smell of her skin and her nasty-ass perfume flooded my senses, and it made me want to kill something. Preferably her. Preferably slowly. Fuck no, I wasn't going to answer her fucking invasive questions. And I especially wasn't throwing Nadia under the proverbial bus to do it.

But the Contessa had given me a command. Disobedience came with a price tag, and Meph would be the one footing the bill.

"Arkay," Nadia said slowly. "Go ahead. Tell her. She probably already knows."

I pried my jaws apart. "Nadia says hello." My teeth were sharp enough to cut my tongue.

"Very good." The Contessa's eyes were wide and dark, and her manicured nails had been almost entirely replaced by claws. She was as affected by my scent as I was by hers. Which made for two dragons holding on to self-control and rationality by the tips of our very sharp fingernails.

I forced myself to take a breath through my mouth. It helped with the smell, barely. "To what do I owe this…" 'Pleasure' was too big a lie. "…visit?"

"You have no one to blame but yourself." The Contessa's grin widened. "Did you really think you could escape me? Did you really think there wouldn't be consequences?"

Oh shit.

"She knows," Nadia breathed.

I backed up. "Listen. Whatever you think this is, it's not."

"Don't waste your time making up stories. They've already been caught in the act." She made a small gesture, and Ivan grunted into his phone. The screen at the far end of the room lit up with a security feed of the interior of an apartment. Three burly rakshasa crowded in the foreground, their backs to the camera. Rosario stood facing them, looking bewildered and betrayed. And backing away from her, a four-fingered hand rising pre-emptively to his throat, was Meph.

Meph. Out and free. With Rosario.

The beautiful idiot had managed to escape one trap and walked right into another one.

"I… I didn't do this," I rasped.

"You're lying."

This couldn't be happening. Not here. Not now. Not like this.

"It's true! I didn't— I had nothing to do with this!"

"I didn't call you here to defend yourself. I called you here to watch." She raised her hand. Ivan opened his mouth to speak.

So did I. "Nadia, pull up the launch codes."

The Contessa narrowed her eyes. "If you're going to bluff, *Schlängelchen*, you must make it believable. You don't have nuclear warheads."

"There's more than one kind of nuclear." Desperation and fury collapsed into a singularity, leaving behind the inescapable gravity of calm. "Anything happens to the two of them, and I release everything on our servers onto the Internet. Irrefutable proof of dragons. The coordinates of every one of your safehouses and strongholds. The names and aliases of all your pets." My lips parted to show my teeth. "Tell me, how long do you think your little tryst with the Archduchess and Commandant Durer will be trending on Facebook?" I tsked. "Teaming up with two different flavors of Nazi. Gotta tell you, that won't go over well."

The Contessa's expression froze onto her face.

Ivan's ears flattened against his skull. "You wouldn't dare."

"Try me."

"Do you have any idea— you'll expose everyone! The humans will launch a genocide on our kind. Thousands of our people will die!"

I turned my eyes to him. "Right now, I'm concerned about two."

He started forward. "Your Grace—"

"Calm yourself, darling," the Contessa said coldly. "There are no such materials on the Hoarde's servers. You've seen for yourself."

I snorted. "You really think I was gonna store that shit here? It's already out there. All I have to give the signal, and it goes global. You've heard about the internet, haven't you? Once something's out there, it never goes away."

"Your Grace!" Ivan was practically begging.

Good.

"That is enough, Ivan," she snapped. "She is lying. She won't burn the whole world for the likes of them."

Ivan stared at her, and back to me. His nostrils flared; his eyes were ringed with white. He knew better than to question my priorities.

I peeled back my lips in a savage grin. "Nadia—"

Ivan vaulted over the chair and charged. His whole body bent double, his head down, his horns forward to maul. Eight feet of solid muscle barreled into me with all the force of a wrecking ball.

But unlike minotaurs, wrecking balls are *stable.*

I braced myself and grabbed him by the horns and the chest, directing all of that momentum up and away from me. For a wild moment he was suspended in the air, and then he came crashing down onto the conference room floor.

I crouched over him, braced one knee against his shoulder, and grabbed his horns with both hands. A good twist and I could snap his neck. Let's see what the Contessa was willing to do to protect her 'darling'.

But when I looked up, the Contessa wasn't at the end of the table. Neither was my armchair.

Before I could look around, the mass of hardwood and upholstery crashed down over my head. Shattered wood sliced my shoulders. Broken springs carved into my back. I lay stunned, buried under loose springs and torn cotton that still smelled like a house fire.

"Arkay?" Nadia sounded like she was running. "Arkay, are you still there?"

I was too winded to reply.

The Contessa's heels clicked vindictively as she stepped over me, the hem of her dress collecting blood and sawdust as it trailed the ground. She bent over Ivan and pulled the phone from his belt, deactivating his Bluetooth.

"I've had enough of this game," she said into the speaker. "Kill them."

I wrapped my hand around the nearest shard of splintered wood and I rammed it into her perfect fucking leg.

She hissed in pain and stumbled forward. I lunged at her, reaching wildly for the phone. I needed to call them off. I had to stop them, dammit!

The Contessa writhed out of my grip, but that only drove the spike deeper into her calf. I scrambled to get on top of her, but this time she slammed the phone into my face.

I fell back, my ears ringing and lightning flashing across my eyes. Blood poured from my nose.

With a guttural snarl, she yanked the spike out of her leg. Then she reached higher, and drew a syringe from a garter belt on her thigh. I recognized the pale blue liquid instantly.

Styx. Of course she wouldn't come here without it.

"You miserable worm." She grabbed me by the hair and dragged me upright. "Your pets are going to suffer for what you've done. I will peel the nerves from their eyes and string them with pearls."

My back was to the screen, but I could hear the muted crack of gunfire.

No. No, no, *no*.

The Contessa pulled me closer, her lips pulling back to reveal fangs. She was going to rip my throat out with her teeth.

"Do it now, Nadia," I whispered. I didn't wait to hear her confirmation. My whole body surged with electricity, and the earpiece erupted into static. The Contessa's back arched, her face contorting in a silent scream as every muscle fired at once, and she fell, twitching, at my feet.

Rosario

"Please extend our apologies to the Contessa. It seems they already know."

That didn't make sense. I knew these people almost as long as I could remember. I knew their birthdays. I'd baked them cookies. And yes, I didn't like that they kept me on such a tight leash, but I still trusted them not to hurt me.

Lakshmi, the youngest of the three, was worrying her tongue over the dental implants where her tusks used to be.

Huge, muscular Deo was looking at me with the same sympathy he'd worn when I told him I'd signed up for Advanced Astrophysics.

But Jay's face had become a stony, unfeeling mask over a face that had once been so very expressive. He was still listening intently to the Bluetooth in his ear, and the hairs prickled on the back of my neck.

"Wait. You really don't work for Arkay?" I asked.

"Oh God," Adam whispered beside me.

"Everything's going to be okay," Lakshmi said. "There's just been some reorganization lately, and—"

"Lakshmi, shut up," Deo said. He looked me in the eye, but there was no softness in his expression. "You're going to die, Miss Hernandez. Sorry about that. It's nothing personal."

I backed up further, bumping into Adam. "I— I don't understand. Why? What did I do wrong?"

"Nothing," Deo said. "You didn't do anything. This isn't your fault."

My voice rose an octave. "But you're going to kill me?"

"Nobody's killing anyone!" Lakshmi said.

"We have our orders," said Jay.

"Our orders were to guard her!"

"Yeah, well, they changed. It's not our problem."

"How can you say that?" Lakshmi demanded. "These aren't just orders, this is Rosario! Do you actually mean to tell me you're just alright with murdering her like this?"

I shifted slightly to get a glimpse of Adam, currently squeezed between me and the window overlooking the lobby. His expression was a storm of panic and military concentration, and just a smidge of indignation. His hand slid along the small of my back toward the Glock I'd stuffed into my pants. I caught his hand in mine and gave it a warning squeeze. Hopefully none of my guards would take the movement as anything more than gesture of comfort. I didn't want them to remember I was armed.

"If you could just tell me why all this is happening," I pleaded.

"Nothing's happening!" Lakshmi said.

"Shut up already," Deo snapped. "The Contessa says she they need to die, so that's just the way it is. It's out of our hands."

"Who even is that?" I asked. "I've never heard of this person. If I've done something to upset her, I'm sorry. Please, if I can just—"

"No, you can't." Jay pulled out a Glock of his own. "We've wasted enough time. This ends—"

It happened in the blink of an eye. Jay took aim. Lakshmi dove at him and yanked Jay's gun aside. The first cracks of gunfire filled the room, but the bullets went wide, lodging in the TV.

Adam reached for my gun, but I was faster to draw. Deo was faster still, but he wasn't aiming at me.

Another two gunshots split the air, and Lakshmi slid to the ground, bleeding from a bullet wound in her thigh.

I took aim.

I was no sharpshooter, but three years regular attendance at a shooting range meant that when I pulled the trigger, I didn't miss. Three rounds tore through the bulk of Deo's winter coat and came to a stop below his right shoulder. Another three hit Jay square in the stomach. The bullets wouldn't penetrate their Kevlar vests, but the force of the gunshots would still send them to the floor.

I whipped around and raised my gun again, this time firing over Adam's shoulder. He yelped, but his cry was drowned out by the sound of shattering glass. I lunged at him, shoving him through the window and diving after him a moment later.

We fell a solid ten feet onto the roof of the lobby. Splinters of broken glass stabbed through my clothes, but right then, I was more concerned about bullets. I rolled to my feet, pulling Adam up beside me.

"Against the wall!" I hissed, dragging him to the bricks immediately underneath the broken window. An instant later, Deo appeared in the window, staring wildly at the rooftop. But the angle was all wrong. He couldn't see us unless he leaned out of the window.

He leaned forward.

"Shoot him," Adam breathed. "Do it now."

I shook my head. "I'd kill him."

"What do you think he's trying to do to us?"

The outburst caught Deo's attention, and he turned to look at us, a gun already in his hands. Before he could pull the trigger, I fired another volley at the window. All three bullets lodged harmlessly into the brick, but Deo dove for cover.

"We need to get out of here," Adam said.

I was struck with a moment of indecision. Should head toward the street, or toward the alley? Or should we split up and divide the chance of Deo and Jay catching us? Could I even trust Adam?

He didn't give me the chance to decide before he grabbed my hand and pulled me to the edge of the roof. I hesitated for a moment, staring at the distance between the rooftop and the snow-covered ground below. Immediately my mind flashed with warnings of broken ankles and damaged knees and all the things that hadn't mattered moments ago when people were being shot at.

Adam pulled me out of my thoughts. "Hey. Take my hand, I'll help you down."

I gave him a side-eye. "I'm heavy."

"I'm motivated."

I didn't accept his help, but the offer was enough to push me over the edge of the roof. It was hard enough doing it on my own; no way could I manage it while trying to navigate some guy's hand, too. He jumped down after me without hesitation, and we took off running.

I heard familiar voices in pursuit a few seconds later.

"This way." I grabbed his wrist and took off down a slush-covered street, cutting through a parking lot and behind the corner of a Mediterranean restaurant. It wasn't great cover, but it would work in the short term.

"You should have shot him," Adam muttered.

"He's my friend! Right up until five minutes ago, anyway."

"They're not your friends, they're weirdly friendly prison wardens. And if you're not going to shoot them, then we need to—"

"I've got a better idea." I grabbed his hand again and made a mad dash across the parking lot, and my guards followed. More gunshots rang out, and suddenly the parking lot was a cacophony of blaring alarms and flashing headlights and a million obvious distractions. I bent almost double to take cover under the cars as we zigzagged between the parking spaces. But my guards weren't making the same concessions, and they were gaining on us. In a few seconds they'd have us.

"Watch your step!" I shouted.

I let go of Adam's hand to leap over a patch of snow that divided the parking lot from the street. Adam followed behind me, leaping over the same snowbank and landing on the street beside me.

Deo emerged from the parking lot half a second after we did, and he was barreling after us like a train on a track, right through the snow drift we'd jumped. He got all of a step and a half, and suddenly he was buried waist deep in slush and snow. Apparently he'd forgotten about the rain gardens that collected the runoff from the city roads.

While Deo dragged himself out of the pit, Jay continued the chase.

"Up here!" I scrambled up a waist-high wall and kept going across a snowy lawn in the shadow of a towering concrete eyesore. It was a riot-proof monstrosity with a tacky rainbow paint job that did nothing to hide its brutalist architecture. The top-heavy building housed a number of offices. Locals just called it the Federal Building, and considering the department offices that were housed inside, that wasn't an inaccurate description.

I slowed my pace to a fast walk and glanced over my shoulder. Deo was reaching for his gun, but Jay grabbed him by the shoulders, pointing at the rainbow tower and, likely, its impressive array of security cameras.

"That's right," I muttered. "Go ahead and try shooting at us right here. Right now. See what happens to you."

Police sirens howled through the winter air. Deo vanished back into the parking lot, while Jay crossed onto the other side of the street.

"We need to get out of here," Adam said.

"You're kidding, right?" I asked. "This is the safest place to be right now."

"It would be, sure. But right now you're the one with a nearly-empty Glock and an arm full of powder burns. What do you think those cops are going to do when they find you?"

Well, crap. "Come on," I said. "I've got another idea."

Arkay

I whirled to face the screen, silently begging any god that could hear me that all those shots were somehow not fatal. Let there still be time to save them.

But the security feed on Rosa's apartment showed a broken window and footprints on a snowy roof. The only body in the apartment belonged to a groaning rakshasa.

But there had been three of them in the room.

"Nadia? Nadia, can you hear me?"

No response. My phone was fried, the case partially melted. There'd be no salvaging it.

Shit. I pried the Contessa's phone out of her hands and frantically pawed at its power button.

By some miracle, there was no lock screen. I blundered through the German text to find the call logs, and dialed the most recent number. On the conference room screen, the wounded rakshasa twitched and looked up. A cell phone lit up on the floor beside her.

I had no idea where the other two were, but I couldn't contact them. There was no chance of calling off the attack from here.

I started dialing Nadia's number, but a clawed hand raked across my back. The Contessa was rising to her feet, disheveled and furious. Unnatural heat radiated off her skin, warping the air between us.

I scrambled away. "Give it up, Contessa. I already gave the order. In a couple of minutes, the entire world will know all about us both. You've lost."

"You don't know the meaning of that word," she snarled.

I didn't have time for a vocabulary lesson. I needed to get to Meph and Rosa before the Contessa's attack dogs did.

The Contessa lunged for me, but I dove to the side, rolling over the wreckage of my old armchair and out of the conference room. I slammed the door shut behind me and raked my claws over the wood. But before I could disrupt the runes that fueled the door's magic, it burst open, throwing me back into the hallway. The Contessa stepped through, ready for a fight, but I had no interest in engaging her. I turned and ran, hurtling through the next door and then the next with barely a glance at where they led. The Contessa's gait was longer than mine, but she was also running on stilettos and a fucked-up leg. I could lose her in the labyrinthine hallways, and then we could isolate her in one of the back halls.

But I'd miscalculated. She tore after me, her claws gouging the floor as she ran after me barefoot, leaving an ever-shrinking trail of blood in her wake as the Styx did its work. The pain of her mangled leg barely slowed her down. With every step, I was losing my edge.

Change of plans, then. I skipped the first several doors I passed and dove through the next. The light of the hallway vanished, and the bright LEDs were replaced by the impenetrable dark of the Forest. As soon as I emerged among the trees, I veered sharply to the right and kept running, weaving blindly through the trees. It didn't matter that the Contessa had a dragon's sense of smell; this whole cavern smelled like me, and without Ivan to guide her, she could wind up wandering for days, assuming she didn't take a wrong door and wind up in Siberia or something.

Behind me came a crackling roar. The forest lit up in shades of red and gold, striped where the light filtered through the trees. Living shadows rushed to snap up the light, but they couldn't keep up before more trees went up in flames. Vast jets of dragonfire billowed through the branches, catching four or five trees at a time, and the fire leaped from the branches to spread even further.

The Forest was lit up like high noon. For the first time, I could see the domed ceiling and the sheer walls, the stripes that marked where there had once been an underground reservoir, the scrapes where Comet sharpened her antlers. The cavern seemed so much smaller without the endless possibilities of darkness.

I didn't stop running, but the moment of distraction was enough to slow me down. The Contessa dove on me and buried her claws in my back. I covered myself in scales and tossed my head back, goring her with my antlers. She pulled back, but only for an instant. When she struck again, she sank her fangs into my shoulder, barely missing my neck.

We rolled and clawed at each other, gaining mass with every slash and snarl. She grabbed me by the ankle and swung me into a tree, and it exploded with a shower of flames and sparks. Searing heat leeched into my back, and when I rolled away, I left a layer of scorched flesh behind. I returned every hit she landed, but the bigger she grew, the less it mattered. The black smoke left me blind and gasping. The hot air was impossible to breathe. My slashes barely broke her skin while hers cracked my bones. I blocked and dodged the worst of her attacks, but that would only save me for so long.

She only needed one solid hit to land home. Just one. And my reflexes were slowing.

A shapeless mass crashed through the burning trees and wrapped around her face, muffling her frantic roars. She raked her claws around the fleshy mass, and mixed bodily fluids poured from the long gouges.

"Terry!" I shouted.

"I got 'er, boss!" Their words were badly garbled, echoing through several fractured mouths as the Contessa carved them into ribbons. "Hurry, get—"

With a final shriek, the Contessa ripped the veil of the eldritch abomination off her face and started after me again. Terry lunged again and snared her ankle. Again she thrashed, momentarily caught.

I had to end this. Terry was hard to hurt, but even they had their limits.

I ran. Blood poured and bones protested with every step, but I had to keep going. I had to get to the door.

The Contessa would chase me. At this point, I didn't think she'd be able to resist even if she wanted to, the instinct to kill was so strong. But out in the open, in plain sight of thousands of humans and their cameras and their phones, she wouldn't dare get all big and scaly, and that meant I'd have at least the ghost of a chance of fighting her off.

I burst through the door and into a snowy road in central Indianapolis. The cold hit me hard, but I kept running, straight into the middle of the street. A white sedan slammed on the brakes, its tires skidding on the ice as it careened toward me. There was no chance to escape. I could only roll over its hood, leaving a smear of blood in my wake.

I lost another moment as I lay helplessly dazed, staring through the horrified driver through a blood-spattered windshield.

She threw open the door, already scrambling for her phone. "Oh God— lady, are you okay? Jesus, you just came out of nowhere! I'm calling 911, just hold on—"

I didn't wait for her to finish before I grabbed her phone out of her hand.

"Hey, that's my—" The rest of her sentence was lost as I threw her onto the sidewalk and slid into the seat of her sedan. The keys were still in the ignition.

"Wait!" she scrambled to her feet. "My car!"

"It's an emergency," I said, and I threw the car into gear and ground the gas pedal into the floor mat. I dialed in a different number. It connected on the first ring. "Nadia, shit just got real."

"I know," she said. "I have Mike on the other line. The videos are being uploaded as we speak. But Arkay—"

There was a crash, and the door to the Felldeep burst into flames.

Behind me, eight inches of snow dissolved into steam around a creature of fire and blood.

Rosario

Almost the second we crossed the lawn of the government building, I pulled Adam toward an enormous war monument, and then he yanked me on a sharp right behind an apartment building.

There were no straight lines. Every move was twisting and turning.

"Where are we going?" he asked.

"Downtown," I said. "We can lose them in the mall." It was big and public and there were plenty of people to witness a potential murder. More importantly, the mall connected to a whole network of tunnels and gerbil tubes that went all over the city. Once we got in, we could keep avoiding Jay and Deo forever. Or at least as long as it took for Kindra to reach us.

I checked my phone.

Just passed Lebanon, she wrote. *ETA 30 minutes. Stay safe.*

I was trying.

But I was so cold it was getting hard to think. I'd expected Adam to meet me inside my apartment where my bodyguards could keep an eye on him, so I was slogging through snow and slush in a sweater, yoga pants, and house slippers, all of which were rapidly soaking through. I kept one hand stuffed in my armpit for warmth, and the other clamped fiercely around Adam's wrist. I couldn't even feel my toes anymore, and my waist was encircled with a constant biting pain from where my shirt rode up to expose my midriff to the wind.

I needed to get inside, so I cut through the Salesforce Tower. It was the biggest building downtown, lined with mirrors and marble. But more importantly for me, it was open to pedestrian traffic, and let out just a block away from the mall. I pulled Meph to a shiny escalator hurried him up the steps before I paused to catch my breath. We were on a landing, out of sight from the street below. It wasn't perfect cover, but it would give us a few minutes.

"Are you alright?" Adam asked.

I caught my reflection in a mirrored pillar. My clothes were soaked with sweat as much as grimy slush, my hair hung in lank tendrils out of its braid, and my skin was a blotchy patchwork of red-brown and puce. By what stretch of the imagination did I seem alright?

"I'll be fine." I rubbed my hands together to get some feeling back into them. "We're almost there. Just give me a minute to warm up."

I wrote up a text to Kindra.

My bodyguards just went rogue. They're trying to kill me. Don't trust them. I'm by Monument Circle now, heading to the mall. Let me know when you get downtown. Be careful.

I love you.

It took me a few tries, and I swore at the screen as the message garbled into incomprehensible word salad. Adam watched me struggle to type with my shaking hands.

"Can I… Do you want some gloves?" he asked helplessly, pulling a pair out of his pocket.

I stared at him for a long moment, incredulous. "Why are you even here?"

"I was trying to warn you about… well, what just happened."

"Great job with that. Very timely of you." I scowled, but accepted the gloves from him. "So you knew that was going to happen? Just like that?"

"I knew the Contessa wasn't going to like me escaping. I figured she'd take it out on you. Guess I figured right."

"Why would she?" I demanded. "Who even is this person? What does she want with me?"

"She's a dragon. A bad one." Adam shuddered. "And I don't think she wants anything from you. Not really. I told you, she had me for months, but she didn't question me or anything while she had me. I was just leverage to her. Nothing else." He was fidgeting with his hands. The first finger on his right hand was gone.

I felt suddenly queasy.

"Leverage for—" My throat was dry. I knew the answer before I finished asking the question. "Arkay."

He stuffed his mutilated hand into his pocket. "What can I say? You matter to her."

"She's got a funny way of showing it. Most people just send a card or something."

He raised his head, looking me in the eye. "I've seen her kill a demon for you. She spared my life for you. She conquered a nation to wake you out of a coma."

"And ever since, she's kept me under constant surveillance, and dictated who I could talk to and where I could live. This isn't a fairy tale. Just because you kiss the princess awake doesn't mean she goes off and—and *marries* you or whatever. I'm not her kid, I'm not her pet, and I'm sure as hell not her prisoner. I'm just some person who did her a favor once. And I really would have preferred a thank-you card."

My outburst had attracted the attention of the security guard. We'd need to get moving soon.

I grabbed his hand and started moving again, down the escalator to the other side of the building. "Couldn't Arkay and this Contessa person just... I don't know, talk it out?"

"They tried that once," Adam said. "They wound up defenestrating each other."

"Of course they did." I sighed and glanced back at him. A few hours ago, the mere possibility of meeting this man was enough to terrify me. The story I'd been told was of a soldier and a traitor. The living incarnation of malicious competence. Up close, though, he just seemed very sad. The guy could barely hold himself together. How the hell could he hold onto a firearm?

I signaled to the doors ahead of me. "We cut through the circle. The mall is on the next block."

Through the glass doors I could see the wide roundabout surrounding the Soldiers and Sailors Monument, a towering obelisk piled high with statuary and surrounded by people. A wedding party was gathered around the base of the monument, snapping photos. Horse-drawn carriages were lined up along the street, ready to take tourists on romantic rides around town. People in business casual filtered through a Starbucks. A homeless woman huddled on the sidewalk, talking into an old cell phone while she nursed a coffee. This space was always decently populated, and that made it a good place to hide in plain sight.

Unlike most of the people out there, though, I wasn't dressed for the weather.

The second we stepped through the glass doors, I got hit by a blast of winter air. Sweat soaked my too-thin clothes and clung to my clammy skin. The wind whistled between the towers and bit painfully at my bare heels.

I grabbed Adam's hand and forced myself to march across the slushy courtyard. Just a couple more blocks. That was all. Then I could get indoors again and wait for Kindra.

But we'd barely reached the base of the monument before Deo stepped out from behind a limestone buffalo and cut through the crowd toward us.

I tried to pull a sharp left and start running, but the cold air stabbed at my lungs and threw me into a coughing fit. Before I could catch my breath, Jay had appeared at the other end of the road, marching inexorably toward us. Deo closed in on us from behind. We were trapped.

Adam stepped close behind me. "Rosario, give me the gun."

"What? No!"

"Listen, I know you don't want to hurt them, but we're out of options here. A headshot will be quick—"

"I said no."

But he was right. We were out of options, and almost out of bullets. We weren't getting out of this without someone getting shot, but it didn't need to be through the head. Jay and Deo were close enough that I could shoot out their kneecaps. It wouldn't be pleasant for anyone, but at least they would still be alive.

I drew the Glock from the waistline of my jeans.

"Oh my god, 'e's got a gun!" somebody shouted, and the wedding party burst into screams. Horses reared and shrieked, fighting their frantic coachmen.

I wanted to pacify the scattering crowd. I wanted to tell them that it was okay, that I wasn't going to hurt them, that this was all for self-defense. But they weren't running away from me.

They were fleeing from Jay, who'd been standing in the heart of the screaming crowd, who'd already pistol-whipped the first bystander who'd tried to tackle him to the ground.

They were fleeing from Deo, on the other side of the street, who was holding a semi-automatic.

Both of them were aiming for me.

Both were in my periphery.

I would only get a chance to fire once.

Whoever I shot, the other one was going to kill me.

The world slowed down. My senses pricked, and I could feel every snowflake melting on my skin. Every drop of sweat beading down my back. I could smell the cold. Hear the approaching rev of an engine.

I turned and I fired.

Arkay

Tires squealed as the stolen car rammed into the rakshasa. His firearm went off with a burst of bullets, but I couldn't see which way it was pointed as he rolled across the hood. Meph and Rosa whipped around to look at the source of the sound. Behind them, another rakshasa lay on the ground, bleeding from a wound in his chest.

The air was split with the screams of a fleeing crowd, and with the approaching wail of sirens. The police were on their way, and according to Nadia, they wouldn't be alone. The Order was scrambling to do damage control, and the Contessa—who even knew where the Contessa was anymore?

The point was, we couldn't stick around.

I threw open the door. "Meph, Rosa, get in the car."

Obediently, Meph started toward me, but he only got a few steps before he realized he wasn't followed.

Rosario stood unmoving, her hands tight on the gun despite her violent shivering. She was dressed in thin sweats, her clothes soaked with dirty slush almost halfway up to her knees.

"We don't have a lot of time," I said. "Hurry. We need to go."

She lifted her chin. "No."

Meph rushed back to her side. "Rosario, that's Arkay."

"I know who she is."

"Listen, I know you've got a problem with her right now, but you two can talk it out later. She's here to help."

"You sure about that?" Rosa asked. "Because the last couple of my friends who came to help just tried to kill me."

"Are you really going to do this right now?" I snatched the keys out of the ignition and threw them into the snow at Rosario's feet. "Drive yourself if you don't trust me. But things are about to go seven kinds of sideways. If you stay here, you will fucking *die*. And I—"

I'd been running my mouth when I should have been running. Meph and Rosario both had their eyes on me. Neither of them noticed the momentary cold as a shadow passed over us. Neither one saw the enormous crimson figure twist through the air.

We were out of time.

I opened my mouth, but my mind went blank. Words were beyond me. There was nothing left in my head but the primal horror-rage-fear that came with looking at another dragon mid-flight.

The Contessa sucked in a massive breath as she wheeled into position. The last remaining horse bolted, dragging a carriage behind it. Somewhere in the distance, a man screamed.

I bolted forward, sliding into scales and claws. My bones elongated, and every added inch lengthened my strides. Every extra pound increased my inertia. I crossed the distance to Meph and Rosa in less than a second, catching them in my claws. There was no time to run. No time to hide. I could only clutch my two humans against my stomach and curl into a ball as the flames hit.

First there was pain, infernal and inescapable.

I clenched my jaws and howled, but I did not thrash. I didn't not spasm. I did not tighten my coils around the fragile little bodies in my grasp. My hind claws dug into limestone and brick as I struggled not to react.

I welcomed numbness as my nerves burned away.

"What just happened?" Rosa asked, frantic, pawing at the safe darkness in the center of my coils. "Adam, what's that smell?"

Burning keratin. Burning flesh. Burning tires, too. Our would-be getaway car was up in flames, along with two very dead rakshasa.

But Meph couldn't tell her any of that. He was huddled against my scales, whispering a cracked litany of "no no no no please God no."

I tried to loosen my grip on him, to give him a few inches more room without exposing him to the flames. A second body brushed my knuckle as Rosa climbed closer to him.

"Adam? Meph? Whatever your name is. It's gonna be okay. We're gonna figure this out, and it's gonna be okay."

No, it wasn't.

I peeked out between my coils with one eye. I couldn't move without leaving Meph and Rosa exposed, and the Contessa was wheeling around for a second attack. She was going to burn me to ashes. If the two little humans didn't asphyxiate inside my smoking corpse, they would be easy pickings after I was dead.

I wouldn't give her the chance.

The Contessa banked sharply and plunged into a dive. Again her jaws opened wide to take in a vast gulp of air. To take aim. But when she breathed in deep, so did I.

I summoned a surge of electricity and let it loose. It hit her dead on— not strong enough to kill her, but enough for a split second's paralysis. Her wings stiffened, her tail froze, and all the minute course-corrections that normally happened mid-flight didn't happen. She sailed past us and careened into the monument, bringing down an avalanche of dismembered limestone statues on top of her.

I unwrapped myself from around my humans. If I was going to fight, it had to be now.

For an instant, Rosario stared up at me, wide-eyed with horror— but only an instant. She grabbed Meph and took off running, pulling him along behind her.

I turned away from them and drew another long pull of electricity from my core. But before I could summon another assault, the Contessa dragged herself out of the rubble. My attack went wide, hitting her wings but leaving her claws free to slice deep into my shoulder. She hit me with all the force of a freight train, and the two of us rolled down the monument's steps in a writhing ball of blood and scales.

I caught her throat between my teeth, but she forced me away before I could break through her armor. I blasted her with electricity, but she didn't give me the chance to stun her again. Her claws raked across my sides, carving through muscle and bone. Instinctively I tried to constrict the life out of her, but she was too huge and I was too small to make a difference.

Unless…?

I whipped my serpentine coils around her upper body just as she caught my throat between her jaws. Her teeth sank into my neck, and with all my strength, I squeezed.

But I wasn't wrapped around her broad, solid chest.

I was clamped around her *wings*.

She threw her head back and howled in agony as long, delicate bones snapped in half and tore through the thin membrane from the inside. She tried to rip my head off, but pain made her desperate and frantic. She could only gouge my shoulders and neck while I ratcheted the pressure ever tighter.

Tighter.

Tighter—

With a burst of insensible strength, she smashed my head against the monument, and I fell dazed beside her. One of her wings fell with me, held onto her back by frayed threads of sinew and the shattered pieces of her shoulder blade.

She collapsed into herself, shrinking smaller and smaller until the blood that covered her blended into the fabric of her dress. Her breath came in hissing gasps as she stumbled out of my reach. Tears of agony poured from her eyes. One arm hung limp at her side. With the other she fumbled at her thigh, grabbing another syringe from her garter.

Clumsily I lunged at her, but my mangled legs couldn't support my full weight. Before I could shrink down, she stabbed the needle into her thigh, and then another.

Wailing sirens broke through the surrounding buildings, suddenly audible without the roar of fighting dragons to drown them out. Overhead came the sounds of distant rotor blades, but I couldn't see the helicopter.

A platoon of black SUVs squealed into the cul-de-sac, blocking off the roads on all sides, some of them skidding to a halt beside the wreckage of a burning getaway car. Order soldiers poured out of the vehicles, all of them heavily armored and armed to the teeth.

The Contessa crouched low, snarling at the newcomers. In that moment of diversion, I shrank down beside her and ripped the garter and its remaining syringes off her thigh.

They couldn't find out about Styx. They couldn't.

But the Contessa didn't care about humans and their petty distractions. She whirled on me, wrapping a clawed hand around my ruined throat.

Her grip tightened.

Her talons carved flesh.

Meph

Rosario and I stood in the middle of a battlefield and watched the world end.

Two dragons fought, ripping each other to shreds.

Around them, the Order rolled in like a tide. A ring of black SUVs encircled the dragons. More vehicles blockaded the street behind us, cutting off our escape. A helicopter circled around the obelisk, swinging low enough that I could see the people inside. The Archduchess, her black veil whipping in the wind like a battle standard. And beside her, another figure holding a camera. Its lens focused on the writhing dragons with a depraved attention to detail, pausing only to linger over the still-burning corpses of two rakshasa.

The Archduchess pointed, and the helicopter dipped closer to the battle. She wanted a front-row seat.

That was how the Archduchess had built her career, after all: stand back and let two dragons tear into each other, and then take credit for the kill. Only now she wouldn't just be rising within the Order. This was happening in broad daylight, in the dead center of a major city. But if nonhumans couldn't be kept a secret anymore, then they could still be painted as savage beasts that needed to be exterminated for the good of mankind.

The dragons were already showing signs of exhaustion, both of them badly maimed and pouring blood. It was only a matter of time before one of them died. The other would be too exhausted to defend herself against an entire army. And just like that, the Order would become the valiant heroes who saved an entire city from a pair of rampaging monsters.

With an earsplitting shriek, the Contessa shrank down to human proportions and Arkay followed after her.

What the hell was she doing? The army was closing in. Their bullets would rip right through her. But when the Contessa turned to snarl at them, they held their fire. Their rifles were leveled at the two dragons, but they remained unmoving. Above, the Archduchess was barking commands into a radio.

She was waiting for a better shot.

It was one thing to slay a pair of dragons mid-battle. But if an army gunned down a pair of frightened, injured women? That was something else entirely.

The standoff only lasted a few seconds before Arkay leaped at the Contessa, and again the dragons were at each other's throats. But this time, the fight lasted only a moment.

Arkay hung limp in the other dragon's grip, her toes swinging nearly a foot off the ground. She batted at the arm around her throat, but her arms were too short to reach the other woman, and her movements were sluggish and weak.

Around them, the Order soldiers were closing in. As soon as the Contessa finished off Arkay, she'd have to go back to her full form. They wouldn't leave her any other choice. And then they would butcher her. It would be slow, to prolong the drama. It would be painful. They would make sure of it. It would be nationally televised until the end of time.

Not even the Contessa deserved that.

I wrapped my hand around Rosario's and pried the gun out of her shaking hands.

I couldn't save her— I couldn't save any of us— but I could do this one last thing.

The crack of the gunshot was deafening. My ears rang as I watched blood spray across the charred steps of the monument. As Arkay fell to the floor. As the other dragon reeled, staggered, and finally collapsed, blood pouring from the hole in her head.

I couldn't hear the Archduchess' shriek, but I could see her following the trajectory of the bullet. I could pinpoint the moment that her eyes fell on me. And when they did, I pulled the trigger again.

The cameraman tipped forward and fell to the street below. The Archduchess still stood, and she was holding a weapon of her own.

I emptied the clip. I couldn't see where the bullets landed, each one lost in her billowing veil. At least some of them must have hit, because a spray of blood hit the air. Her posture slumped. But she didn't go down.

Not without firing off one last round.

Rosario

I didn't even feel the shove. One second I was on my feet, the next I was on the ground. The helicopter veered sharply to the side and lifted up and away, vanishing beyond the rooftops. Adam watched it leave, his expression stony, his face gray.

"Adam?"

He looked down at me, but it took a moment for his eyes to focus on mine. Blood welled from a hole in his shirt.

"Shit!" I whispered. He was in shock. I grabbed for my phone. I needed to call an ambulance. He needed a doctor. But when I looked up again, the phone dropped from my fingertips. We were surrounded by armed soldiers, and every last one of them was staring down their sights at the two of us.

Slowly I climbed to my feet. There was no point in running. We were dead either way.

I took a deep breath. *I'm sorry, Kindra.*

Behind me, an engine roared. Tires squealed on pavement, followed by the deafening crash of metal on metal. The soldiers who had been preparing to gun us down dove out of the way as an armored van punched through the line of SUVs. The vehicle hadn't even come to a full stop before its doors burst open and a dozen men and women in the Hoarde's deep blue uniforms leaped out, guns blazing.

Right now, that didn't make me feel nearly as relieved as it should have.

"They're all on Arkay's side, right?" I asked Adam. "They're not trying to kill us, too, right?"

Adam didn't answer. He didn't seem to notice the firefight erupting around us, not even when a spray of bullets shattered the cafe windows behind us. More Hoarde vehicles were ramming through the line of Order SUVs, spreading the war zone in every direction.

We needed to get out of here, now. But there was nowhere to go. No matter where we went, we risked getting flattened by crashing vehicles. Every direction would put us in the line of fire.

Almost every direction.

"This way!" I grabbed Meph by the wrist and took off running toward the monument. A ring of street lamps and concrete posts would keep the vehicles from running us down. Hopefully, the soldiers would be too busy shooting at each other to bother coming after us.

Nearby movement caught my eye, and I almost dove for cover. On the steps of the monument lay the red dragon, identifiable mostly by her ruined gown. There wasn't enough left of her face to corroborate. I swallowed down the taste of vomit and averted my eyes from the gray matter that spilled across the steps. Beside her, Arkay dragged herself toward us, an inch at a time.

"...Rosa...?" Her voice was small. Her clothes were shredded, and the body beneath them was slashed and charred almost beyond recognition. One arm was clutched to her chest. Her legs didn't look like they should rightfully be attached anymore.

But for all of that, a faint smile brushed her face when she looked at me.

"...you're okay?" It sounded like her breath was coming from a punctured lung.

We had to get out of here. We had to run. And Arkay— she was dying. There was no saving her now.

But dammit, I couldn't just leave her. Not like this.

"Hold on," I said, and I scooped her into my arms. She whimpered, but she didn't struggle as I hurried up the stairs, behind the relative cover of crumbling limestone and broken statues. I dragged Adam by the wrist. He was moving more or less of his own volition, but his movements were stiff and mechanical. His expression was dazed with shock.

I threw open the door at the base of the monument and shoved him inside, slamming it shut after me. Inside the monument lay a gift shop, full of off coffee table books and Civil War hats, and in its center, a rickety little elevator to the top. I snatched a canteen off a display and wrapped the thick strap between the handles of the brass front doors as best I could, and then hurried to do the same to the doors on the other side. It wasn't a fantastic lock, but it might buy us a minute or two.

I dragged Adam into the elevator and squeezed in after him, then slammed the button to take us to the top floor. By some miracle, all the damage to the monument hadn't broken the internal mechanisms.

Arkay was bizarrely light, but already my arms were burning from the strain of carrying her. I tried to adjust my grip, but the slight movement made her hiss in pain.

"Sorry," I muttered.

"Don't... don't worry about it." Slowly, gingerly, she opened the hand that had been tucked against her chest. Inside her fist she was clutching... either a very short ammo belt, or a woman's garter belt, fitted with several syringes. She pulled one of them from its fastening and jabbed it into her side. "Put me... put me down. I can stand."

"You sure about that?" I asked.

She gave a faint nod and emptied a second needle into her thigh.

I set her down as carefully as I could manage in the tight space. She wobbled, but she didn't fall. A few seconds later, the elevator door rattled open and I squeezed into the impossibly narrow stairwell. Even if I wanted to carry her any further, there wouldn't have been enough clearance to let us both through the passage.

"There's a few more steps," I said. "Can you make it?"

She nodded and dragged herself up the iron railing, and then abruptly turned back. With a burst of strength she shouldn't rightfully have anymore, she raked her claws across the mechanisms of the elevator. When she continued up the stairs, the metal was twisted out of shape and slick with blood.

I pushed Adam up behind her, and I brought up the rear. There weren't many more steps, just one last turn before we emerged onto the sunlit observation deck at the top of the monument.

It was an awkward place to make a last stand, but it was the best I could do right now. If someone came after us, they'd have to climb an endless staircase to reach us, and we'd have the higher ground. The passageway was narrow enough that they'd have to go one at a time, and the first person who got shot would be a pretty effective barricade against anyone who came after them. Only problem was, there was only one way out. No matter what happened, we'd be at the mercy of whoever won the battle down below.

Kindra was on her way here right now, if she wasn't here already, and she'd be driving right up to a warzone.

She'll be fine, I told myself.

Unless she decided to come looking for me.

My thoughts were interrupted when Arkay started to sway, and she latched onto Adam to keep her from falling. He seemed to welcome the touch, because he grabbed her so tightly that she cringed.

"Hey!" I started, but she shook her head.

"It's okay. It's okay, Meph. You did a good job."

His grip relaxed slightly, but he gave no other signs of having heard. Arkay slid to the floor, pulling Adam down beside her.

"He's in shock," I said. "He got shot. If we don't get him to a doctor soon…"

"He'll be fine." She drew another syringe and emptied it into his chest.

I looked away. My first memories were of a hospital, and getting repeatedly jabbed with needles was not one of the happier ones. Instead I diverted my gaze through the scratched glass of the window. From up here, I could see for miles. Most days it must have been a lovely sight. Right now, though, I could only see combat and carnage. Below, the Order and the Hoarde had turned downtown into a warzone, using buildings and vehicles for cover as they traded fire.

"So that's the Order I've been hearing so much about?" I asked quietly.

"Yeah." Arkay stroked Adam's hair, but her eyes were on me.

The soldiers had the monument surrounded, and some of them had already vanished inside. The elevator strained against its broken machinery, responding to a call down to the ground floor.

"How many bullets do you have left?" Arkay asked.

I pulled out the magazine and gave it a quick glance. "I'm out. Even if I did have any, it wouldn't be enough to win a fight against all them."

"Enough to buy us some time, maybe."

"I think the Order is doing a good job of that themselves."

"Well, yeah. Three hundred thirty steps is a long way up."

I frowned. "You know that off the top of your head? Is that like a dragon thing?"

"You counted them, in another life. I wanted to see the view from the top, but two dollars apiece to take the elevator… that was a lot of money for us at the time. So we took the stairs. You hated every single step, but you did it anyway. You hated a lot of the things I put you through." She let out a harsh laugh that turned into a coughing fit. "Sorry about that."

"For which part?" I asked.

She gave a defeated shrug and wiped a trickle of blood from the corner of her mouth. "All of it."

"No." I repositioned myself to look her in the eye without taking my peripherals away from the stairwell. "You don't get to do that. You don't get to drag me into all of this and then make a blanket apology for shit I don't know or don't remember. That isn't fair."

She grinned ruefully. "If you don't know all the shitty stuff I did, I get to look like the good guy."

On the ground below, the battle raged on. Beyond the wreckage of Hoarde and Order vehicles, ordinary people were fleeing the sounds of gunfire. Lines of civilian cars clogged the roads. Some of them trying to race away; others lay abandoned while their owners fled on foot. But one car was fighting against the flow of traffic: a beat up old red Mustang. When it couldn't get any closer, its driver threw open the door and started running. Half a dozen city blocks away, I couldn't see her face, the glint of her piercings, the bounce of her bleached braids as she ran. I could only guess by the way her hand hovered at her side that she was packing heat.

Kindra.

Oh, God, no.

I wasn't where I said I'd be. With my phone somewhere on the battlefield, I had no way of calling her to tell her I was okay. And she was already armed and ready for a fight.

I was struck by a sudden, crippling sense of *deja vu*. I knew this story. This was the part where the brave knight fights her way through impossible odds, climbs the tower, and battles the dragon to save her princess— or she dies trying.

Fuck that.

I never agreed to be part of this story. I never agreed to be anybody's damsel. Like hell was I going to sit here and wait for my girlfriend to risk her life trying to save me.

I started marching toward the stairwell.

Gingerly, Arkay sat up. "Did you hear something?"

"I'm leaving."

"We just got here," she said. "And they're not exactly throwing us a parade downstairs."

"Kindra's down there," I said.

"So are they." Arkay growled at the ceiling. "Rosa, there are people coming up those stairs right this minute. Are you going to… what, kick them to death?"

"If I have to."

"And what if it doesn't work?" Arkay asked. "What happens if they shoot you? How are you going to rescue your girlfriend if you die before you get to her?"

"I don't know!" I shouted. "And honestly, I don't fucking care. You two just stay up here and… and try not to die."

"Sure, I could do that. Or I could help you."

"I don't want any more of your protection," I said with more acid than I had intended. "I can —"

"I know you can," Arkay said, dragging herself to her feet. She seemed steadier now, her breathing less ragged. "But I also know that sometimes you've got to work with the people you hate to protect the people you love." She flashed an odd smile, halfway between gentle indulgence and a grimace of pain. "I can help you."

I hesitated. "What's the catch?"

"Before you go down there, I want you to use this." She drew another syringe from the belt.

I eyed it suspiciously. "Why?"

"For my own peace of mind," she said. "It might save you if you get hurt. Just try not to get hit in the head."

I stared at the eerie pale blue liquid. Styx. This was why I couldn't remember any of my life before the coma.

"Not going to happen," I said, stepping back. "You can help me if you want, or I can do this on my own. But I'm not using that stuff again. Ever."

She took a deep, steadying breath, and then let it go. "Okay. In that case, try really hard not to get shot."

Because this wasn't her fairy tale anymore. It was mine.

And in the end, the princess doesn't belong to the dragon who kept her, or the monarch who woke her, or even the knight who saved her.

Whether she lives or dies, the princess belongs only to herself.

Arkay

I'd only had Styx in my system for a short while, but it had done enough of its work. My wounds weren't gushing blood anymore, my tendons weren't completely severed, and my punctured lung seemed to actually be doing its job again. I still wasn't at my full strength, but right now, I didn't need to be. I just had to not drop dead in the next ten minutes or so.

The butt of the gun was enough to shatter a pane of the observation deck's windows, and I dragged myself outside. A cold wind whipped at my skin, and I scrambled for purchase on the icy glass and stone.

Below me, the Hoarde and the Order traded bullets and blows. Both sides had brought in reinforcements, but now that I was looking, I realized just how fucked we were. For every soldier wearing the Hoarde's blue fatigues, there were four in Order black. The scorched ground was littered with bodies from both sides, and the body count was rising by the second. Nadia danced among them, set apart by graceful movements and blood-splashed white fatigues, drawing the enemy away from her soldiers and onto herself.

But she wasn't the only one who could paint a target on her back.

In a blink of an eye, I slid into full big-and-scaly mode. And in case anybody missed the fact that forty feet of charred scales and claws were suddenly bear-hugging a bronze statue of Victory, I threw back my head and let loose a roar.

Then I spent a solid thirty seconds coughing and hating myself for taking such a deep breath of cold air. But while I regained my bearings, the Order's soldiers pulled back, some ducking for cover, some freezing up as the thing of their nightmares— the monster they'd been raised to fear above all others— asserted that I was very much alive. My roar was answered by whoops and shouts from the Hoarde as they pressed on, encouraged by a second wind.

While they were occupied, I reached into the shattered window and lifted Meph out of the observation deck with one claw, careful not to crush him or the garter belt full of Styx currently wrapped around his bicep. Rosa climbed out after him and wrapped herself around one of the few patches of my back that wasn't covered in burns.

"I'm on," she said, burying her hands in my scorched mane. "Whenever you're ready."

Dozens of the fighters broke away from their stations to storm the monument. Some of them were heading to the brass doors, probably hoping to come up here and shoot me from the observation deck. Others took positions on the base of the monument and took aim.

I roared again. But this wasn't an attention-getting roar. This wasn't an intimidating roar. This one meant something. And down below, Nadia knew exactly what that was.

I couldn't hear the command she gave, but I could see the blue-uniformed soldiers retreat from the monument. I didn't give them any more head start than that.

My fight against the Contessa had been all frantic, desperate flailing. Up here, I had the chance to think things through. Up here, I had the time to properly pool the electricity within my body. Up here, I could savor the sizzle and crack of it between my teeth. And when I unleashed it, it came down like the wrath of a god. The thunderclap that followed was deafening. Windows shattered in the surrounding buildings, and broken glass rained down around us. The lightning left a crater where it hit the ground, then continued to spread outward in every direction in a flash of purple and blue, arcing through everything in its path. It took a fraction of a second to burn out, but in that instant it left behind a massive circle of charred stone and fallen soldiers. I didn't know how many of them were unconscious and how many were dead, and right then, I really didn't care.

I unwound and scurried three-legged down the side of the monument, with Meph clutched against my chest and Rosa clinging to my back. When I neared the base, I took a flying leap from the obelisk and landed on a pair of Order cars with enough force to crumple them beneath my weight. Soldiers scattered in every direction to avoid being crushed.

Maybe they didn't see Rosa rolling off my back. Maybe they didn't notice her running alongside them, dragging Meph by the arm. Maybe they assumed she was some civilian who picked a really shitty time to evacuate the area.

Whatever the reason, none of them made a move to stop her.

And so I did what I should have done years ago.

I let her go.

Instead, I turned my attention back to the battle. I tossed my head, scooping up a handful of Order soldiers in my antlers and throwing them across the building. I knocked a few more over with a swipe of my tail. And yet there were always more of them. The Order was like a colony of ants—no matter how many I stomped flat, more kept coming to take their place, and they just kept coming. The roads were clogged with black SUVs and green jeeps and—

Wait. The Order didn't use green vehicles. Their doors weren't painted with fancy stars. And their soldiers didn't wear olive drab.

Shit shit shit shit shit!

I raised my head high into the air. More green jeeps were rolling in on every side, creating a perimeter around the warzone. Soldiers in pixelated cameo emerged from the vehicles, rifles raised, awaiting orders.

Where are you where are you where are you— there!

I'd never kept up with the ranks and tiers of the American military, but I recognized the leader by the way he carried himself, the way he took in the scene before him, the way his soldiers orbited around him. Some things needed no translation.

I signaled to Nadia with a shake of my head, and I rushed at the captain. Order soldiers opened fire on me as I passed, but I shrugged off their bullets and kept moving. The American soldiers took defensive positions, raised their rifles, took aim—

Before the first volley of shots could be fired, I slid to an abrupt stop. In the same instant I shrank down until I looked entirely human. My knees were on the charred ground. My hands were on the back of my head.

"Hold your fire!" I shouted, the instant my mouth could form words. And again, louder: "Nadia, hold your fire!"

I didn't need to look to know she was behind me, close enough to hear. My eyes were on the captain.

"I surrender," I said. "My soldiers and I surrender. Don't shoot."

The captain stared, but he recovered himself in reasonable time. "Drop your weapons!"

"Nadia, do what he says."

I could feel her gaze scorching into the back of my head. It was hardly the worst burn I'd felt there today. A moment later, I heard the clank of a firearm falling onto the street.

"Put down your weapons and get on your knees," she commanded. "Don't argue. Just do it."

I glanced over my shoulder. Nadia was on her knees behind me. Behind her, more soldiers in Hoarde uniforms were doing the same, their eyes wide and their hands shaking as they put their faith into their Fext and their dragon. Members of the Order hesitated, looking at each other in confusion. In the entire history of this conflict, I doubt anybody had ever surrendered before.

And probably for good reason.

A crowd of Order soldiers rushed toward me, high-powered rifles in hand.

I turned my back on them. My knees remained on the ground. My hands on my head. My eyes on the Army captain.

I didn't take my eyes off him when I heard the Order open fire, or when I felt their bullets rip into my back.

Only when the captain shouted an order that I could no longer understand. Only when his soldiers returned fire. Only when my vision smeared into a senseless void of green and gray and endless, boundless dark.

Only then did I close my eyes.

Epilogue

The room on the other side of the magic door was small, barely the size of an average bathroom. A thin mattress over a slab of solid concrete formed the bed, and another, thinner slab took the place of a writing desk. The rest of the cramped space was shared by a toilet, sink, and shower. The stale air was helped somewhat by the scent of flowers— blue alstromeria, the same shade as a dragon's scales. The flowers were suspended from the ceiling and walls with sticky tack, and their dried petals trailed on the floor, crinkling softly underfoot as I stepped on them. I set a new bouquet on the desk, along with laptop and a paper sack, and glanced at the bed.

Arkay lay curled on her side, her eyes fluttered shut. Her right arm was tucked under her pillow. Her left was gone, amputated at the shoulder. The Order's last stand had taken its toll on her; it had been a miracle that the doctors had been able to save as much of her as they did. Maybe, if we could ever track down Doctor Magbantay, or if we could find the last of the Contessa's strongholds, we might get enough Styx to regrow her arm. Repair the damage to her spine. Heal the map of scars that covered her skin.

She didn't seem too concerned about it, though. The way she was acting, you'd think she'd gotten off easy. And honestly, maybe she had.

"You're doing that thing again," Arkay said. Her eyes were still shut, but a sly smile tugged at her lips. "I swear, Nadia's a bad influence on you." She leaned up on one arm, and I eased her into an upright position.

"I'm afraid Nadia can't be here to watch you sleep, so she asked me to do it for her. I hope I'm a suitable substitute."

"You've done an excellent job so far," she said airily, before tilting her head to one side. "So what's got her so busy?"

"Aside from negotiating with Mara, you mean? She's in a meeting with the Prime Minister of Canada about using the doors to get supplies to First Nations communities in Nunuvut. Hopefully that'll get Canada's support behind the Hoarde."

It was no longer a secret that the Hoarde had access to magical doors. They'd been part of an object lesson when Arkay and her soldiers had first been taken into US custody.

One night, during a changing of the guards, all two hundred and fifty-three Hoarde personnel had vanished from inside their cells without a trace. Only Arkay remained in solitary confinement, drinking a gas station Slurpee and playing on a Nintendo DS that she hadn't had a few moments before. But that was more than a year ago. By now, the guards were used to seeing her entertaining guests who didn't use the front door. It was a minor inconvenience compared to an angry dragon.

As the leader of the Hoarde, Arkay took full responsibility for the events surrounding the Battle of Indy last January, and she stayed of her own volition. Nobody could keep her a prisoner here against her will. Nobody.

I grabbed the sack off the desk and settled beside her, handing her a paper-wrapped burger.

"Has Congress voted yet?" she asked, unwrapping her meal with more dexterity than I had once thought possible. "Or are they throwing it to yet another congressional committee?"

"Last time I checked, they were still debating semantics. But it's moving forward. Just give it time."

Congress had spent the last eight months chewing on a series of bills that, if passed, would label the Order of Saint Michael of the Sun a terrorist organization. Other bills had been proposed— and then amended, and reworded, and amended again— proposing to guarantee full citizenship to Americans regardless of species. Or outlaw non-humans entirely. It was a bit of a hot-button issue.

Colorado and Nevada had passed legislation protecting non-humans from discrimination, and other states were following suit. Other states barred non-humans from working in schools or government institutions, demanding they be put on detailed registries. It was much the same elsewhere. Around the world, people found themselves suddenly having to form an opinion of people that they had up until now considered creatures of myth.

But they had supporters now, more than anyone had ever thought possible. It seemed like every day there was another news story, another trend on social media, another march on another capitol. Every day another celebrity came forward and declared themselves nonhuman. Every day their numbers grew. It was still an uphill battle, but there was no denying the cause had momentum. But for now, it was out of our hands.

"So what have you got for me tonight?" she asked, scooting forward.

"Well, you have been going on about how I haven't seen the Twilight Zone." I settled into the bed behind her, and she relaxed against my chest.

"Sounds perfect."

Someday it wouldn't be. Someday she'd get bored with prison and frustrated with letting other people play politics. When that day came, she would walk out of this cell and take back the Hoarde for herself. And when she did, I'd be right there at her side.

Until then, I would keep sneaking into a maximum security prison and break the terms of her solitary confinement.

Until then, I would sit beside her and eat contraband takeout and watch pirated TV shows while the world found its footing. Until then, we would heal.

Acknowledgements

Tanya Poliakov, who gave me her passion, enthusiasm, and beautiful drawings.

Stacy Simpkins, who gifted me with encouragement and stories that were at times sweet, scary, sexy, and hilarious (and sometimes all of them at once).

Angie Sandro, who offered me invaluable advice.

EF Jace, who let me bounce my ridiculous ideas off her.

TJ Loveless, who gave me the push I needed.

Jackie Knake, who has a gift for inspiration and honesty.

Jishan Qiu, whose comments always made me smile.

And **Andrew Troemner**, without whom none of this would have been remotely possible.

Thank you so much. All of you mean the world to me.

About the Author

JW Troemner was born in Germany and immigrated to the United States, where she lives with her partner in a house full of pets. Most days she can be found gazing longingly at sinkholes and abandoned buildings.

www.ingramcontent.com/pod-product-compliance
Lightning Source LLC
Chambersburg PA
CBHW030519190726
48283CB00006B/1687